"You're a goo~~d~~ ~~co~~p."

"Sometimes."

Kylie wanted to argue with h~~im~~ ~~abo~~ut that, but figured she couldn't. He had memories ~~he'd~~ never share with her, memories that clearly tr~~oubled him.~~ She just hoped that someday he would ~~one d~~a~~y~~ believe that he was a good man. Because he was.

He ran his palm lightly up and down her arm, from shoulder to elbow. Tingles of pleasure began to run through her, warming cold and hollow places inside her. Because of her amnesia, she didn't know how long it had been fo her, but she knew how desperately she needed this feeling now. Good, normal feelings. Nice feelings. As naturally as breathing, she turned into him and smiled up at him. "I like that."

His gaze jumped to her upturned face, then a slow smile was born. "Dangerous words, lady. And a dangerous time to have them."

But despite his warning, he bent his head a bit so he could brush a kiss on her lips. Sparklers ignited inside her. Just that light, soft touch and she was sizzling.

"Wrong time," he murmured.

"Is there ever a right one?"

* * *

**Be sure to check out the rest of the
Conard County: The Next Generation miniseries!**

* * *

*If you're on Twitter, tell us what you
think of Harlequin Romantic Suspense!
#harlequinromsuspense*

Dear Reader,

I have always been fascinated by the way memory works. Or perhaps the way it doesn't. Who among us has not had a conversation with someone we know, only to discover they remember an event quite differently than we do? Absent videotape, no one can say who is right.

I have some selective amnesia myself, periods of my life that I absolutely cannot remember. I could so identify with Kylie and her sense of having lost something she should remember. In her case, it was all her studies, and with it the future she had planned. With me, it was more personal, but it's troubling sometimes to have people discussing something I was involved in and simply can't remember.

However, in Kylie's case, that amnesia proves to be dangerous. If she can't remember the man who attacked her, how can she know that he is close? Coop, a marine on leave, is all that stands between her and more horror.

Enjoy!

Rachel Lee

CONARD COUNTY MARINE

Rachel Lee

———

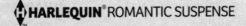

HARLEQUIN® ROMANTIC SUSPENSE

Recycling programs
for this product may
not exist in your area.

ISBN-13: 978-0-373-28148-0

Conard County Marine

Copyright © 2016 by Susan Civil Brown

Printed in U.S.A.

www.Harlequin.com

Rachel Lee was hooked on writing by the age of twelve and practiced her craft as she moved from place to place all over the United States. This *New York Times* bestselling author now resides in Florida and has the joy of writing full-time.

Books by Rachel Lee

Harlequin Romantic Suspense

Conard County: The Next Generation

Guardian in Disguise
The Widow's Protector
Rancher's Deadly Risk
What She Saw
Rocky Mountain Lawman
Killer's Prey
Deadly Hunter
Snowstorm Confessions
Undercover Hunter
Playing with Fire
Conard County Witness
A Secret in Conard County
Conard County Spy
Conard County Marine

Visit the Author Profile page at
Harlequin.com for more titles.

Prologue

The talk in town said Kylie Brewer was returning to Conard City with no memory of what had happened to her. That should have made the man who had tried to kill her feel good, knowing she couldn't identify him, but he didn't trust her amnesia. He was going to have to keep an eye on her in case she started remembering. The possibility terrified him.

And then there was the fact that she was still alive. That bugged him. She was supposed to have died, vanishing forever from his life. Instead she still breathed and walked and talked.

And she might remember.

He was galled by the fact that he had a score to settle with her. He thought he'd done it when he left her in that alley. Apparently not. Or maybe he had. He couldn't quite make up his mind about that.

Regardless, the need to take her out hadn't been

satisfied, not completely, and it still nagged at him, made him itch. Kylie Brewer should be dead as physically as her memory had become.

He pushed ideas around in his head, trying to square his needs with reality. She had survived, but she'd lost all her plans and a chunk of her life. Kylie was now damaged goods. Surely he could leave it at that. But part of him wasn't pleased and probably never would be. An unfinished job.

As long as she didn't remember, maybe he could live with that. Much as he didn't like to soil his own nest, if she started remembering, he'd have to act even though it would be harder to cover himself in such a small town.

But he'd deal with that if it became necessary. In the meantime, he just had to remain one of her friends. He had to find ways to be around her, to listen to her, to make her trust him.

In case she remembered.

Somewhere deep inside, much as the possibility frightened him, he hoped she would because then he wouldn't have to argue with himself anymore. The decision would be made for him; the internal uncertainty would be gone.

He'd have all the reasons he needed to finish the job, no matter the danger to him.

But it occurred to him that a little misdirection might be useful. A little scare that would have everyone looking in a different direction. Something that would distract him from the nagging fear that Kylie would remember. Something that would distract everyone else from Kylie.

Humming, he set about changing his appearance with a wig and ugly cheap sunglasses, then went to get one of the old, unrecognizable cars from the barn where his dead father had left them. All he needed now was to find one little girl walking home from school alone.

Chapter 1

Riding into the outskirts of Conard City finally released the awful tension in Kylie Brewer. Her sister, Glenda, was driving, and Kylie had been uneasily aware since they left the hospital in Denver that nothing looked familiar to her. Nothing.

And yet she had lived in Denver for the last three years. She'd even been treated in the hospital where she had worked part-time. The violent assault that had landed her in the hospital at death's door had stolen those three years from her, and all she wanted was to see and touch something, anything, that was truly familiar.

Now she saw familiar sights at last. The Olmstead ranch, green and lush with the spring, caught her eye and filled her with a sense of peace. Cattle and deer both grazed amid the deepening grasses. She wondered vaguely if Mr. Olmstead minded the deer grazing, but couldn't recall if she'd ever heard a word about it. Another gap in her memory? She hoped not.

Conard County, Wyoming, was home, and Conard City was as familiar to her as yesterday. Maybe more so, given how much she had forgotten. She had grown up here, and despite all the fear and despair that had dogged her since she awoke in the hospital, now she felt excited, hopeful. At peace, however temporarily.

"A word of warning," Glenda said, speaking for the first time in the last fifty miles.

"What?"

"I've got a houseguest. You remember Connie Parish? She used to be Connie Halloran?"

"Of course I remember her." It felt so good to be able to say that.

"Well, her cousin is on leave from the marines, and he's in town for a few weeks. I couldn't see letting him stay at the motel when I have a perfectly good room to let him use."

In an instant, all the tension returned to Kylie. "Glenda... I don't know him."

Glenda patted her thigh before returning her hand to the steering wheel. "It's fine. He's not a threat. He was overseas when you were attacked. He only got here two days ago."

That was supposed to be comforting? Kylie's hands knotted into fists. Sharing her sister's house with a stranger? While it was true she had no memory of the attack on her, and no memory of most of the last three years, she didn't feel at all comfortable around strangers. Even the hospital staff, some of whom had worked with her before she was attacked, had presented a constant sense of threat simply because they were now strangers.

"They never caught the guy," she said dully.

"I'm telling you, it couldn't have been Coop. You want to check his passport?"

Kylie glanced at her sister, feeling irritated, noting that Glenda had become sharper since her divorce. Realizing she was probably being unreasonable herself.

"Look," said Glenda, "the doctor explained your fear is normal. I understand that. You can't remember, although I'm not really sure how remembering would help. It's natural to be uneasy around strangers. That's what he said. But Coop is Connie's cousin and he won't be a stranger for long, okay?"

Kylie managed a stiff nod. All she had wanted to do was come home and sink into the comforting familiarity of a life she *could* remember, and now a stranger had been thrown into the mix. She nearly felt betrayed by Glenda. Then she tried to tell herself that meeting a *real* stranger, one she couldn't possibly remember, could be beneficial itself because she wouldn't have to rack her absent memory. Somehow she didn't quite believe her own argument.

Turning her head, she stared out at the passing countryside, picking out the ranches she remembered, realizing they were only minutes from driving into town. She had no idea how much or little had changed about Conard City during the years she couldn't remember, but she guessed she was going to find out. It would probably be almost the same. Little changed as slowly as Conard City.

The center of town looked pretty much as it always had. There was the courthouse square, surrounded by storefronts, where a handful of retired men regularly met to play checkers or chess at the stone tables in the front park. A few were there now, though the afternoon was still chilly. It was like a snapshot, familiar her entire life long. The picture never changed much, although the faces at the tables did with the turning of the years.

"Brick sidewalks?" she asked suddenly, noticing.

"The resort up the mountain put them in. They were going to paint, too, but the landslide halted everything."

Small change, an attractive change, but she remembered nothing about a landslide at the resort, although she remembered hearing it was going to be built. Another gap. She wondered if she should bother asking about it. It hardly seemed worth the effort at that moment.

Everything else remained solidly familiar, including her sister's driveway and the house. It was the family house, a two-story Craftsman style painted white, left to both of them by their grandparents a few years ago. Their parents had both died years before on holiday in Guatemala. Their tourist bus had been attacked by some bandits.

But that had been a long time ago. Fifteen years?

Glenda pulled up to the side door and switched off the ignition. Kylie didn't move. After a minute, Glenda turned in her seat. "Kylie, if it's really too much, I'll ask Coop to move to the motel. I'm sure he and Connie will understand, under the circumstances. But give it a try for me, okay?"

Kylie managed a stiff nod. "I will."

Glenda sighed and reached for the door latch. "This has got to be hell for you, not remembering the last few years. I can't imagine it. So be patient with me, okay?"

Kylie felt a rush of warmth for her sister. "If you'll be patient with me."

Glenda smiled. "The house is pretty much the same. I think you'll remember most of it."

All of a sudden Kylie reached out and touched her sister's arm. "Glenda?"

"Yeah?"

"I may have forgotten other things, too. I have no way to know."

Glenda nodded. "I guess we'll see. We'll talk about it more, but let's go inside and make you some coffee or something. And you must be hungry by now."

Maybe. Her stomach was still knotted with the trepidation that never quite left her anymore, but she forced herself to get out of the car.

The back steps were concrete, and still had the crumbled corners she remembered. At some point a larger crack had been patched, the concrete a different, lighter gray. The screen door still screeched the same old protest. The glass-topped inner door opened soundlessly on well-oiled hinges.

One step into the kitchen and she paused, looking around, dragging in the familiar smells with a deep breath. Little had changed indeed. The cabinets had been repainted, but the same white. A few new appliances sat on the counter, but otherwise it carried her instantly back to her childhood. She smiled for the first time in ages. "Do I smell marinara?"

"I made some last night. If you want, we can have it later. Let me get your suitcase."

A suitcase. She had a whole bunch of possessions from an apartment in Denver, but most of them might as well have belonged to someone else. She'd brought a few keepsakes she remembered along with her, and Glenda had ruthlessly put everything else in storage until Kylie decided what she wanted to do with it all.

Gratitude toward her sister once again flooded her, and she made up her mind to do her best with this Coop guy in the house. Besides, he'd probably spend an awful lot of time visiting Connie, Ethan and their children. She probably wouldn't have to see much of him at all.

Glenda rolled the suitcase inside. "You get your old room," she said. "It's always been yours, but you know that."

"Thank you."

Glenda smiled. "You don't have to thank me. What are sisters for? Anyway, this house belongs to both of us."

Glenda was a few years older than Kylie, which, when they were children, had always given her a superior position. It didn't feel that way anymore, Kylie realized as Glenda parked the suitcase in one corner of the kitchen and waved her to sit at the old table. The years had at last made them equals…at least to some extent. Kylie definitely felt at a disadvantage with her memory loss, but those were years she hadn't lived here, anyway.

Glenda buzzed about. For a woman of thirty-four who'd been through an ugly divorce, she looked good, Kylie thought. Even with the gap in her memory she was barely able to note changes in Glenda. She still wore her light brown hair in a ponytail and moved with the ease of someone who was fit, and still seemed to prefer scrubs to jeans. But then Glenda was a nurse, too, like Kylie.

A sharp contrast there, Kylie thought with a touch of humor. Kylie herself was moving much more cautiously these days, since parts of her were still healing. Almost there, she assured herself. Soon she wouldn't feel the hitches of scars from all the knife slashes, or the ache in her ribs from the beating. Soon she'd be almost normal again.

If she'd ever be normal with a three-year hole in her memory. Three years that had included her own long-awaited training as a nurse-practitioner. Stolen from her by some creep on the street.

As she sat at the table waiting for Glenda to make the coffee, she closed her eyes and listened to the house. It still sounded the same, she realized. An odd thing to notice, but she did. Sounds moved the same way through the structure, echoed in the same way. Even the sound of the refrigerator turning on carried her back in time.

At last Glenda joined her at the table. "Tired?" she asked as she poured the coffee and pushed a plate with toasted bagels closer to Kylie.

"No, not really. I was listening to the house."

Glenda arched a brow. "Listening? It's awfully quiet. Not like when we were running around here constantly making noise."

"That was a long time ago."

"Yeah, it was." Glenda sighed. "So three years are missing?" Until now, Glenda had devoted herself to dealing with each matter that arose, but they really hadn't talked between them about Kylie's amnesia. As if Glenda needed some time to deal with it, too. Or maybe Glenda had just been glad to have a chance to rehash her divorce with someone who didn't already remember every detail of it.

"Pretty much. I can't remember my training, or my apartment, or anything else. Denver seems like a place I've never been before. But the truth is—" Kylie bit her lip "—I can't be sure I've forgotten everything. Or even sure that I haven't lost even older memories."

"Memories are a funny thing," Glenda said, reaching for a buttered bagel. "We rewrite them all the time. So my suggestion to you is that you not get wrapped up in knots over details. It's not like I could tell you every minute from a day four years ago."

For the first time Kylie felt like laughing, so she did. "That's a good point."

Glenda grinned. "I'm full of good points. I know it must be disturbing, but the doc said there's a good chance you'll get at least some of it back. I hope it's just the good parts."

Kylie heartily agreed with that. She definitely did not want to remember the attack, although she felt bad that she couldn't identify her attacker. It might have protected some other woman from the guy.

"And you can always start your training again," Glenda added cheerfully.

That was exactly the wrong thing to say. Kylie battled back a sense of darkness that threatened to swamp her. She'd been pursuing her master's in nursing with an eye to becoming a physician's assistant. She couldn't do that here. To do that would mean going back to Denver, to the program that had promised to reinstate her entire scholarship so she could afford it, and she couldn't imagine any possible future path that would take her back to that city. Not now. Not ever.

She heard Glenda sigh and opened her eyes.

"Sorry," Glenda said. "I was trying to be positive and I guess I put my foot right in it. But there are other schools in the country."

"It's okay." But it wasn't okay. In the broad daylight of a late afternoon, Glenda had brought the nightmare back. Usually the evil darkness pursued her only in her sleep, but now here she was wide awake and she felt as if a demon were looking over her shoulder. God, she hated the feeling.

Just then, causing her to start, there was a knock at the side door.

"Coop," said Glenda, pushing back from the table.

Kylie could see only the silhouette of a man on the other side of the sheer white curtains, and her heart hit an immediate gallop. *Stop it*, she told herself. *Stop it.* She was safe. She was not alone. She was home.

Glenda opened the door. The sun was at a perfect angle to bathe the man standing on the top step in golden sunlight so brilliant that Kylie had to blink. For an instant she couldn't make out any details while her eyes adjusted to the brightness.

Then, stepping out of that halo came a tall man dressed in jeans and a blue polo shirt. His impact was instant. He was big, muscular and still golden from the light, even his dark brown hair.

"Is my timing bad?" he asked immediately. A deep baritone voice that seemed to go along with his size.

"Kylie and I are having some coffee. Join us?"

Kylie realized she was gripping the edge of the table as if it were a lifeline and she was about to drown. She tried to tell herself she was being ridiculous, but she couldn't loosen her grip. She *did* manage what felt like a wan smile.

Coop stepped farther into the kitchen while Glenda closed the door, but he didn't come close to Kylie. "Hi, I'm Evan Cooper. Everyone calls me Coop, obviously. And if you want, I'll just disappear upstairs. I...heard you've had a bad time."

Kylie didn't want to be rude, much as she wished she didn't have to face this, not yet. Not before she got her feet beneath her and felt more comfortable about being home. But she also didn't want to be discourteous, and Glenda had asked this man to stay here. Absent three years, she still knew that Connie and Ethan Parish had three kids who probably filled their house to the rafters.

Be civil, she told herself. *You can always run upstairs if you feel overwhelmed.*

"Please," she said quietly. "Join us. You just got back?"

So Glenda rearranged things, putting the table between Coop and Kylie, and settling herself at the end between them. Then he smiled at Kylie, speaking easily. "I arrived in Baltimore three days ago, then flew out here to see Connie and the kids."

"Where were you before?" Thank God she hadn't completely lost her ability to make casual conversation.

For the first time she noticed how blue his eyes were, maybe because they almost twinkled at her. "I was here and there. Lately in Afghanistan and then Germany."

She was relieved to feel her fingers starting to relax. Just in time, because they had begun to ache. "You must travel a lot."

"I rarely get to hold still. Say, listen."

Reluctantly she looked at him again and saw that he was addressing her. "Yes?"

"If me being here makes you uncomfortable, there *is* a motel. I'll gladly move. Glenda told me you're… recovering, and having me around might not be restful. I can understand that."

She glanced at Glenda, and saw her sister looked unhappy. Was Glenda interested in this guy? Oh, hell. "No, of course you can stay here. I wouldn't dream of asking you to move out."

"As long as you're sure, because I'm used to far worse digs than the local motel."

A little laugh escaped Glenda. Relief? Kylie couldn't tell. Glenda spoke. "Yeah, like rocky ground?"

"Yeah, like that. Cold, too. So really, neither of you need to worry about me."

"I like Connie," Kylie said, reaching for the old self

she still retained. "I've known her all my life. It only seems right that if we have an extra room, you should be able to use it."

Speaking the words had an odd effect on her. Maybe because it was the first time since she woke in the hospital that she'd made a real decision for herself. Taking control again, in a small way. She sensed a smile form on her lips. It felt good.

"Well, if I get to bothering you, just send me on my way." He shook his head, smiling. "It wouldn't be the first time my butt has been booted out of a place."

"Why," asked Glenda, "do I think there are some stories there that I'd love to hear?"

"The ones you'd most like to hear are the ones I will never share." He winked at Kylie.

God, he was charming, she thought, and let her face relax into a small smile. Such a relief to be able to smile naturally again, not just because it was expected. There'd been too much of that in the hospital and while Glenda had helped pack up her forgotten life. Pretense. No pretense this time, and she simply smiled.

Coop wasn't immune to that smile, not by a far sight. With eyes used to assessing men's condition, he scanned Kylie. Still recovering, still not at full strength and still very much uneasy. But dang, when she smiled it was as if the sun lit the room.

She looked a bit like Glenda, and they'd always be recognized as sisters, but despite all she'd been through, Kylie still looked softer. Not physically softer, but emotionally softer. Of course, he'd heard all the bad stuff about Glenda's divorce from Connie, but this was different. Whatever Kylie had been through, apparently she didn't remember it, and failing to remember it had perhaps saved her kinder side.

Or maybe he was imagining it. All he knew for sure was that he felt the punch of attraction in his gut, both unwanted and dangerous. This woman needed to be sheltered for a while, and she didn't need some guy like him coming on hot and heavy.

Still, it didn't hurt to admire her wide hazel eyes, her small pert nose or the smile that hinted at an ability to hit the megawatt range when she was truly happy. Her light brown hair was almost blond, lighter than her sister's. With effort he turned his attention back to Glenda.

"You're working tonight, right?"

"Yeah."

"So let me run over to Maude's and bring you both back something for dinner. Connie's patrolling tonight, too, and Ethan begged me to stay away so he could get the younger two kids to bed on time."

A laugh escaped Glenda. "You're a problem?"

Coop shrugged a shoulder, laughing himself. "Apparently I'm still new and exciting. I swear I don't try to get them wound up."

"Right," said Glenda with a touch of sarcasm.

"Well, okay, they like to wrestle with me. So what do you two want for dinner? My treat."

Glenda twisted around and pulled a paper menu from the diner off the fridge bulletin board, and a magnetic memo pad. "You need something solid to eat," she told Kylie. "You've been pecking at your food like a bird and the doc said you need to eat more."

"I eat what I can," Kylie answered, sounding defensive.

"Then pick something with a lot of calories."

Coop watched with amusement, sensing the older-younger sister dynamic at work. Kylie looked a bit rebellious, and Glenda was every inch the knowledgeable nurse.

"Say," he said, "just order what you want and let Glenda yell at me. I'm not force-feeding anyone."

Kylie looked at him and her smile returned, just a small one. "A brave man."

"Who me?" He laughed.

Glenda spoke. "He doesn't know me well yet." Then she tapped the menu. "Pick whatever looks good. Just don't go for another salad. You're going to turn green."

Kylie pulled the menu over in front of herself, and Coop noticed for the first time how fragile and small her hands were. She'd been a nurse? There must be more strength there than was immediately obvious. Of course, from what he'd heard, she'd been to hell and back. He figured her amnesia had to be a good thing.

But what did he know? he asked himself as he stepped outside at last with the list. The late-afternoon sun still bathed the world, though the air was growing chillier as evening approached.

He noticed the light. Light could be a good thing, providing clear sight lines and plenty of warning of bad things that might come. On the other hand, darkness had its advantages, too, like lots of cover. Odd to reflect that there'd been a time when he hadn't much noticed the passage of hours or light, but over the years in the marines he'd become alert to its every shift and change. Just as he'd become highly attuned to changes in the wind, the barometric pressure, the movement of clouds, the whisper of even slight breezes. Acutely attuned to sounds, constantly cataloging them as natural or not.

He figured it would be a while before he settled into comfortably walking streets without being on guard.

But even as he noted the late-afternoon changes in the light and the town around him, his thoughts kept trailing back to Kylie Brewer. He'd seen that look in other eyes, that look of a terror that wouldn't quite go away no matter how safe the situation. He'd seen that terror break grown men when it wouldn't quit.

He hoped it wouldn't break Kylie. Hell, she couldn't even remember what had put it there, but that fear had evidently been stamped on her soul at a level so deep no memory was needed.

He hoped Glenda understood that. But how could she? She'd probably never dealt with anything like this.

But he had. A sigh escaped him as he pulled up in front of the diner. He would only be here a few weeks, but he felt an unexpected need to try to help Kylie in some way.

Fear like that wouldn't just wash away. Sometimes it took years to drain. But maybe he could help it on its way.

Then he wondered if he was going to spend his time off by setting himself a new mission. It wouldn't surprise him. He could have laughed at himself.

Glenda used the time to get Kylie settled into her old bedroom. She noted the way Kylie moved around, touching things, items that Glenda had taken care to put exactly where they had been before Kylie had moved out, including her pile of stuffed animals. The doc said she needed familiarity, so Glenda had ensured it was there.

She was relieved to see her sister's face relaxing as she caressed various items. "I can't believe it's still the same."

"No reason to change it," Glenda half lied. "Your house, too."

Kylie sat on the edge of the bed. "I don't remember," she said finally. "I barely remember Brad, except what you told me about him, and your divorce..."

"Was about as ugly as they come," Glenda answered frankly. She sat in the Boston rocker facing the bed. "I wish I could forget it."

"But why so ugly?"

"Brad." Glenda shrugged. "Apparently it wasn't enough to leave me—Brad wanted to gut me, too."

"Did he succeed?"

"Maybe a little. Anyway, he's gone."

She watched Kylie look down and run her fingers over the quilt that their grandmother had made. Then Kylie spoke. "You interested in Coop?"

Glenda blinked, then laughed almost helplessly. "Hell, no. He's nice and everything, but Brad kind of killed my interest in the whole idea of happily-ever-after."

Kylie sighed and returned her gaze to her sister. "That seems so wrong."

"I'll get over it. Once the stitches come out of the scars."

That elicited a small, welcome laugh from Kylie. "Still? What an image."

"Well, I'm a nurse, and that's how I feel sometimes. I'm glad you weren't around for it. I'd probably have soured you on half the human race."

"You were angry?"

Glenda had to remind herself that Kylie wouldn't remember any of this. Not a thing. All those furious phone calls, nasty texts, the bellyaching...all of it erased for Kylie except for the brief updates Glenda had given her while she packed Kylie for this move. And there didn't seem to be any point in filling in more of the blanks. Some things were better forgotten.

"I was very angry," she said finally. "Still am sometimes. But it doesn't matter. What was it Grandma used to say? Good riddance to bad cess?"

Another sound of amusement escaped Kylie. "I'd almost forgotten she said that."

"Well, I've had a million reasons to remember it thanks to Brad. At least he had the decency to move to San Francisco. Although I guess that means I'll never visit the place now."

Kylie tilted her head, smiling faintly. "It's a big city. You'd probably never run into him."

"Just my luck that I would." But Glenda noted that despite her smile, a shadow moved over Kylie's face. Probably thinking about visiting strange cities didn't feel good right now.

While she spent a lot of time with Kylie being upbeat and cheerful, she was concealing a whole lot of concern for her sister. The amnesia was a worry because it resulted partly from brain damage. And while the neurologists had felt that the brain would reconstruct a great many connections with time, there could be repercussions that nobody had discovered yet. And then there was the whole big future facing her, with the loss of her dreams and no apparent desire to start them over again.

Aw, hell, Glenda thought. Too bad life didn't provide magic wands. Somehow she didn't think this journey of recovery was going to be easy for Kylie. Not one little bit.

It wasn't as if Kylie could even go back to work as an RN. Not yet. Not until they could be sure what she'd forgotten and what she hadn't, and whether there were other as yet undetected problems.

But that could wait. In the meantime, Glenda decided,

her sister needed some kind of equilibrium, and she hoped she could provide it here.

Then they could worry about everything else.

Chapter 2

After Glenda left for work, Kylie sat in the living room and found herself wishing Coop was there, stranger though he was. She hadn't been alone for more than a minute or two since her attack. Either in the hospital, or later when Glenda had brought her back to her apartment to pack, the only solitary time she had experienced had been in the bathroom or when her sister went out to grab food.

She wasn't enjoying it. As the evening shadows lengthened and day faded into night, her skin began to crawl. She knew she was safe here, in her own home, miles away from the attacker who had nearly killed her, but some part of her seemed unable to believe it yet.

Time, she reminded herself. Time would help her get past the unreasoning fear. There was no reason whatsoever to believe that her attacker would even look for her again. None. The cops had told her that. It wasn't as if she could identify the man who did this, and they'd made sure word had gotten out through the press that she had amnesia. To protect her. She should feel grateful for that, but instead she felt as if her failings had been announced to the world. *See Kylie Brewer, the woman with amnesia.* God.

The knock on the front door shocked her, and a spear of terror ripped through her. For long moments she couldn't even move as her heart raced and her mouth turned dry.

"Don't be ridiculous," she said aloud in a muffled voice, her tongue practically sticking to the roof of her dried mouth. "You're home. No one outside this town knows where you are. It's just a neighbor."

The knock came again. She had to answer it. Someone might be looking for Glenda. It could be important. Or maybe it was Coop, locked out. She had no idea whether Glenda had given him a key.

On stiff legs that didn't want to move easily, she rose and walked toward the front door. Her feet felt leaden. Shaking, she finally turned the latch on the dead bolt and opened the door.

A familiar, smiling face greeted her. Todd Jamison, a man she had known most of her life, one she had dated in high school. Surprise replaced shock and she gaped at him. "Todd?"

His smile was warm. He was still a handsome man, with light brown hair and dark brown eyes. He wore a white dress shirt with his jeans. "Hey, Kylie. I heard you were back and I wanted to see with my own eyes that you're okay. Is that all right?"

Knowing him eased her fears. Not that she felt entirely comfortable—in fact, she felt edgy—but she couldn't blame him for that. Nor could she slam the door in his face when he'd been kind enough to come by and check on her.

"I'm tired," she admitted honestly, "but a few minutes is okay."

So she let him inside, reminding herself of all the years Todd had been part of her life, whether as a classmate or briefly as someone she had dated. Somehow, however, when she closed the door behind him, the ants began to crawl along her nerves again. God, she had to stop feeling as if threats hovered in every moment of the day. She'd never be able to do anything with her life if she became a hermit terrified of other human beings.

She didn't offer him coffee or tea because she hoped he wouldn't stay long, and she tried to remind herself that she'd just been wishing she weren't alone. Now she wasn't alone.

"I read the papers," he said as he perched on the edge of the couch. "Maybe it's dumb to mention it, but I just want you to know how happy I am that you're okay. Except...you can't remember? That's a good thing, right?"

She'd already heard that more times than she wanted to count. Not being able to remember the attack was a blessing. Losing three years of her life fell into an entirely different category. She cleared her throat, not wanting to delve into this. "I'm glad I don't remember the attack." *Leave it alone, Todd. Please leave it alone.*

"I'm sure you are." He frowned faintly. "I'm sorry, I just don't know what people are supposed to say. Never did this before."

"Me, either."

Then his smile returned, the smile that had once, all too briefly, attracted her. "I guess we're all going to be ham-handed for a while. So are you glad to be home? Or is life around here too boring now?"

"How would I know?"

Kylie looked down, realizing she had just rudely ended the conversation. Worse, she didn't even feel like apologizing for it. What was wrong with her?

But before she could figure out how to ease her blunt question, she heard the side door in the kitchen open. Fear slammed her yet again.

Feeling like an extra wheel, Coop had left the ladies to eat their dinner, saying he needed a stroll before dining himself. Walking the streets of Conard City was slowly becoming a pleasure for him. No need to wonder what was around every corner or behind every building. Just nice people, when he ran into them, who smiled and gave him a friendly nod. A lot of them seemed to know he was Connie's cousin, which he suspected eased his way. At least he didn't get regarded with suspicion.

He toyed with the idea of moving to the motel, to give Kylie space, then cast it aside. Glenda had generously offered him a place to stay while he visited, and he didn't want to offend her in some way.

As for his cousin and her brood...every time he thought of those three high-energy kids—two of their own and a daughter who was older, from Connie's previous marriage—he had to grin. They were a handful of boundless energy, especially the two youngest. Connie and Ethan both worked, and by the time the evening was drawing to a close, whichever of them was around for the bedtime chores had started to look exhausted.

He tried to help, but Ethan was right: his presence seemed to excite the youngsters more. He hoped that would pass as they got used to having him around or Connie was apt to beg him never to visit again.

He suddenly realized that light had almost faded from the day and he switched course to head back to the house. Glenda would be at work, and Kylie would be alone. While he wasn't sure Kylie really wanted him around, Glenda had mentioned that *she'd* feel better if Kylie weren't left in solitude, at least for a while.

Coop understood. Regardless of her inability to remember, Kylie had lost her basic sense of safety. The unimaginable had happened to her. Being alone, even in a familiar house, might be difficult for a while.

So he'd play it by ear. If she wanted him to disappear, he'd go up to his room. She'd still know someone was in the house if something frightened her.

Glenda's car was gone when he got back to the house, but a different one was parked out front. An old friend? Nevertheless, he sped up his pace, just in case Kylie was nervous.

When he got to the house, he let himself in the side door and heard voices coming from the living room. A man's voice. Kylie's rarer and quieter. He made no secret of his approach. A big man, he could be stealthy or noisy as the situation demanded. Right now he chose noisy.

Two lamps had been turned on in the living room. Kylie sat nearly huddled in an armchair, facing a handsome man of about her age, maybe late twenties, who sat on the couch with legs splayed and his elbows resting on his knees. Leaning toward her. In an instant Coop gathered that Kylie was subtly leaning away as best she could. Body language spoke volumes.

"Am I interrupting?" Coop asked.

"No...no..." Kylie said tautly. "Come in."

The man on the couch stood immediately, smiling

broadly. "Todd Jamison. Kylie and I grew up together. Just thought I'd see how she was doing."

Todd offered his hand and Coop returned the smile as he shook it. "Evan Cooper, just call me Coop." But even as he made the pleasant greeting, he was also ticking off a catalog. The guy was a little over average height, fit and looking like he could have stepped off the cover of *GQ*, rancher's edition. Jeans, a white shirt, all neatly pressed, and boots that had been highly polished. Brown hair artfully tousled. A fashion plate.

But then Coop met his dark gaze, and felt the back of his neck prickle. He'd seen eyes like that before, the emptiness of men who'd seen too much on a battlefield. "You military?" he asked casually.

"Never had the honor," Todd answered easily. "No, I'm a financial adviser. I work from home here but have to travel a lot. I just got back in town and wanted to check on Kylie."

"I'm fine," Kylie said, the slightest edge in her voice.

It struck Coop as a dismissal, but not Todd apparently. Instincts were kicking in, and although Coop already had the lay of the land, he scanned the room quickly again. Cabbage-rose couch from a past era, the armchair in which Kylie sat, reasonably new, a recliner that was old enough it creaked when it was extended, a glass-fronted bookcase, a flat-screen TV...nothing out of place. He was probably overreacting, which wouldn't surprise him given the last few years of his life, but then his gaze settled on Kylie again, the way she seemed to have shrunk. Todd might be an old friend, but she wasn't welcoming him with much warmth.

Wondering if he should try to do something about what was clearly an uncomfortable situation for Kylie, his thoughts were interrupted by the ringing of the front doorbell. He looked at Kylie. "Want me to get it?"

"Why not?" She didn't exactly sound happy about it.

Shrugging inwardly, he went to open the door, wondering if maybe all Kylie had wanted tonight was to be by herself. Maybe Glenda worried too much about her being alone.

He opened the door and a strawberry blonde breezed through. Two steps in, she froze and scanned him head to foot. "My, my," she said, "you must be Coop. I'm Ashley. Ashley Granger. Kylie knows me from way back."

Before Coop could do anything but close the door behind her, Ashley had stepped into the living room, and he was relieved to hear genuine pleasure in Kylie's voice as she said, "Ashley!"

"It's been too long, girl," Ashley answered.

A moment later he rounded the door frame to see the women hugging. Todd stood to one side, smiling faintly.

A regular convocation. Suddenly feeling like an intruder, Coop decided to go make some coffee. It'd give these three old friends some time together.

But just as he was turning away, he heard Ashley address Todd, and her tone caused him to hesitate.

"I'm surprised to see you, Todd. You avoided Kylie for a long time after she turned you down for the prom."

Todd laughed easily. "Sheesh, Ashley, that was a long time in the past. I got over it ages ago. Of course I wanted to make sure Kylie is okay."

"Me, too," said Ashley, then turned back to Kylie. "So I want to know everything."

Kylie blinked, her face tightening, then sank into her chair again. "Everything? I don't remember *anything*!"

Ashley dropped to a knee beside her and took her hand. "I don't mean about that, Kylie. You know that."

Her voice had gentled. "I mean about now—how you're feeling, are you glad to be home? That's okay, right?"

Coop had to resist the urge to throw everyone out right now. Not his decision, not his house. But he didn't like the way Kylie was looking. And these were her friends?

But Ashley remained gentle and concerned and Kylie began to relax a bit. Todd on the other hand seemed to get a different message.

"I'll be going," he said. "Call me if you need anything at all, Kylie. I'll see you again soon. You just take care of yourself."

One problem solved, Coop thought as Todd let himself out. Then he looked at the women. "I guess I should make myself scarce."

Kylie shook her head and Ashley looked directly at him. "I don't mind you being here. It's up to Kylie."

"Stay," Kylie said, sounding stronger. "I was just shocked to see Todd. We haven't had much to do with each other since high school. I mean, we've been casual friends, but he's not the first person I would have expected to show up."

"Curiosity visit," Ashley said sharply. "You'll probably get a lot of those. But not me," she added with a smile. "I promise. I just want to know how you are *now*, and Marisa, Connie and Julie designated me." She looked up at Coop. "We've been a gang forever. And would you please sit?"

"You could take a seat yourself," he answered humorously, but accepted the hint, settling onto one end of the couch. Towering over the women probably wasn't very comforting to either of them. "Oh, I wondered about coffee. Anyone?"

"No thanks," came two prompt responses. Ashley sat on the other end of the couch. "So everyone wants to know how you're feeling. Still worn out by everything? Getting your energy back? Julie wanted to have a Scrabble night but decided we ought to find out if you were up to it yet."

"Not yet. Thanks. These big waves of fatigue just wash over me from time to time."

And waves of fear, Coop suspected. Then he took the bull by the horns. It had to be hard for Kylie to dance around things, and she already looked tired. "It's a lot to deal with, not remembering the last few years, recovering physically, moving home with your sister. It'd wear anyone out, I'd think."

Kylie surprised him with a crooked smile. "But aren't you always on the go?"

"Well, yes," he admitted. "But I've had years to get used to it. You're probably used to being more settled."

"I was. Once. I don't know about recently."

The stark honesty drew silence from both Coop and Ashley. They exchanged a quick look, then Coop rose. "I want that coffee. I'll be back in a few."

The least he could do was give Kylie the time to talk freely with Ashley. If she could. No question that he was the odd man out, and acutely aware of it. He listened to the murmur of their voices from the kitchen and nodded to himself. Give the ladies some time alone. It might do Kylie a world of good.

"He's a hunk," Ashley remarked after Coop walked away.

"I guess." Which was kind of an evasive comment, Kylie thought as she heard herself. She *had* noticed he was a hunk. She just wasn't interested in hunks or much else right now except the constant wondering about all she'd forgotten. The memory loss left her feeling unsettled. Uneasy. Unable to really trust herself, never mind anyone else.

"So what's the hardest part and what can I do?" Ashley asked. "Anything?"

Kylie rose at last and walked slowly around the living room, touching familiar items as if they could connect her to the past that had a great gaping hole in it. Her ribs still ached, and she felt scars on her body stretch a complaint, but it wasn't that bad anymore. "I honestly don't know, Ashley. All I know is that it's scary to have forgotten so much. I didn't even recognize my own apartment, or most of what was in it."

"That would be…eerie. Weird."

"It is. I mean, I could tell I lived there, the signs were everywhere, but I couldn't remember it. The only things I recognized were things I had before I moved to Denver."

"Creepy," Ashley said. "My God, that's got to be a scary feeling, Kylie. I can't imagine it."

"Don't even try. It's hard enough to explain." Weariness washed over her again. It had been a long day. She returned to her chair and tried to smile. "Some of it may come back. In fact, they seem sure that some of it will. The thing is, it probably won't be enough to make up for those semesters in school that I can't remember now. I don't know if I even want to try again."

Ashley nodded sympathetically. "The nice thing is you don't have to decide now. Glenda is thrilled to have you back. In fact, I think she's thrilled to have someone in the house who isn't Brad. Do you remember him?"

"Yeah. Sort of."

Just then heavy steps alerted them and Coop appeared carrying a coffeepot and three mugs. "Want to join me?"

Kylie felt Ashley look at her. Apparently it was to be her decision. A moment of amusement passed through her. Glenda swore she wasn't interested in Coop. Now she wondered if Ashley was. "Love to," she answered. Regardless of how she might be feeling, she could see no point in interfering with Ashley's romantic interest.

Coop poured and passed the coffee around and set the pot on a coaster. "If I'm a fifth wheel, tell me."

Kylie shook her head. "You're fine. We were talking about my amnesia. We might as well talk about it. It's kind of lying there in the middle of everything."

Coop sat on the other end of the couch. "So…how much did you lose?"

"About three years for sure," she said honestly. "All my time in Denver, all my schooling and training there… it's a big blank. I don't even remember people who were apparently my friends. The thing that also worries me is I don't know if I have other blanks from earlier in my life."

He lifted one corner of his mouth. "I think we all have *those* blanks."

"That's what Glenda said." But she felt a burst of resentment. Having amnesia wasn't something to be minimized. Not being able to trust your own memory at all wasn't something to be brushed aside. But railing about it would only make these people feel bad, and all they were trying to do was make her feel better. God, this whole thing had turned her into some kind of mess.

Apparently Coop was better at understanding people than she would have expected from a marine. He spoke quietly. "I'm not trying to be dismissive, Kylie. Not at all."

"No," she agreed, the irritation remaining with her. "Everyone's trying to be reassuring. And, yeah, I get that most of us don't have the best memories, and that we all forget things, but it's different when you lose three whole years!"

She heard her own voice rise with vehemence and didn't care. Let them deal with it. It stank. All of it stank. Being attacked and nearly killed would have been bad enough all on its own, but losing a big chunk of her life? Losing all that work toward her master's degree?

It was as if some part of her brain had simply shut down the sections labeled "Denver" and "Grad School." She hoped she never remembered the attack. If that was all she had forgotten, she'd gladly live with it. But she had lost a whole lot more, and now she had to wonder what other things were lost that shouldn't have been. Sure, everyone had holes in their memories, but usually they forgot unimportant things. She couldn't be sure she hadn't lost the important ones.

Then shame pierced her. "I'm sorry. You're both trying to be so nice."

"Well, maybe," Ashley said, "us being nice isn't what you need. Do you want me and the girls to stay away for a while, give you a chance to settle? Because honestly, Kylie, I've never dealt with anyone with amnesia before. You're going to have to tell me what you want and what you don't want."

"That's just it. I don't think I know." Kylie dropped her head against the back of the chair and closed her eyes. "It's weird, Ashley. I keep feeling like I'm meeting myself for the first time and I don't know who I am anymore. I remember who I used to be. But who am I now?"

Coop spoke slowly. "I realize I'm a stranger here and should probably just keep my mouth shut…"

Kylie opened her eyes and looked at him. "Just say it." At this point she had no idea who might hold a key that would unlock the tension inside her and just allow her to move on. Because moving on was her only choice, and she really couldn't understand why she was resisting it, fighting it, as if nothing mattered but remembering.

"There are a lot of ways life can give us that feeling," he said quietly. "I've had it a few times myself. An experience that completely changes you. Now admittedly, I knew exactly what I'd been through that caused it, but I *do* understand the feeling. It'll pass, Kylie. Whether you regain your memory or not, eventually you accept that who you are now is all you are now."

"Wise words," she said quietly.

He shook his head a little. "I'm no sage. I'm just trying to tell you that what you're feeling is a natural response to a huge change."

She propped her chin in her hand and closed her eyes, thinking about it. He was right. But so was she. Life had stolen something priceless from her, and she didn't think she was going to be happy about that anytime soon. But wondering who she was? Maybe that was a pointless exercise.

Ashley spoke. "You're looking tired, Kylie. I'll leave now and let the girls know you're okay. Or Coop can tell Connie."

"You go ahead," Coop said. "I've been temporarily banished for the crime of overstimulating kids."

Ashley laughed. "The two young ones wind up faster than a top. How long is your banishment?"

"Only until tomorrow morning. Then I'll be in demand again."

Kylie watched Ashley rise and head for the door, Coop right behind her, playing the host. Or maybe he was interested in her, too. Ashley was beautiful, all right, with that strawberry blonde hair, a color no one would ever get out of a bottle. Next to her, Kylie felt plain, not that she'd ever minded before.

But then Ashley was gone and it was just her and Coop. She hadn't touched the coffee he'd poured, but he grabbed the mugs and carried them to the kitchen, and when he returned with them, he poured more for both of them.

"You want me to be scarce?" he asked. "I do know how."

She looked at him and envied him. "Right now I wish I were in your skin."

A surprised sound escaped him. "What?"

"You look so comfortable with yourself. Like earlier, when Ashley was here, you just sat there looking like you belong right here."

He hesitated, then sat, legs splayed, elbows resting on his jeans. "I'm not sure I'm following."

"I don't feel like I belong anywhere anymore," she admitted, feeling as if her heart were tearing. "I don't know why. I practically grew up in this house, but I don't feel like I belong here, either. And...I'm scared all the time!"

There, she'd admitted it and she wasn't happy with her own outburst. She felt weak, silly, maybe a little crazy. The only Kylie she remembered was the one from years ago, before life had stolen so much from her. That Kylie hadn't lived in fear. That Kylie had been happy being Kylie and had felt comfortable in this house, in this town...

"God," she whispered, "what did that man do to me?"

Chapter 3

Coop didn't know how to respond. All the appropriate words sprang to mind about traumas, major life changes, all of it, but speaking them wasn't going to fix a damn thing for Kylie, and she'd probably heard it all already from the medical people. He understood what she was trying to say—he could even identify with some of it— but he had no handy-dandy answers to offer.

Finally, carefully, he said, "I'm not as comfortable as I look."

That brought her head up, and her reddening eyes fixed on him. "You look like you own your space."

"That's easy to do when you're a big guy and a marine. But it's all on the surface."

She started to shake her head, and he could tell she didn't believe him.

"Look," he said. "I'm living in your sister's house for a few weeks. Nice offer and all that, and I wouldn't want to offend her or cause my cousin to feel bad, but frankly I'd be a whole lot more comfortable in that motel no one wants me to stay at. Instead I'm a guest in a stranger's house."

The disbelief began to fade, and interest leavened her face a bit. "That makes sense to me."

"It probably does. I'm just sorry you're feeling that way in a house you grew up in. That's wrong. Anyway, what did that guy do to you? He stole from you, and he stole things that no one should ever have to lose, but unfortunately people get robbed of them all the time. You might be fairly unique with your memory loss, but lots of people lose their sense of safety. I don't know what he did to you physically, but I can see the emotional results and, while they're normal, they stink. And they're something you're just going to have to ride out."

He wished he had more to offer, but all he could give her was honesty. Call it what she might, Kylie had some grieving to do, and grief was never an easy road. More like a roller coaster—it would come in waves and just when you thought maybe you were on top of it, it would slam you once again.

Then he decided to change the subject. It was all he could think of that wouldn't make her brood more about her situation. "So this Todd who came earlier. Old friend?"

Kylie shrugged. "We went to school together. We dated a few times but…" She sighed. "What can you say about dating someone in high school? Relationships change fast. I think he was mad at me for not going to the prom with him, but by then we hadn't dated in months. I was surprised he even asked."

"You liked him?"

"Sort of." He was relieved to see her expression

lighten a bit, and hear a small laugh escape her. "We were kids, Coop. He's good-looking, and that got my attention, but when it came to the actual dating part... We just didn't hit it off. It was a relief to move on. I enjoyed time with my girlfriends more."

He nodded. "Well, it was nice of him to stop by."

"I suppose. Ashley might have been right about curiosity, though. I wonder if I'm going to get a lot of that. Maybe I should charge admission. Come see the woman who lost her memory."

Then she really did laugh, and a prickle of unease ran through him. Her mood seemed to be swinging fast. But instead of worrying him further, she simply leaned back, smiling. "Well, I can still remember high school, including giving Todd his letter sweater back."

"You only had a couple of dates but he gave you his letter?"

"I know. We moved fast back then, didn't we?"

Coop didn't remember it that way, but after a moment's thought he could remember a few couples who had. For his own part he'd never dated much until after he'd left home and joined the corps. Even then his job and tastes had limited him.

"Anyway, he did seem mad at me for a few months after I refused to go to the prom with him, but it blew over. It was hardly the end of the world, after all, and he went with another girl, so he didn't miss out on anything."

"And you?"

"I skipped it." She shrugged. "It wasn't just Todd I didn't want to go with. I didn't want to go at all."

"Well," he said, feigning surprise, "now I'm shocked. I thought every girl wanted to go to the prom."

"I didn't. It all seemed so plastic. A rite of passage

left over from another era. For some it may have been a high point, but for me I was already focused on starting my nursing classes, and that seemed like a much bigger deal. It wasn't like I was going to settle down with one of the guys from high school…although quite a few girls did. But that wasn't me."

He smiled. "Memory check good."

At that a small laugh escaped her. "I guess so." Then she swiftly changed subject. "So what did you do in Germany?"

"I was on leave. I had some extra time built up and decided to see a part of the world where bombs weren't flying. And since there was a military transport flight headed that way and they offered me a bucket seat, I went."

He almost ached at the way she seemed so eager to think about something that had nothing to do with her situation. While he was used to feeling sympathy for people—it came naturally to him—he wasn't used to feeling something deeper and stronger, but Kylie seemed to be pulling that out of him. Dangerous. He was supposed to be taking some R and R, not giving himself a new mission. Or creating new problems for anyone, himself or Kylie.

"Anyway," he said, deciding his boring little travelogue would at least distract her, "I was only there a few days but I got to see a couple of castles. I fell in love with their bratwurst and German cooking in general, and they have the most wonderful public transportation system."

"Really?"

He didn't know if she was feigning interest, but he plunged on, anyway. "Trams in town, trains to almost every place you could want to go. I got chills touching old Roman walls."

She perked up. "Chills? Really?"

"Think about it. I touched stones that had been cut and laid by Roman soldiers nearly two thousand years ago. It was like I could feel this connection to those long-ago workers. Of course, I had the same reaction to a few places when I was in Iraq. Call me crazy, if you want, but it was like stretching across the millennia and reaching out to people long gone who had left a real mark of their passing."

Her gaze grew almost dreamy. "I don't think that's crazy. I like it. Maybe you should be an archaeologist."

He shook his head a little. "I may be past making such a major life change. But that doesn't mean I can't appreciate it. Maybe it meant more to me because my job doesn't involve building much."

He liked the way she was brightening as she listened, and he sought other stories to tell her that might please her. Unfortunately, the kinds of jobs he'd had to do were best told only to other combat vets. And maybe he had enjoyed those ruins more because his job involved a lot of demolition and destruction. On the other hand…

He spoke quietly, almost forgetting her for a moment. "Roman soldiers had to be builders, too. They built their own forts, their own barracks. Eventually they helped build towns. The modern military doesn't require that of most of us."

"Do you think it should?"

He stirred and finally drank some of his cooling coffee. "I guess that depends on what you're trying to accomplish. The Romans were making their forts a permanent presence—establishing outposts for an empire. That's not our goal."

"Maybe not," she answered tentatively.

He summoned a smile and tried to leave reflection

behind. Now that he was evidently home for good, he'd have more than enough time to sort through his own baggage. Right now all he was concerned about was making one woman feel comfortable with him. "Anyway, I hope to go back to Germany for a longer visit. And if I do, this time I'm damn well going to see Paris, too."

That elicited a chuckle from her. "I guess you missed all the good stuff in your travels."

"Yeah, it was very mission oriented. Go here, do that. Not a whole lot of time for sightseeing."

"And probably not safe, either."

"Rarely." He tried to study her without staring, wondering if she was trying to bring up the subject of her own fears.

Then she answered his unspoken question. "How do you live with being afraid all the time?"

Ah, crud. He stared at her openly now, thinking that she was truly lovely and life had dealt her a hellacious hand, and seeking some kind of answer that wasn't trite.

"Do you ever get over it?" she asked.

Another good question. "Some people do," he answered finally. And others got sucked dry by it, depending on the intensity and persistence, but he wasn't going to tell her that.

"It must be different for you," she argued. "You must have gone into a lot of scary situations."

"You mean I had practice at it?"

She bit her lip. "I guess that came out wrong. I just know I've never felt this way before, and I can't shake free of it. Which is really strange, because I can't remember what happened, and it's obviously over and I'm mostly fine. How can I be scared of what I can't remember?"

He hesitated again. This woman was making him

very hesitant, and he wasn't used to that. He felt like he needed to tiptoe, to be very careful he didn't say the wrong thing. He was no professional, and he had no idea how psychologically vulnerable she might be. The last thing he wanted to do was add to her problems.

"We don't just remember with our brains," he said after a moment. "Our entire bodies remember some things."

That caused her to draw a sharp breath. "I didn't think of that."

"And fear can be a good thing."

"It's awful," she said bluntly.

"But if there's a reason for it, it's useful. So you never want to lose your ability to feel it. It can be directed, it can be protective. Or…it can overwhelm you."

"So how do *you* deal with it?"

"Like a warning system."

"But I have nothing to be afraid of!"

At that moment he would have liked to gather her into his arms and hold her, as if he could soothe her. As if. But a hug wasn't going to take care of the invisible demons stalking Kylie. Certainly part of the problem was that they were invisible. If she could see them, name them, face them…he suspected her fear would find direction and maybe even ease somewhat.

"You don't *know* that you don't have anything to be afraid of," he pointed out. She might be trying to believe it, but she didn't actually know it. Whole different thing.

She nodded slowly. "You're right. That man is still out there. I can't remember him. What if he wants to finish what he started? What if he walked up to me right now? I wouldn't even know it!"

That was the crux of her problem, at least in part, and

for this there was nothing he could say or do. "That's rough," was all he offered when she remained silent.

"And maybe a bit crazy, too. I'm home in a safe place. And I'm willing to bet Glenda asked you to keep an eye on me. You don't have to, you know. I'm not going to do anything crazy."

"I never thought you would. Would you rather be alone?"

Her face froze, paling a bit. "No," she whispered. "Coop, I don't want to be alone."

Kylie hadn't been alone for more than short periods since she emerged from a medically induced coma in the hospital nearly two weeks after the attack, once her brain had stopped swelling. Not really. Even in the middle of the night when her room had been darkened and the door closed, she could still hear the voices in the hallway outside, the voices of medical staff moving around. A hospital was never completely silent, and solitude was the illusion of a door.

Then Glenda had been there almost every minute. After the hospital, Glenda had taken her back to her apartment to help her pack, and at most she'd been alone for twenty or thirty minutes when her sister ran out to get more boxes or something for them to eat. Those minutes had seemed endless, her nerves crawling every single second, impatience for Glenda's return driving her nearly nuts. How many times had she come close to hiding in a closet during those interludes?

The memory of that could shame her, but the feelings had been overwhelming. Were still overwhelming. The idea of coming home had looked like the answer to everything. Apparently not.

She sat in the house she had spent a lot of her

childhood in and she still felt the crawling fear, still felt that if she just looked over her shoulder she'd see…what? Something. Something bad. God, she must be crazy.

Coop stirred finally and came to sit cross-legged on the floor at her feet. "I won't leave you alone," he said. He held out a hand, palm up. Asking, not demanding. Apparently aware that he was a stranger and she might fear a man's touch.

That careful, gentle invitation called to her, however, and she reached out, laying her hand in his. He squeezed gently, but in no way made her feel trapped. She could slip her hand away as easily as she had given it.

"You can't promise me that," she said finally.

"Not every minute of the day, obviously. I need to visit Connie and her kids. But I can do that when your sister is home, which is most of the day usually. And tonight, for sure, I can be right here in this house."

She started to feel small. "I'm sorry. I don't have the right to ask that of you. You came here to see family, not to babysit me."

"Who said I'd be babysitting? You're an attractive, interesting woman. I won't mind at all." He smiled, but only with his blue eyes. They crinkled at the corners, and his expression was warm.

For a few seconds, Kylie didn't answer. In those moments she was suddenly a girl she'd almost forgotten, one who had once thought it would be wonderful to share her life with a man, a man like this one who could be powerful and gentle at the same time. She had the worst urge to climb off the chair and curl up in his lap. To let him take care of her. Almost at once she rebelled. What the hell was she thinking? The Kylie she had been before the amnesia had been strong, capable of taking care of herself. She couldn't let this weaken her like this.

She spoke, dragging her thoughts back to reality. "I don't know what could be interesting about me. All I've done is whine."

"I hadn't noticed. Look, you're dealing with a tough problem. Talk about it as much as you want."

"Do you talk about your problems?" She watched him start.

"My problems?"

"You've been in combat, haven't you? Surely you've got some wounds from that."

He looked down, but didn't release her hand. "I don't talk about that much, for obvious reasons."

"But you've learned to live with it?"

He glanced at her, his expression almost rueful. "I'm still learning. I'm good at hiding it."

She sighed, feeling the warmth of his hand. This wasn't wise, not in her current state. She was letting a man get too close—worse, a stranger. What was she thinking? Had she become that desperate for comfort? The only comfort she was going to find evidently had to come from within herself. "Maybe I should hide it, too."

"Why? I talk with other people about my experiences. I've just found it's wiser to reserve them for other combat vets. We're all on the same page. Unfortunately, I don't know who else would be on the same page with you."

Except him, she thought. He probably came closest. He'd undoubtedly been under attack. Maybe even wounded. He might understand better than anyone.

"I don't like being scared," she said quietly. "Especially of something that's over. I don't like the fact that my whole career plan blew up. If I had to forget something, the attack would have been quite enough, without forgetting all the time I put into school. But that's where I am, and I'm already sick of feeling sorry for myself. I need to move on."

"Of course. But you're scared. So…it'll take a little time. You'll grow comfortable again. Promise."

Then he smiled and astonished her by leaning forward to drop a quick light kiss on her hand. Then he rose and stretched. "I want more coffee. You?"

She hadn't even touched hers and it had grown cold, but it sounded good now. "Thank you."

Then she was alone again, although not entirely. She could hear him in the kitchen, but it was as if her internal vision was shattered somehow. She could look around the room and recognize every single item except the new TV. Her grandparents' living room, hardly changed over the years except for the chair she sat on. It should have felt like home. Except something was preventing her from feeling that. In its silent emptiness it had become part of the threat that stalked her. An unresolved threat. The man who had tried to kill her was still out there, and from things she suspected she hadn't been intended to hear, they thought she'd been attacked by a serial killer. Someone who had done this before and would do it again.

So how could home even feel safe?

Coop stood in the kitchen making a fresh pot of coffee. The last one had mostly gone down the sink drain. He liked his coffee, but he didn't like wasting it. Like when he was in the field, and he'd be lucky to get an opportunity to make one lousy, warm cup of instant coffee. Precious coffee.

Thinking of Kylie was opening a can of worms inside him, too. He couldn't imagine how alone she must be feeling. She was walking a path that no one else could walk with her. Everyone was trying to make her feel better and take care of her, but that wasn't enough. She needed to face that demon, or at least talk to someone who understood it.

As he waited for the coffee to finish, he wondered if he should open his own can of worms for her benefit. Just a little. To show her that someone really *could* understand. Holding things inside rarely did much good, which was why he'd been taking full advantage of various veterans groups where folks could get together and share those stories that couldn't be heard by other ears. That *shouldn't* be heard.

But Kylie wasn't going to find a support group for the surviving victims of a serial killer, or any kind of killer, around here. And he doubted there was a whole lot of support anywhere for the victims of amnesia.

Which left him, he guessed. Maybe he could find one story to share with her that would let her know he understood what it was like to live with crawling fear even when you were safe. Yeah, he was getting better at it, but that didn't mean he was fully past it.

He returned to the living room with two mugs, saying, "I guess I should have asked if you want tea. That seems to be Glenda's poison."

She gave him a wan smile. "I like coffee, too. Thanks."

"It's the staff of life for me." Then he volunteered a bit to see what kind of reaction he got. "When I was in the field, we had packets of instant coffee. I was lucky if I could warm it up a little. These days I'll take a real cup of coffee any time I can get it."

"I'd imagine so." Her eyes followed him as he returned to the couch. He could feel her gaze, an instinct as deep in the human race as it was in any prey animal, but honed in his case by experience. When he sat facing her again, he got socked once more by how pretty she was. But it wasn't just that she was pretty. His body had chosen a very inopportune time to react to a woman. This one was in no condition for *that*.

But how to reach her? He scoured his memory for a way to relate his experience to hers. Maybe generalities, he decided. "I have some idea what you're going through, Kylie. When I was in a dangerous area, the only way I could tell friend from foe was by a uniform. People who seemed nice and welcoming could turn into killers in an instant. Not always, but often enough that I stopped trusting."

She nodded, and he thought she was looking almost hungry for what he might say, as if it would help her to feel better in some way. "So, yeah," he said after a moment. "I know what it's like to be wondering what's around the next corner, what's right behind you, where the threat might be."

"And now?" she asked.

She wanted more hope than he knew how to offer. "It's getting better," he answered truthfully. "It still sometimes hits me hard, but it's getting easier."

She bit her lip, then asked, "So you feel it even at home?"

"Of course. Those feelings don't let go easily." And sometimes they never let go, but he didn't add that. The repeated experiences of war were different from a single attack, and if anyone had a decent chance of getting past this, she did. He didn't want to discourage her in any way.

"But I'm not crazy?"

Shock rippled through him. "Hell, no. Who made you think that?"

"Me," she admitted. "I can't remember any of it. But

I'm sitting here in a house I know every nook of from my childhood and it's like… I can't explain it. It's like the coziness went away."

He waited a moment, seeking words that might help without making her more uncomfortable. "When I come home," he said presently, "I can't tolerate narrow streets. In fact, I sometimes have trouble driving."

Her gaze grew intent. "Why?"

"Experience. A narrow street is the perfect setup for an ambush, with no place to run. And driving…well, at times when I drive I see oncoming traffic as a potential threat. It's like I'm dealing with what's really there, and what I used to have to fear."

"But you get past it?" she asked eagerly.

"Eventually. It eases. I get occasional flashes, but just flashes. It doesn't consume me anymore."

She nodded, absorbing what he'd said. He didn't tell her how hard-won that emotional equilibrium was, or that he could still, though rarely, have a really bad flash. She had only one experience to deal with. There was no reason to believe she wouldn't eventually get almost completely past this.

"But," he added, "sometimes it's like living in two worlds, where for a few moments here and there I'm not sure where I am. So if I do something weird, you'll know why. I haven't been back very long." Although the time in Germany had helped ease the transition.

Finally, she sipped some coffee, but he thought she was looking as weary as if she hadn't slept in a week. Which brought another question to his mind. "Are you sleeping okay?"

She shook her head slowly. "The anxiety hits the minute my head touches the pillow. Finally, I fall asleep, but I wake up again almost every hour with my heart pounding. That'll pass, too, right?"

"I'm familiar with that. It passes." Eventually. God, he was beginning to feel as if he were talking to another vet. She might not have had the same experience, but she was having the same fallout. Maybe it was worse for her because she had forgotten so much. He knew a lot of guys who forgot the trauma of their injuries, but they didn't forget the rest. How much harder might it be when you couldn't remember anything for such an extended time frame? Imagination failed him.

He spoke. "Did they give you any medicines to help with this?"

She shook her head. "I had some brain damage. I got the feeling they'd rather I didn't take anything at all, at least not yet. They sure didn't offer me anything."

"Tough." Absolutely tough. He had plenty of friends who were on all kinds of meds to help them over the hump of PTSD. Plus counseling and support groups. He looked at Kylie and realized that family and friends aside, she was more alone than anyone he'd ever known. No one to turn to who could really understand. No real medical support.

And he was getting in deeper by the minute. For a guy who'd come here to take a break and visit his cousin's kids, he was starting to become involved in more dangerous waters. He wanted to help this woman but he didn't know how. Not really. All he could do was listen and assure her she wasn't crazy. And she certainly wasn't crazy.

He passed his hand over his mouth, thinking again about how pretty she was, how beaten she was and how frail she looked. Where did he find a wedge to start prying her out of the prison the attack had created around her?

Damned if he knew. Hell, he didn't even know if she had shared any of this with anyone else. Did he seem safe to her because he was a stranger who'd be leaving soon?

He didn't know. And he wasn't sure he liked that idea, either. What was happening to him?

At some level, Kylie had been listening to herself, wondering at her own frankness, surprised that she felt as if Coop was some kind of kindred spirit. Really, they had little in common, yet here she was spilling her fears to him. She hadn't even done that with her own sister.

Think about something else, she told herself. *Talk about something else. Pretend to be a normal person talking about normal things.* God, every time he told her he'd experienced some of what she was going through, she was probably stirring up bad things for him. That wasn't very kind of her. At any minute he'd probably find a reason he needed to stay at the motel, just to escape her whining.

She sighed and shook her head. "Sorry. I seem to be totally self-involved. And don't tell me it's understandable. We both need other things to think about than trauma, yes?"

"Only if it works." One corner of his mouth lifted. "Don't apologize. I've done my own share of this over the years. It's normal. The brain processes things in bits when they're overwhelming. Give yourself the processing time."

"I may be processing for a long time."

"And maybe not. So Glenda said you're a nurse, too?"

"I was."

He leaned forward. "Was?"

"With this memory loss... I was studying to become a physician's assistant. I can't remember any of my studies from the last three years. And right now, I doubt anyone would let me take care of a patient as a nurse until they're sure I haven't forgotten important parts of that."

He nodded. "I guess I can see that. And I guess that was exactly the wrong change of subject."

Her mood shifted a little. Where it came from, she had no idea, but she laughed quietly. "Quite a conundrum. This is one of those wait-and-see things, I guess. Ashley is beautiful, isn't she?"

Now why had that popped out? One of the disturbing things she had noticed since she awoke was that occasionally things would just pop out of her mouth, things she never would have spoken aloud before. It scared her, because it showed she had lost a basic form of self-control. Thank goodness it was apparently rare. She just hoped it didn't become permanent.

"Yes, she is," he answered. "But *you* were the one I noticed."

Her jaw dropped a little and she felt an astonishing kernel of warmth blossom inside her, driving back the cold that had been consuming her for weeks now. Just a little lifting of the curtain that reminded her she could have normal feelings.

Then he said something more. "You look exhausted. If you don't want to go up to your room and be alone, how about you stretch out on the couch here and I can keep watch over you. If you won't feel awkward. Or…you can put your head in my lap for a pillow. I'd kinda like that."

"But how would you sleep?"

"Lady, I can sleep standing up or hanging off a cliff. No worries."

It proved to be an offer she couldn't refuse. Not to be alone. Even after Glenda had come to her apartment they'd slept in separate rooms, leaving her to face the nightmare alone each time she woke.

It would be miraculous not to be alone when she woke in terror. The invitation was irresistible.

Five minutes later, she had a blanket and took the offer of his lap. His thigh was warm and powerful under her head, and his hand reassuring on her shoulder.

Until now, she had believed she would never want to be touched again. Instead, with Coop at least, it felt like the most wonderful thing in the world.

Her heart didn't slam into high gear; her mind didn't start racing trying to recover the forgotten nightmare. She focused instead on his warmth, his strength, his caring.

And sleep found her gently for the first time since her coma.

The killer was growing increasingly agitated. Why couldn't Kylie have remained in Denver? Getting to her there would have been so much easier. Instead she was living in a town with few secrets where everyone knew her, and that Coop guy was an added wrinkle.

He told himself over and over that he'd gotten even, that he didn't need to finish her. But there was a part of him that needed that resolution, knowing that his victim was gone for good, and that he'd made sure of it.

How had he screwed this up, anyway? That bugged him as much as knowing his victim was still alive, however damaged. He'd failed.

He hated to fail. He was a winner by nature; he expected everything to work out the way he wanted, including this.

But he'd messed up, and he was pretty disgusted with himself. Utterly disgusted. A great big failure.

Maybe he'd settled the score, but he hadn't settled himself. He'd gotten an F on the ultimate test and it chafed him constantly.

He had to find a way to remedy this. Even if she never remembered him, he still needed to finish it. And the longer he waited, the more likely it was that she'd remember something.

He didn't know what upset him more sometimes, failing to kill her or fear that she might remember him.

But there was one way to settle it all. He just needed to figure out how.

Closing his eyes, he allowed himself to savor the minutes when he'd tried to take her life, running them like a movie through his head. It felt like a power surge, unequaled by anything in his life. He could do it. He could do anything when he put his mind to it, and killing the woman whose rejection haunted him, and whose memory might snare him, seemed like something he needed to put his mind to.

Kylie might be a slipup, but that was temporary. He could do it.

Chapter 4

The hardest part of the next few days for Kylie was when Glenda came home from her shift at seven in the morning and a short while later Coop would leave to visit Connie and her family. Yes, Glenda was in the house, but she still felt horribly alone.

But Coop…he'd kept her company every night while she'd slept, and for the first time she began to feel she was catching up with herself. She no longer felt as exhausted.

Her loss of memory haunted her, riding her like a monkey on her shoulder. The problem was, every time she fought to regain any part of her life in Denver, a violent headache came on, as if her brain were warning her away from that area.

How was she supposed to get on with anything with a gaping hole in her memory? With a memory she simply couldn't trust? Hell, a memory no one could trust enough to leave her alone with a patient's care.

More had been stolen from her than her sense of safety. She'd lost the job she loved and might never get it back. That hurt as much as the rest of it.

Glenda awoke from her sleep in the late afternoon, refreshed and ready for another shift, or a night off depending. She always came down the stairs energetic and smiling, and seemed determined to keep things light and even for Kylie. They cooked dinner together. Glenda even coaxed her out to the grocery, which managed to turn into an overwhelming experience for Kylie. She saw familiar faces everywhere, but everyone wanted to stop and speak to her, to ask how she was doing.

She finally reached the point where she wanted to scream, "Just leave me alone!"

She knew they were just being kind and concerned, but when she'd agreed to Glenda's notion that being among familiar surroundings might make life easier for her, she hadn't planned on the dozens, if not hundreds, of people around here who would feel obligated to express concern.

"I guess we won't do that again for a while," Glenda said as they drove home. "I'm sorry, I never thought about how people would bug you."

Kylie, her hands knotted on her lap, turned toward her. "Was it that obvious? I hope I wasn't rude."

Glenda shook her head. "No, but I could feel how tense you were getting. So I'm sorry. We need to go places where we're not apt to run into half the town until you feel comfortable again."

"What I don't get," Kylie admitted, "is why I feel uncomfortable to begin with." This was home. She knew these people. She ought to feel comfortably wrapped in all this concern, not annoyed or scared by it.

"I admit I'm surprised," Glenda answered. "It seemed like such a good idea in Denver. I guess your fears came with you, and there I was thinking we could leave them behind."

That bothered Kylie even more. She knew she was afraid all the time, but Glenda was right. Shouldn't she feel safer here?

But the only time she felt safe was at home with Glenda. And with Coop, who somehow made her feel as if he could hold the hordes of hell at bay if necessary.

Crazy thought. The killer was in Denver. He'd done what he wanted. No reason to think he wasn't hunting someone else by now. No reason to think he gave a fig about where she was or how she was.

No reason at all. But the fear wouldn't leave, as if it had been branded on her soul. She had to close her eyes and draw a deep breath to prevent a self-pitying tear from leaking out. Would anything ever be the same again?

Coop showed up that afternoon earlier than expected. Kylie felt her heart lighten at the sight of him, and tried to batter down the feeling. Coop was just passing through. It would not be good to become dependent on him for any reason, certainly not her sense of security.

In fact, she told herself sternly, she needed to find that security inside herself somehow, not from without. Recovery would truly begin when she could walk out the front door alone and feel at least reasonably comfortable. Until then she was the prisoner of fears she couldn't control, perhaps in part because she couldn't remember them.

Sometimes she wanted to pound her head on something until she shook a memory loose. Crazy urge. Was she growing nuts, as well?

"I got evicted again," Coop announced. "I hope you don't mind that I'm here so early."

Glenda waved him to a seat at the table. "Get comfortable. I'm making a stir-fry and there's enough for a crowd. Did something happen?"

Coop slid into a chair, a big man who seemed to dwarf everything around him. He smiled. "I guess I need to learn. I was talking about taking the kids to a matinee one day, just sort of generally. Apparently I took the lid off the pressure cooker. They're now so excited they can't wait. But it's not like I can take the words back, or take them tomorrow. School."

Kylie felt a giggle slip past her lips. "And Connie evicted you? Wouldn't it have made more sense to let you deal with the excitement?"

He flashed a grin. "There's something about the way Connie tells them to settle down. She says it works better when I'm not around." His grin faded. "I love those kids and Connie, but I had no idea I was going to make life more difficult by visiting."

"I don't think you have," Glenda said firmly. "The kids wind up easily because of their age. She's been working hard, though. The deputies are pulling double shifts. She's probably just trying to reduce the amount of confusion she has to deal with at any moment. Too many balls in the air. And Ethan's been putting in long hours at his dad's ranch, too."

Glenda brought coffee to the table, leaving bowls of cut vegetables on the counter, the wok still sitting on an unheated burner. "You remember when her daughter was kidnapped?"

"Sophie? Hell, yeah. And I was halfway around the world. I didn't hear about it until it was over. Why?"

Kylie spoke. "I remember even though Connie is older and I wasn't in her circle then. My God, I was still in high school, and I was petrified. Deputies everywhere, being warned not to walk alone...and then Sophie vanished. Thank God Ethan was able to track her."

Coop looked at Glenda again. "Why did you bring that up? Did something happen?"

Glenda hesitated. "Well...the deputies are working overtime because a stranger has been hanging around near the school and he spoke to one of the girls. After what happened to Sophie, do you think Connie is in the best of moods? I think she's wound up tighter than her kids. It's not you, Coop."

He drummed his fingers briefly on the tabletop. "I read you. I guess I didn't pick the best time to visit."

Kylie felt sympathy for him. "Like you got to pick your time? I'm sure this wasn't on anyone's calendar. Glenda? Is this a big deal?"

"Not yet. They're kind of keeping a watch on it. The guy could just be passing through and there hasn't been another incident in three days. But—" she shrugged "—nobody wants to take the chance."

"And the threat would really hit Connie hard," Coop offered. "No wonder she's acting like her plate is too full. I'm just adding to it."

"Well," Glenda replied, "spend as much time here as you want. Kylie doesn't mind." She eyed her sister.

"I don't mind at all. Coop's been helping me sleep."

The smile he gave her then lit the room. "I'm so glad," he said quietly. "So very glad."

He offered to stir-fry under Glenda's watchful eye, and an hour later they were sitting down to a wonderful meal that exploded with the flavors of ginger and soy sauce.

Conversation hovered around the edges of Glenda's job, a safe topic, but after they'd finished the dishes, Coop asked a question that almost left Kylie gasping for air.

"Wanna try a stroll with me after dark?"

The formless, shapeless nightmare of terror about things she couldn't remember slammed in on her then. The room went nearly dark, and as her vision gradually returned she realized she had two very concerned people hovering over her. Glenda kept calling her name. Coop cussed quietly.

"That was dumb," he said to no one in particular.

But as the world began to settle, as her heart started to slow down and she caught her breath again, she looked straight into the heart of the darkness that stalked her. Was she ever going to face it or was she going to cower forever?

Coop squatted beside her. "I'm sorry," he said, touching her forearm. His fingertips on her skin almost felt like an electric shock that raced to her core. "Too soon. I don't know what I was thinking."

She managed to meet his gaze. "You've been here."

He nodded slowly. "I'm still there at times."

"But you take walks."

"It's the only way I know to beat it down. But maybe it's not the right way for you."

She drew a long shaky breath. Glenda immediately started to say, "She's not ready—"

"No," Kylie interrupted. "I want to try. My God, Glenda, I've got to keep trying or you might as well put me in a rubber room for the rest of my days. I won't be alone." She turned to Coop again. "If it becomes too much…?"

"I'll bring you right back. Promise."

She hesitated a little while, drew a deep breath and gathered herself, clinging to every shred of courage she could find. "I want to try."

Todd had parked just down the street and was astonished to see Kylie come out of the house on Coop's arm. Man, that guy moved fast.

Kylie wore a light jacket; Coop seemed content with a fleece shirt. Her arm through Coop's bothered Todd more than anything. And now he'd have to wait until they came back to find out what was going on. After a moment, he decided to follow them at a distance. Maybe this was nothing. Maybe Coop was poaching.

Because for some reason it felt to Todd that he had far more right to Kylie than some guy just passing through town.

But then Kylie had broken it off with him years ago. They'd been just casual friends since. Poaching? He tried to tell himself he was being ridiculous, but the anger wouldn't subside.

He climbed out of his car and followed. It was as if a cord linked him and Kylie, a cord he could cut only one way.

Glenda had clearly been nervous about this walk, but she hadn't protested. With her arm through Coop's, tight to his side, Kylie felt his strength like a huge wall around her. He could keep her safe from almost anything, she thought.

"I hadn't realized how much I missed being out in the dark," she said.

"Not making you too nervous?"

"A little, but not as bad as I feared."

He tightened his arm, bringing her more firmly against his side. "Good."

She took another few steps, then asked, "What's it like for you?"

"Being out walking in the dark, you mean?" He paused, evidently giving it some thought. "In my job, light conditions are extremely important. Nighttime provides cover, both for me and for the enemy. So I'm cautious about it. But I still like it. That's why I take so many walks. I guess it's a kind of immersion therapy. The more I do it, the less nervous I get about it."

She thought that over, and decided it might be the only way she could handle all these pointless fears. The breeze rustled the spring leaves gently, like the whispering voices of nature. The air smelled fresh and alive. To miss this for the rest of her days? No way.

But they'd barely rounded the second block when she froze in place, her skin crawling.

"Too much?" Coop asked immediately.

She didn't want to sound crazy but blurted it out, anyway. "Do you ever feel like someone is staring at you?"

"How so?" He faced her now, his face in shadow despite the streetlights.

"I don't know. It's just… I keep feeling watched. I thought it was just my nerves, but now I'm not sure. That's crazy, right? We're in town. Anyone could be watching."

She was right about that, but he silenced his other thoughts, nearly every one of them a screen to keep away the memories that so often haunted them, and opened his senses in a way he tried to avoid when he was home.

Living on constant alert only made him dangerous to innocent people.

He felt it. Eyes were on them. He couldn't believe he hadn't felt it immediately. Turning his head slowly, as if glancing around casually, he tried to see another soul. The street appeared empty. No one stood at any of the lighted windows he could see.

Imagination? Combat experience had taught him never to ignore the feeling. But he wasn't in combat and he had a woman to reassure.

"I don't see anyone."

"I'm probably imagining it, then."

But he didn't want her to dismiss such feelings. That could be dangerous, too, even if he didn't believe her to be facing any real threat right now.

"I never ignore that feeling," he admitted.

"Are you having it?"

"Just a bit," he said honestly. "Let's keep walking and see what happens. It's probably just someone else out for a walk."

But her arm tightened around his and he was sure she didn't quite believe it. Years of experience had taught him not to quite believe it, either, but he kept reminding himself with each step that they were in Conard City, a safe little town, a place where threats didn't stalk every shadow and corner, unlike too many places he'd been.

She'd brought it back, he realized. All the buried things, all the instincts that had no place here. She felt watched, and as soon as she said it he had wanted to kick himself because he'd been ignoring the same feeling on purpose, telling himself it was nothing to worry about.

But what if it was? That was the devil in the instincts he had learned the hard way. You couldn't just put them on a shelf and ignore them because you thought you were safe. Safety was never guaranteed, and he knew it.

But he didn't want Kylie to feel that way. He gathered from his cousin and Glenda that people here spent most of their lives feeling perfectly safe. Kylie hadn't lived his kind of life, and he wanted her to rediscover the security that was her birthright here.

He just wished he knew how to help it along. He wouldn't be here forever. He couldn't watch her every night as she slept, couldn't take every stroll with her. At some point she would have to be able to retake her life, as if it were a fortress in the hands of invaders.

Already he was regretting his impending departure. Kylie appealed to him in ways few women had. Maybe that was because she shared some of the same feelings he lived with. She understood, sad to say. But she was also an appealing woman, and he seldom looked at her without feeling the stirrings of sexual response.

He was also quite certain that she wasn't ready for that kind of attention from a man. Her trauma was too recent, and it made him feel special that she had come to trust him so much so quickly. He didn't want to risk damaging that.

So they kept walking, he with his eyes and ears on high alert, and the feeling of being watched remained with him. There was something wrong.

He knew it in his bones. Casual surveillance should have come and gone, possibly to return as someone else saw them. This didn't go away. It might just be someone strolling somewhere behind them, but when he glanced over his shoulder he saw no one.

Covert surveillance. A curse word rose silently in his mind. They were being stalked. He had no proof, no good reason to mention it to anyone, but he knew it with honed instincts.

Now who the hell would be following them?

In that moment he knew in his heart that Kylie wasn't safe yet and that he had a mission.

"I think I'm going to extend my leave," he remarked casually as they rounded the last corner that would take them back to the house.

"Why? Can you do that?"

"Yeah, I've got more time. As for why?" He looked down at her as they passed under a streetlight and summoned a smile. "I'd like time to get to know you better. A whole lot better."

The smile she gave him then lifted his heart, even though his spirit darkened with worry.

When they entered the house, they found that Connie Parish had dropped in. Connie still wore her full deputy's uniform, except for her hat, and her blond hair was caught up in a ponytail. She was seated at the kitchen table with Glenda. Coop bent and dropped a kiss on her cheek. "Something wrong?" he asked.

"First," she said, "I want to give Kylie a hug, if that's okay with her."

It was okay. She'd known Connie forever, and they had been part of the same group of friends until she left for Denver. The hug felt good, and then the four of them gathered at the table.

"So what's up?" Coop asked. "Escaping the hellions? Sorry I unleashed them."

Connie waved her hand. "It doesn't take much to excite the younger two. No, I'm going back on duty in twenty minutes. I just wanted to check on Kylie and ask you if you'd walk the kids to school in the morning,

Coop. Ethan has to be out at his dad's place early. Some late lambs will be here soon."

Coop nodded. "Sure. Glad to do it, Cuz."

"I thought you would."

Glenda leaned forward a little. "Still worrying about that stranger?"

Connie nodded, compressing her lips. "There hasn't been another contact in this case, but after Sophie..." She shook her head. "I was lucky. It was my ex who took her, criminal though he was, but we found her and she wasn't hurt. But I've never been able to quite escape the fear that it could happen again, and not just to one of my children. And then we did have that serial killer a couple of years ago, although he went after young boys, not girls. Anyway, I probably won't get past this for a few weeks. To be safe, we're pulling double shifts in case."

Kylie spoke, admitting to another gap in her memory, difficult as it was. "When did Ethan stop being a deputy?"

Connie smiled gently at her. "Two years ago. Micah started needing a whole lot more help at the ranch. As he's getting older, balancing his work as a deputy with the sheep is becoming more difficult. And Ethan likes the work. I think he's happier looking after sheep and horses than he was as a deputy."

"And Micah's other kids?"

"All grown up. The twin boys work on the ranch, too. The girls had bigger ideas. They're in college."

Kylie was grateful to Connie for filling in the blanks so easily, as if she were talking to a stranger. No expression of surprise that Kylie didn't remember, just simple acceptance. Something deep within her relaxed a bit, let go of some of the tension that never left her. Then she asked a question to which she needed an answer.

"Connie? Are you still afraid a lot?"

Connie tilted her head, smiling faintly. "Not like I used to be. It's not constant, it's not every day. Most of the time I don't think about it anymore, but every so often... I've got two little ones again, Kylie. So yeah, it hits me every so often, and this incident is so similar to how it started with Sophie that I'm scared to death. I don't want my kids to be alone at all. Ethan and I have a schedule pretty much worked out, but tomorrow..."

"You can count on me," Coop said. "As much as you want or need. Maybe Kylie can help me take the kids to school tomorrow."

He eyed her and Kylie knew he was remembering her fear when they'd walked just a little while ago. Did he really think this would help? But it would be broad daylight and she wouldn't be alone, and she wanted to see Connie's kids again. Three years were missing, and those children must have grown up a whole lot during that time. "I'd like to help," she said, sounding braver than she felt.

Connie's smile widened. "Thanks. I'm sure none of this is easy for you. I hate the way life can teach us to be afraid."

Good way of putting it, Kylie thought. Lessons of life.

When Connie left, Coop excused himself to walk her to her car.

"Okay," Connie said as they reached the driver's side of her official vehicle, "what's working on you? I can feel it, Coop."

He kept his voice low, so it wouldn't carry. "I took Kylie for a walk. Glenda probably told you."

"Yeah. I gather Kylie is pretty scared most of the time."

"She's afraid to be alone, understandably."

"Very understandably." Connie leaned back against her car door. "And?"

"She felt she was being watched. Which wouldn't worry me except that I started to feel as if we were being stalked. Not casual glances. Stalking."

Connie hesitated, chewing her lower lip. "You're sure it's not…"

"It's not PTSD," he said flatly. "I self-checked. Now, you can brush it off, but someone was following us."

"You didn't see anyone?"

"Not a soul, which makes me even more uneasy."

"Hell." Connie tipped her head back and stared up at the night overhead. "There's no reason to think…" Then she shook her head. "And no reason not to think. She didn't die. The bad guy might be unhappy about that."

"Exactly." Coop folded his arms and looked down, testing everything inside himself. "It's not much to go on. I get it. But I can't afford to ignore it."

"Absolutely not. Okay, let's make sure she's never alone. And I'll mention it quietly to the sheriff. I'm not sure what we can do with all this uproar about the stranger, but we'll try to think of something."

Suddenly she reached out and laid her hand on his arm. "Some vacation, huh?"

He laughed quietly and shook his head. "We do what we must."

She turned and opened the door of her car. "Call if anything grabs your attention. See you in the morning at seven, okay?"

"You got it."

He closed the door for her and watched her drive away. A stalker? He wanted to dismiss it, to tell himself he was overreacting because of past experience, but he couldn't do it.

Somebody had tried to kill Kylie once. That sure as hell didn't mean they wouldn't try it again.

He stood outside awhile longer, feeling as if the weight of his field equipment were settling onto his shoulders, familiar with its weight, straps, pockets and tools. He had the worst wish that it was really there with him.

Then he felt the prickle again. This time he didn't bother to look around.

"Stare you, SOB," he muttered. "Stare all you want. Because if you try anything, you're biting off more than you can chew."

Todd wished he could have heard that conversation, but since Connie and Coop were cousins it had probably been about her kids. Then he picked up the bouquet from the back of his car, and once Coop disappeared inside, he headed for the door.

He'd been too abrupt in his visit when Kylie got home. Time to make amends. Time to make her feel he wasn't a threat.

But after only five steps, he stopped. Something was wrong. He could feel it.

Not tonight, he decided. He'd pay his visit tomorrow, in the daylight when it wouldn't seem as unusual, an easy-to-explain drop-in and an apology for turning up so unexpectedly the night she arrived home. He looked at the bouquet in his hand and decided it would survive overnight.

Yeah, tomorrow, under better circumstances, he'd work on persuading her he was just a friend, not a threat.

Because he wasn't. Yet.

* * *

When Coop returned inside, he found Kylie and Glenda had moved to the living room. When Glenda beckoned him with a nod of her head, he joined them, taking the remaining end of the couch.

"That was a nice visit from Connie," Kylie remarked. "I'm glad I'll see the kids in the morning. With three years missing...I can't imagine how they've changed."

"They change fast at that age," Glenda agreed. "But you'll still recognize them. Taller, mouthier and looking like clones of their mom and dad."

Kylie smiled. "I'm looking forward to it."

But she wasn't really, Coop could tell. The tension that had returned on their walk still rode her and hadn't really let go. It would probably remain with her in the morning, as well. If he didn't understand what she was going through so well, he might have sighed.

But he understood it perfectly. He went through some version of this every time he returned from a combat zone. And no matter how you adapted and settled in, you could never return to the old normal, the innocent kid you'd been when you started out. Your life remained haunted, your sense of security and safety permanently damaged.

Sometimes he'd wished he could forget it all ever happened, but now, considering Kylie, he had to accept that forgetfulness would never do the job. The scars went beyond memory, beyond the conscious mind, to a place too deep to restore. The best you could ever hope for was to make peace with it.

Kylie was a long way from that, and as he listened to her and Glenda talk casually about safe and unimportant subjects, he wondered what the hell would happen to Kylie if she recovered her memory. Would she be able to deal with it? If it came in small bits, maybe. But what if she got slammed with the whole thing at once? She might drown in it.

At least his experiences, awful as many of them had been, had mostly been parsed out over time. There'd been breaks, times he'd been able to hunker down in relative safety at a base and deal with it. And the rest of it…well, there was a certain acceptance and adaptation to being at war when you dealt with it day after day. Adjustments made. A change in the way of thinking.

Kylie wouldn't get that, however he looked at it. Her trouble had apparently come out of nowhere, an attack in the night without warning. No time to prepare, no time to deal or adjust, and then…nothing but the remaining terror.

He hoped she never remembered that attack. Never. While he understood she felt she'd been robbed of her future, maybe she could get back all the missing stuff that was good and skip the bad things.

Yeah, how likely was that?

He raised a hand to rub his chin and realized he desperately needed a shave. But not tonight. The rasping sound of his skin against the stubble drew Kylie's gaze his way. He saw the fear pinching her eyes even as she offered a small smile.

"I need a shave," he remarked, trying to keep things light.

"Thus speaks the marine." Glenda grinned. "You're not on duty, Gunny. Let it go."

"I often did when I was on a mission." He seized on something that might amuse them both. "For a while I had a beard halfway down my chest. I blended better that way."

The eyes of both women widened and he could tell they were trying to imagine it.

"Seriously," he said, making a blade of his hand across his chest. "Down to here once."

Kylie tried to imagine it. "But wouldn't your uniform give you away? How was that blending?"

"I wasn't always in uniform."

Simple truth. There were times he'd looked more like a mujahid than most of the mujahideen. Like an Afghan rebel. But he wasn't allowed to talk about those times he'd been slipping around in places he wasn't supposed to go, so he dropped it. No need to get into any of that. It wouldn't help him to remember it and it wouldn't help Kylie with any of her problems.

Then Kylie turned the conversation back to their walk. "Was I crazy to feel I was watched? Coop?"

He didn't even hesitate. "No, I felt it, too. Most people can feel eyes on them. It was probably just folks looking out windows or whatever." Lie. He didn't believe it, but he didn't want this woman any more frightened than she already was.

"Yeah, probably," she said quietly. "God, I hate this fear. I just wish it would go away. There's no point to it. I'm safe here. How much safer could I be than being with you and Glenda?"

Coop nodded in agreement, but he was sickeningly aware of how little *real* safety there was. "I don't know if you'll ever entirely shake it," he admitted. "Look at Connie."

"Right," said Glenda. "You heard her. Most of the time she forgets about it, but nearly losing Sophie… well, it still comes to mind from time to time. And now with this new incident, it must be like reliving her worst nightmare."

"She seems to be handling it well, though," Kylie said.

"She's had more time," Coop answered. "It'll get easier, I promise."

Kylie seemed to wander off in her own thoughts for a few minutes, then shook herself and smiled. "I need to stop being such a baby. Worse things happen to people and they survive. I will, too."

"Of course you will," Glenda said swiftly. "I don't doubt it for a minute. You were always strong. That hasn't changed."

Except in one important way, Coop thought but didn't say. Later Kylie decided she wanted to try sleeping in her own bed by herself. He was sorry about that. He'd started to really like the long night hours with her head on his lap, stirring from sleep any time she moved or murmured.

He wondered how many people looked as good as she did when they were sleeping. He doubted he looked good at all racked out with his face slack and probably snoring. Not that he snored, as far as he knew. No one had ever complained about it or mentioned it, and there'd been plenty of times when he would have been kicked awake by his buddy for making that kind of dangerous noise. No kicks had ever come his way.

But still, he'd watched enough people sleep to know it wasn't always pretty. But Kylie was. In sleep all the tension left her face and she looked almost like an angel. An angel he felt an increasing desire to make love to. This desire he felt for her was different, though. Women had revved him up before, made him nearly lose his mind with hunger, but this one...it was different.

Softer. Kinder. Gentler. Growing as if it would blossom in its own time, not just kick-start. It was a new experience for him, and he decided to just enjoy it. He wanted her, no question about that, but she was far from ready for that kind of contact, and everything inside him seemed to understand that this was special somehow, and different.

It felt good, the simmering desire, just waiting for the right time. Once or twice he thought he'd seen sexual recognition in Kylie's gaze, but it had vanished swiftly. Too many problems on her plate right now to leave room for that.

When the women headed upstairs, he stepped out onto the front porch to test the night. Silent. The breeze had even died away. In the distance he heard a barking dog, and nearer he heard a couple of cats holding a yowling concert. Normal sounds.

Most importantly, there was no feeling of being watched. Stretching his senses, he sought even the slightest thing that might be wrong, and there was nothing. He'd quickly memorized this town, its usual sounds and smells, and the night was exactly as it should have been.

That didn't keep him from patrolling the outside of the house, checking everything out. At last he came back to the front porch, convinced the night was safe. For now, at least.

But thinking back to his walk with Kylie, he was equally convinced he hadn't been wrong when he told Connie he'd felt they were being stalked.

Folding his arms and leaning against the porch railing, he watched the street with highly trained eyes, senses remaining on alert.

Why would someone stalk either of them? In this place? Only one reason came to him and he didn't want to admit it, but he was too well trained to ignore it.

Kylie had survived. She hadn't been meant to survive. Somebody might feel he had a mission to finish.

He dropped his arms and his fists knotted briefly. Well, he wasn't going to let that happen, was he.

When at last he went back inside, he chose to spend the night on the couch, not in his bed upstairs. He knew how to choose his ground, and the couch was it.

Whatever might be out there, it wasn't going to get to the two women he'd decided to put under his protection.

Chapter 5

The trip to school in the morning was fun. Apparently deciding to spare Kylie any unnecessary exposure on the streets, Coop drove his rental car and all three of the children were delighted to get a ride.

Sophie, the eldest and from Connie's first marriage, was in her senior year and trying to appear to be above all the excitement. She looked so much like Connie it was almost heartbreaking. The younger two looked more like their father, their Native American heritage dominating their dark hair and facial structure, although it was still soft from their youth. James was six and Sara was eight, and Glenda had been right—Kylie recognized them both immediately from before and was astonished mostly by how much they'd grown and how much they had to say now. The thing was, they remembered her from visits during the years she had forgotten, and evidently no one had told them not to bring up the subject. She squirmed a little and pretended she knew what they were talking about.

After leaving the kids safely at their schools, Coop asked if she'd like breakfast at Maude's. Her instinct was to say no, but then she stiffened her spine. She had to get past this, and she wasn't going to do that if she couldn't take a few baby steps. "Sounds good," she answered.

At least he didn't ask her if she was sure, because she probably would have changed her mind. Already she missed sleeping with her head on his lap, and the solitude last night had not eased her fears any. The nights with her head on Coop's lap had given her comfort, had kept the panic at bay when she happened to wake. In fact, sleeping like that had kept her from waking much at all. Last night had been a return to the restless sleep and the haunting demons. So she was still a 'fraidy cat, feeling safe only with someone nearby. Well, she couldn't let that extend to going out among people. It would cripple her forever.

At the early hour, the diner was full of older men, mostly retired ranchers, but also a few people clearly on their way to work at the shops around. Everyone nodded and smiled at her, addressing her by name, but at least no one crowded in to question her.

"Wondered if you'd get around to showing up," was Maude's grumpy greeting as she slapped the menus down.

"I'm definitely home," Kylie murmured to Coop, smothering the giggle. Maude's temperament was as famous around here as her food, and probably as unchanging as Mount Rushmore.

"She's something else," he agreed. "I'm glad Connie warned me."

To her surprise, she felt a real appetite for the first

time since leaving the hospital, so she ordered an omelet and toast. Coop added home fries to his, and asked for bottomless coffee.

"That's the only kind we serve here," Maude groused. Two mugs clattered onto the table, and moments later her daughter, Mavis, was filling them. Mavis shared her mother's sour disposition and said nothing as she finished pouring and moved to the next table.

"I'm surprised," Kylie remarked. "I thought Sara and James would be shier with me..." Then she trailed off.

"What?" Coop asked.

"Well, I realized that even though I don't remember the past three years, they do. I apparently visited often. Of course they'd remember me."

She felt her stomach sinking once again with the realization of all she'd lost.

"Don't," Coop said mildly. "You don't need to go down that rabbit hole. It won't help a damn thing."

She drew a steadying breath, acknowledging that he was right. No point in feeling bad about something she had no control over. "I wonder if I should have people write down things for me. Like how often I visited. What I did with the kids. That kind of thing."

"Would it help?"

She turned it around in her mind, disturbed only when their platters of breakfast were slammed down in front of them. "It might," she said. "At the very least I'd know what people were referring to."

"So ask. Obviously I can't fill in any gaps."

The way he winked when he said it caused her to smile again, and once more she let her tension ease. "You're a nice man, Evan Cooper."

"Hey, that's a secret. I'm a marine, remember?"

"I thought marines were gentlemen."

"Only sometimes." He wiggled his eyebrows, drawing a laugh from her. "You're stunning when you laugh, Kylie Brewer."

That cost her her breath. "Oh, my," she murmured weakly, and unexpected drizzles of hot honey seemed to pour through her veins to her very center. Well, she hadn't lost that part of herself at least.

He seemed to recognize it, the corners of his eyes crinkling. "You're as safe with me as you want to be."

While one part of her hated to drag her attention from his face, it seemed necessary if she was ever going to breathe regularly again, or feed herself. He'd changed her mood in a flash, and all the things that had been consuming her for so long had blown away as if in the hurricane wind of the desire he'd just awakened in her.

Not good, she told herself. Not the feelings, they were great, but this guy would be leaving in a few weeks and would probably never look back until he decided to visit his cousin again. And since she was fairly certain she'd never seen him before, it was something he evidently didn't do often.

"What made you decide to visit Connie?" she asked. "I don't remember you visiting before."

"Connie, poor woman, is now my last living family. I haven't seen her in years, and I got to thinking it was high time we put some kind of family back together. You remember Julia, her mother?"

Kylie nodded. The omelet was even better than she remembered. "She was in a wheelchair. That was so hard on Connie at times."

"She never complained, at least not to me. But when pneumonia took her a few years ago, Connie and I were it. Julia was my father's sister, and I was an only child, like Connie. So we started talking on the phone and here I am. Aren't you lucky?"

He said it jokingly, and she appreciated it because it gave her another reason to smile. "I think so," she answered honestly. "What happened to your parents?"

"Mom died when I was a kid. Breast cancer. Dad… well, Dad didn't retire as early as he should have and he took one helicopter ride too many, right after we went into Afghanistan."

"Oh, Coop, I'm sorry."

"It was a long time ago."

"Was that why you've stayed in the marines?"

She watched him pause, forgetting to chew the potato he'd just popped into his mouth. He didn't speak until after he'd swallowed. "They're family now," he said quietly. "My brothers and sisters, all of them. I know some of them as well as I know myself. Hell, I even grew up with some of them."

His honest statement touched Kylie, and her throat tightened. "That must be special."

"It is." Simple answer. "I'm thirty-five now, and I'm giving some thought to retiring when I reach my twenty. I'm still not sure, though."

"You've got time."

His eyes creased again, but this time there seemed to be little humor. "Maybe. If there's one thing this life has taught me, it's that the only minute you can count on is the one you have right now. The past, the future… figments. Gone. Just right now."

His words struck Kylie. She returned her attention to eating because she wanted to think about that. Past and future were figments. The future part she understood, of course. But the past? Memories? Were they in their own way as ephemeral as the future people were always thinking about?

Life is what happens when you're making other plans. That had been bandied about so much that it was almost trite, but she remembered another one as well: *If you want to make God laugh, make a plan.*

Then her mind took an unexpected hop back to high school Spanish class, when their teacher had read them a fable to explain why Spanish people so often said, *Si Dios quiere.* If God wills it. In other words, whatever your plans, something could go wrong. It might never happen.

Well, hadn't she run smack up hard against those truisms? Her plans had vanished with her memory, she felt helpless sometimes with a fear that she couldn't control and she sat in Maude's diner with a man she'd only recently met and wished she could just forget everything in the world except him.

Oops. There went all her planning, such as it had been. All she'd wanted to do was get back here, feel familiarity wrapping her in its comforting grip and hope like hell enough of her memory would return so that she could pursue her dream again.

Now this. Oops indeed.

Feeling strangely shy, she looked at Coop once more, but he was absorbed in cleaning his plate. He'd just be a complication, she argued with herself. Even though he'd let her know he found her attractive, what did that mean? Nothing long term. Nothing that would last.

She needed to get her own house in order before she could deal with anything else. But it still felt good. She was smiling again as she looked down at her own plate.

Good indeed.

* * *

Glenda's car was gone, but the rental being used by that Cooper guy was parked out in front of the house. Todd hesitated, then realized that the chance of seeing Kylie alone would probably not happen for a while. The woman was still recovering, and Glenda seemed to have made certain that someone was almost always around.

He didn't have a lot of options left. He might have to go on a business trip for a few days, and if he did, he needed to know if Kylie had started remembering. That would affect everything. He looked at the flowers on his seat and decided a short visit would do what he needed for now. Later he could deal with the rest of it.

He pulled up behind Coop's car and climbed out with the flowers. Now, he thought with some amusement, he just had to get past the current gatekeeper.

He climbed the steps, feeling the whisper of a warmer spring day on the way, and rang the bell. He was not surprised when Coop answered the door.

"Hi, Coop," Todd said pleasantly, although he was not so pleasantly aware of Coop's size and strength. A man-mountain. "I just wanted to drop in on Kylie for a second. I didn't get much of a chance to see her the night she got home."

"Let me check," Coop said, but he left the door open and Todd could hear him talking to Kylie in the living room. Moments later Coop was waving him inside.

Kylie gave him a small smile. "Hi, Todd."

"Hi, Kylie. You're looking better." He held out his bouquet. "Just checking in. I've been worried about you. The last time I saw you we met at that small park outside the hospital."

He watched Kylie stiffen a bit, and it pleased him. She really *didn't* remember.

"We did?" she asked hesitantly.

"Sure," he answered breezily, putting the flowers in her nearly limp hand. "I know you've forgotten a lot, but a couple of times when I was in town on business we met for coffee. For old times' sake."

"Oh." She looked down.

Coop spoke. "I don't think this is helping, Todd."

Todd wanted to glare at him, but instead maintained his best business smile, the one that oozed trustworthiness. "Maybe not. How am I supposed to know?" Without being asked, he took a chair near Kylie. "It doesn't matter that you can't remember. I just thought I'd mention it because we haven't been strangers all this time, so naturally I'm concerned about you."

"That's…nice to know," Kylie answered hesitantly. "I'm sorry I don't remember."

"Not to worry. It was just casual, and only a couple of times. You were always so busy with school and work. Anyway, I just want you to know I'm thinking of you. I'll be in Saint Louis for a few days on business, but I'll see you when I get back, okay?"

She nodded and gave him a thin smile. "Thanks, Todd. The flowers are lovely."

"The best the grocery has to offer," he said with a shrug and a laugh. "Stay well, Kylie. See you soon." Then, with a nod to Coop, he left.

He figured he'd handled that with a light enough touch, and paved his way for a return. He was a good planner.

Whistling, he climbed into his car and headed out of town.

After Todd left, Kylie sat very still in her chair, staring down at the bouquet of flowers. A cheap bouquet, Coop thought, but it was indeed probably all he could find at the local grocery.

He could tell she was disturbed by the visit. "Did Todd's mention of meeting with you bother you?"

She lifted her head slowly. "I don't know. I mean, I don't remember the last three years, Coop. But without them, I'm kind of surprised. Todd and I kept a distance after high school. I guess if he was in town, catching up with him would be a natural thing if we happened to meet…" She trailed off, but he didn't miss the little negative shake of her head. Then she said, "I've forgotten so much."

Coop was having a very different reaction, one he wouldn't share. If the woman hadn't wanted much to do with Todd before she left for school in Denver, would she have changed her mind? He supposed she might have just thought it the polite thing to do.

But he didn't think she'd appeared honestly happy to see him the first time or this time. Weird. It was almost as if Todd were trying to shoehorn himself back into her life.

Which seemed crazy considering what Kylie *did* remember about him. "You don't really like Todd, do you?"

Her head raised, and he didn't like the way she looked haunted again. They'd come so far this morning and he wanted to bring back that genuine smile.

"I don't hate him," she said.

"No, but…?"

"But…we dated just a couple of times. I never got really comfortable with him for some reason so I called it off. After I turned him down for the prom, it was as if we went our separate ways. Polite but distant. No big deal. Meaningless."

"But you're surprised you met with him a few times?"

"We're older now," she said. "Maybe I got over whatever it was. I mean, I'd probably agree to meet with almost anyone I knew if I ran into them. Have coffee, whatever. No biggie."

Maybe. But he remained troubled, anyway. Something about Todd put her off, although maybe she was right that it was because she didn't remember meeting him during the last few years. She might be reacting to the distant past.

"What does he do again?"

"He's a financial adviser, I think."

And maybe oily and smooth. Then Coop caught himself. Was he judging the guy from jealousy? He had absolutely no right to be jealous over Kylie. Zip. *Control yourself, man*, he told himself.

She sighed, looked at the flowers again, then rose. "I'm throwing these out. I don't want them."

He watched her walk to the kitchen and thought that reaction may have spoken louder than any words.

But it was not his problem. An old flame, an old breakup, a friendship that Todd for some reason wanted to bring back to life. Kylie was the kind of woman who could make a man feel that way.

Look at him. He laughed silently at himself. His own reaction was enough to turn him into a jealous jerk, and he had absolutely no right whatsoever to feel that way. Of course Todd was taking another swing at it. Who wouldn't?

Todd's visit had the oddest effect on Kylie, but she didn't know how to express it. He'd left her feeling down, but also something more than that. Uneasy? Why in the world would she be uneasy about Todd? Because he remembered something she had forgotten? Maybe that was all it took.

Except she hadn't reacted to Connie's kids' remembrances of her that way. It had disturbed her that she couldn't remember those visits, but not like this.

Maybe it was nothing except that she and Todd had had no real relationship after the prom incident. That alone was enough to make things a bit awkward, especially if she couldn't remember patching up things with him when he happened to be in Denver. *He* certainly seemed to think they had.

But as she returned to the living room after dumping the flowers, waiting for Glenda to come back from her hair appointment, she found Coop pacing. "What's wrong?" she asked.

He stopped and faced her. "Me, I guess."

"You? Something haunting you, as well?"

"No." He looked almost sheepish. "I just don't like your friend Todd."

"He's not my friend." The statement burst out of her, and she felt its truth all the way to her heart.

"Really? He's trying awfully hard." Coop's sheepishness had vanished.

"I know. It's pushy." There, she'd said it.

At that a quiet chuckle escaped him. "I thought so, too, especially after you trashed his flowers. But I thought maybe I was overreacting."

She shook her head. "Maybe *I* am. He said we met a few times when I was in Denver. Maybe we smoothed it all over. I don't know. That's what bothers me—I don't know. I just remember very clearly that for a long time we were acquaintances and not *friends*." She emphasized the word deliberately. "I used to wonder sometimes if he hated me because I turned him down. Evidently not.

But right now I feel like he's trying to take advantage of the fact that I don't remember a whole lot."

Coop seemed to freeze. "Wow," he said quietly. "That's quite a charge."

She shrugged one shoulder. "Maybe I'm crazy. God knows, with the brain damage, I could be. But that's how I feel and flowers didn't make it go away."

Now she was the one who paced and he gave her the floor, perching on the arm of the couch. "What do you want to do about him?"

"Him? Nothing. He lives here. I can't avoid him indefinitely. No real reason to, I suppose. I just... I don't like the way he made me feel, talking about things I don't remember, giving me flowers. Man, Coop, flowers? Am I wrong or was that over-the-top? If I were still in the hospital..."

She didn't complete the thought, but he followed it, anyway. The flowers *were* over-the-top. Her girlfriends hadn't come rushing over with them. "Maybe he wants to strike an old flame."

"That's never going to happen. We had our moment. It didn't work. I just... Coop, I don't know what it was about him, but it just wasn't right. Not for me, anyway. I'm surprised he didn't find someone else. It's not as if he's unattractive. He probably even has some money, given what he does. I can't imagine why he'd be interested in me after all this time."

"Maybe," Coop said quietly, "he never really got over you."

She stopped pacing and stared at him. "Give me the willies, why don't you? It's been over ten years."

There *was* that, he admitted. Okay, so the Todd guy was a bit of a creep. He'd met the sort before. Harmless enough, stupid enough and the type that women wanted nothing to do with, although they'd never understand why. Coming on too strong, not knowing when to back off or let go... Creeps.

Finally she sighed and sat down again, curling her jeans-clad legs beneath her. "It was fun with the kids this morning. I want to see more of them. It was fun going out to breakfast with you." She smiled. "I didn't know I was ready to do that."

"But you did."

"I did. And the thing is, nobody crowded me. Everyone greeted me, but nobody pestered me, and some of them probably would have liked to ask questions."

"Common courtesy," Coop remarked.

"Which Todd clearly lacks." She ran her hand down her thigh as if smoothing something. Coop watched the movement and felt hunger stir in him again. He was getting dangerously near the creep designation, he thought with self-amusement. That woman kept pulling his thoughts in one direction. Maybe he should feel more sympathy for Todd.

She spoke again. "Yeah, Todd lacks it. Maybe he always has. Maybe I should feel sorry for him."

"Whoa," he said swiftly. "That could be dangerous."

At that she finally laughed. "Yeah, I don't want to encourage him." She arched a brow at him. "Do you know how easy it is to talk to you? I feel so comfortable."

Well, he was glad to hear that. Now he just had to keep her that way. "I'm happy to hear you say that."

"Are you really thinking about extending your leave?"

He nodded. "I really am. I have the time, I'm enjoying Connie and her family and I'm really liking getting to know you. Unless that puts me in the Todd category."

She laughed then, a full-throated laugh that lightened

his heart. "You could never do that, Coop. I don't think you're capable."

He wished he was as sure.

Okay, he thought later that night. Glenda was at home, her night off, with Kylie, and he'd sought the excuse to take a long run. Coop was feeling cooped up, he thought, making a groaner of a pun.

But the simple fact was, he was used to a lot of physical activity and exercise, and he didn't feel good when he missed it for too long. Before Kylie's return, he'd worked off a lot of energy teaching Connie's two youngest how to kick a soccer ball around and telling them stories about how he'd played with the Afghan children on fields made of dry dirt and with nets made out of whatever they could find that their parents could spare.

He'd loved those times. Kids were the same the world over. Give them a ball, play with them, and the joy would bubble to the surface, no matter how bad everything else might be in their lives.

When he thought of those children, he always felt his own heart lift. What he refused to do was think about what had probably happened to some of them after he left.

But someday he'd tell someone about the rebel soldier who had let him live simply because he remembered playing soccer with Coop a few years earlier. Just let him go, sending him off into the night and telling him to stay away.

He didn't like to think about the youth of many of the people he'd had to fight. Some things were past bearing.

He also knew that eventually he was going to deal

with all that stuff he kept socked away in his emotional and mental backpack. Someday. Just not yet.

His feet pounded the pavement in a rhythmic stride. A few people peered out to see what was going on, then waved. He'd become familiar. He liked that.

His thoughts turned to Todd, however, a more present problem. Kylie's reaction to him was troubling. She didn't remember the past three years, so perhaps she didn't remember cozying up with him, but her overall reaction said she was troubled by the man.

Maybe it meant nothing. Or maybe it meant something. He just knew he had to keep an eye on the guy, at least while he was here. He wondered if he should put a bug in Connie's ear, although he wasn't sure she had room for another bug when she was so worried about a stranger approaching a little girl.

It had been a few days, though; it might have been meaningless. Not that anyone was going to act on that yet.

When he thought about Kylie, however, he was disturbed. She was inclined to dismiss her reaction as crazy from her head injury. He was not so inclined. Life had taught him the hard way that dismissing instincts could be fatal, even if you didn't have a single hook to hang them on. He was not prepared to dismiss Kylie's uneasiness at all.

When he got back to the house, pleasantly tired, he discovered he'd been missed. Glenda needed to run to the grocery, and Kylie didn't want to go with her.

"It was too hard the last time," Kylie explained.

"I get it," Glenda answered, "but I won't leave you alone. So, Coop? Do you have time?"

"All the time in the world," he answered. "I can shower when you get back."

"Thanks." Glenda buzzed out the side door, leaving the two of them alone.

"I'm sorry," Kylie said to him. "I'm complicating life for everyone. Why should I be afraid to go to the grocery?"

"I don't know, but you are and that's enough for me. And you're not complicating my life at all."

Not in any way that really mattered. His continuing desire for Kylie Brewer was something he could manage. As for the rest, being a guard dog came naturally to him, given his background. Whether he was protecting a unit or an individual made little difference.

Protecting Kylie. The thought gave him pause as he realized that he was doing exactly that, and felt a strong need to do even more. But protecting her from what? A creepy ex-boyfriend? Or something more? He couldn't do anything about her lost memory and how uneasy that made her feel. So what more was there? Lending an ear? At least she had said she felt comfortable talking to him.

But he was the kind of man who wanted to do more. He knew that life couldn't be fixed—there were no magic wands to make it all better—but he still wanted to offer more than his presence.

But damned if he had an idea how.

Kylie made a valiant effort to pull herself out of the funk Todd's visit had cast her into. It was ridiculous to let old feelings about him mess her up. He shouldn't have that kind of hold on her. So she made some popcorn and pulled a DVD off Glenda's rack, a comedy that she hoped would make her laugh.

Coop seemed content to join her in front of the TV, and his frequent laughter made her feel good. The shadows that haunted her pulled back, receding into the night outside where they belonged, for a little while leaving her feeling almost normal and cheerful.

God, she needed to feel happy again. She remembered the happy woman she had once been, seldom down about anything unless it was a patient she couldn't do much to help. Everything else, though…well, she'd been a little like a cork, always bobbing up again.

She hadn't been like that since she woke up in the hospital and she didn't much like this new, darker, frightened version of herself.

The contrast to Kylie before disturbed her deeply. She wanted that person back, and hoped the new Kylie wasn't a result of the brain damage. Because there had been brain damage.

After the show was over and she cleaned up the popcorn bowls, she returned to sit with Coop. "I must bore you," she said.

His blue eyes widened a shade. "Not at all. Never."

"Well, I bore myself. I don't even like myself anymore. Did Glenda tell you I had brain damage?"

"I don't think so. You don't seem like it."

"Well, it's part of the reason I lost my memory. Now I'm wondering if I lost my personality along with it."

"I'm not the one to answer that, but I don't see anything wrong with who you are now. You're recovering from a severe trauma, but the flashes still come through of a Kylie who enjoyed life, who laughed easily. Trust yourself."

She sighed, propping her chin on her hand. "I guess it's all I can do. I sure can't change anything."

"For a fact." He leaned forward, resting his elbows on his knees and clasping his large hands. "I was stationed for a year in Okinawa. There was a *Go* master near the base and I went to him for instruction. Do you know what *Go* is?"

"A game?"

"Right. You move colored stones around the board, and the goal is to capture swaths of territory on the board. A strategy game. The details don't matter. What matters is what my sensei said to me. I asked him if I'd made the right move at one point and he looked at me and said, 'Right move, wrong move, all is *next* move.' I thought about that for a long time, but he was right. It's all about the next move, Kylie."

All is next move. The phrase glued itself to her brain, and she pondered it. She couldn't go back in time. She couldn't change anything that had already happened. So it made sense that what mattered was the next move.

Grieving for a woman who was no more—and she couldn't really be sure of that, given how recent her trauma had been—might be necessary, but it wasn't very useful.

In fact, trying to reach that woman only made her feel worse, and enough had happened that was bad. She didn't need to add to it with her own resentment and self-pity.

Bad enough that she couldn't shake the fear that haunted her, as if the demon that had attacked her would once again emerge from the darkness to finish the job.

Coop had already told her that it might be a while before she shook the fear. He ought to know—he'd been in a lot more deadly situations than she had.

Words popped out again, that new distressing tendency of hers. "Do you feel afraid walking down the streets?"

He looked up from studying his hands or the floor or whatever. "Yeah. Sometimes. It gets easier, but I think

I told you. There are situations where my skin crawls, anyway."

She bit her lip. "The whole night frightens me. And look what happened when we took that walk. I was scared the whole time with the feeling that somebody was watching. Of course someone was watching. Probably a dozen people looked out their windows or around the corners of their houses as they walked their dogs. It was ridiculous. But you were so nice about it."

"Because I don't think it's ridiculous," he said firmly. He wasn't about to tell her that he'd felt they had been stalked. It would only scare her more, and for all he knew it was just some ambling idiot who was curious. Being watched was not necessarily a threat. "I told you, we feel it when someone watches us. Instinct."

"But it doesn't necessarily mean anything."

"No," he agreed, hoping he wasn't misleading her. "In most situations it doesn't mean anything at all."

Then, surprising both of them, she rose and came to sit right beside him on the couch. Almost as if it were an instinct, he draped his arm around her shoulders.

"You'll get past this, Kylie. I swear. It'll take time, but you'll find your normal life again." Another lie? He hoped not. God knew, he had to fight these same battles every single time he emerged from a combat zone. Maybe they never really quit, just got more controllable.

She felt so good as she leaned into his side, making it entirely too possible to forget she was wounded in some important ways. His whole body leaped in response to her curves, her closeness, her scents.

"Am I bothering you?" she asked.

"You're making me crazy."

"Crazy?" Her head snapped up and she looked directly at him. "Should I be sorry?"

"No. I can deal with it. You're one hell of an attractive woman, Kylie, but I won't take advantage of you."

He was pleased to see a small smile begin to tickle the edges of her mouth. "What if I said I wanted you, too?"

"Tell me that again in a few days. Right now..."

Her smile faded. "You don't trust me."

"No, I don't want to hurt you. How can either of us be sure you're ready for a fling?"

Because a fling was all it would be. He could extend his leave, but he'd have to depart eventually. Leaving her behind. He didn't want to leave more wreckage.

"A fling, huh?" She rested her hand on his chest. "You have no idea how good that sounds to me right now."

"Why?"

She closed her eyes. "You. Escape. I don't know."

"This is never a good way to escape. Unfortunately, it doesn't work for long. But a little later...I'm definitely open to the possibility. I want you. I just want it to be good for both of us."

"You're saying I'm fragile."

"Aren't you?" He caught her hazel eyes and saw sad acknowledgment there. Yeah, she knew it, too. She was fragile and too open to being hurt again. God, he wished he could fix this.

She rested her head on his shoulder. "This okay?"

"Fine." It was more than fine. He liked it a whole lot.

"Tell me more about yourself."

"Sanitized version only."

"Fair enough."

"I've been a marine since I was eighteen. And by the way, we resent being called soldiers. The army are the soldiers. We're marines."

"Got it." He heard the faintest hint of humor in her response.

"Anyway, I've been in Iraq and Afghanistan, and I wouldn't want to send any postcards home. Let's just say it was a bad experience for everyone, no matter what side they were on. Yes, I have nightmares—sometimes when I'm awake. But I had some good times, too, like a year in Okinawa, and a vacation in Japan. And believe it or not, I developed an unquenchable love for Korean food in Okinawa. There was a restaurant near the base that I went to as often as I could afford it."

"That sounds yummy."

"Oh, it was. The family that owned it were really nice to me and introduced me gradually to their delicacies. When I got home from that assignment, I was disappointed that I couldn't get rice with every meal."

"And then?"

"Some time at Marine Corps Barracks Eighth and I. Then the Middle East. Mostly when I came home from there I came back stateside. And I'm young to be a gunnery sergeant."

"Gunny," she said slowly. "Glenda called you that."

"Anyway, that's the condensed version. There's a whole lot I'll never talk about, and even more that I'd prefer not to remember. But it wasn't all bad. I was thinking earlier about the kids I played soccer with in Afghanistan. Give kids a ball and they have a ball, if you don't mind the pun. I loved those times."

She stirred and he could hear the smile in her voice. "I can picture it. You're one big guy."

"Mostly I played a whole team unless one or two of my buddies joined in. Then they often played against me, which gave the kids no end of delight."

There was a knock at the door and Coop immediately pulled away. "I'll get it. Seems kind of late for an unannounced drop-in."

She stayed on the couch, but a glance at her told him she'd tightened up completely. Her face had that pinched look again. Damn the SOB who'd done this to her.

He opened the door and found a five-year-old boy standing there holding out an envelope. The kid was cute with tousled brown hair and eyes too big for his round face. "What's this?"

"It's for a lady who lives here. A guy asked me to bring it tonight."

Coop stared at the envelope, and all his instincts zoomed into hyperdrive. "Can you wait here for a few minutes? I'll leave the door open."

The little boy said, "Sure. I live just down the street."

Coop pulled out his cell phone and called Connie. "Cuz, get over here right now. We've got an interesting, very young messenger at the door."

Chapter 6

Connie arrived fast in her official vehicle, but without lights or siren. Kylie waited in the living room doorway, wondering what was going on and why Coop had called her. He wouldn't say anything except that he wanted Connie to talk with the child.

Kylie didn't know the boy, but that was hardly surprising. Given her amnesia, she wouldn't have any memory of him much past the age of two. But he looked vaguely familiar, and she wondered why Coop didn't ask him his name. In fact, all he said to the boy was, "My cousin will be here soon. You know Deputy Parish?"

"Which one?" the boy asked.

Coop chuckled quietly. "The lady."

"Yeah, she's cool. She came to talk to us at school a few weeks ago."

"Well, she's my cousin and I'm sure she'll be interested in the envelope. Okay by you?"

The little boy grinned. "Sure."

So the kid was okay with whatever was going on. Kylie was not. Her level of anxiety was pushing to new heights. She tried to tell herself not to overreact, but the simple fact was, these days she was afraid of almost everything, even little boys at her door holding an envelope. Who could possibly have sent him and why?

It had to be some innocent thing, a note from a neighbor perhaps. She hadn't heard the beginning of Coop's conversation with the boy, however, which left her wondering why he'd felt it necessary to call Connie.

But then Connie arrived, in full uniform, and the smile on her face was friendly as she approached. "Hey, Mikey, what are you doing out so late?" When she climbed up the porch, she squatted in front of the boy.

"A man asked me to bring this envelope to the lady who lives here," Mikey answered.

"A man you know?"

Mikey shook his head. "He was kind of funny looking, though."

"Funny how?"

"Too much hair." Mikey wrinkled his nose. "His sunglasses were big enough for a clown."

Kylie couldn't mistake the way Connie tensed. Her tension snapped to Coop like lightning, and then hit Kylie with a fresh wave of her own.

"I see," Connie said. "And what did we say about talking with strangers?"

"I didn't talk to him," Mikey said defensively. "He just handed the envelope out the car window and said he hoped I'd take it to the lady at this house tonight."

"He was definite about the time?"

Mikey furrowed his brow. "He gave me a dollar and said I could keep it if I came right after dark."

"Okay. And which lady is it supposed to go to?"

"The one who just came here."

Kylie's heart jammed her throat. She tried to drag in air, and was glad that she was able to reach the chair and sit. *Don't overreact*, she told herself again and again, but the advice didn't take root.

For a little while, she seemed to drift far away to where the activities around her receded into the distance. Mikey's parents came. Mikey got a talking-to about strangers again, then a couple more cops arrived.

And the contents of the envelope remained unknown.

Finally she was drawn back into the moment by a pair of khaki-clad legs standing right in front of her. "Kylie?" Connie said.

Slowly Kylie raised her head. "An envelope for me."

Connie nodded. "And a stranger approached another child in this town."

Kylie felt nearly punched. How could she have overlooked that in the midst of her own self-preoccupation? Connie must be worried beyond belief. "You must be half out of your mind."

Connie shook her head. "Not yet. I may get there. Anyway, we're taking this envelope as evidence. We haven't opened it yet. Maybe we'll get some prints on whatever's inside, okay?"

"Take it. But...you'll tell me what it says?"

Connie flashed a humorless smile. "It's probably some sappy love poem. Who knows? It could even be empty."

Kylie's heart jerked again. The idea of an empty envelope seemed somehow more threatening than a note. "But the little boy is okay?"

"He's fine. The only fear he experienced came from his mom and dad. Which is a shame. Sickens me to raise our children with fear. But sometimes..."

Connie started to turn away, then paused. "I need to get to the office. You'll be okay here with Coop?"

"Absolutely."

"All right. Count on a visit from me tomorrow. Meanwhile, we've got a stranger to nail."

A stranger. The words rolled around in Kylie's head like lead balls. A stranger who had the town on alert for its children, and had now evidently sent something to her by way of one of those children.

None of it made any sense at all. If someone wanted to reach her, why come through a child? And if some creep was after a kid around here, why send something to her?

Coop brought her a mug of hot chocolate and sat on the couch. He patted the space beside him invitingly, but she wasn't ready to take it. "What do you think about all of this?" she asked him.

"It's weird. Maybe Connie will figure out something."

"But you called her as soon as you saw the child?"

"As soon as Mikey said a man wanted him to give you something. That's a bit different."

Indeed it was. And it told her that the fears she'd been experiencing weren't merely nutty. "You think... you think that guy could still be after me?"

Coop frowned. "I don't know. How can I know? I'm just not willing to take chances, that's all."

She closed her eyes, trying to deal with it. For weeks she'd been told and had been telling herself that she no longer had anything to fear. The fright had remained, but everyone had treated it like a leftover scar from the attack.

Now someone was saying it was possible she had something very real to fear. That she might be unfinished business.

She felt as if she might shatter into a thousand pieces.

* * *

Coop had been doing pretty well since his arrival back in the States. Few nightmares, few moments where time collapsed and put him back on the battlefield. All that changed when a little boy showed up bearing an envelope for Kylie.

He'd seen kids that age used for nefarious purposes before, and it always blackened his heart when innocence was corrupted or abused. This kid Mikey now had a new reason to fear strangers, and while Connie had been gentle, his parents had not. Just as bad, the child had been used to strike fear into Kylie's heart. Of that Coop had not the least doubt, even if he couldn't prove it yet.

Fury bubbled in him, just one instant away from turning into a cataclysmic eruption. Mikey's visit had clearly gotten to Kylie. She was sitting over there in the chair practically trying to disappear inside herself, and she wouldn't come sit beside him where he could at least remind her she wasn't alone.

Oh, yeah, he wanted to erupt. But he had no target, the most maddening thing of all, and he had to find some way to make this easier on Kylie. He couldn't promise safety that she wouldn't believe now, nor could he even be sure she needed protecting. Or that he could provide it.

But, God, he needed to do *something*.

The urge to action was familiar to him. So was waiting. And with effort he tried to push himself into a premission mindset, when time moved like sludge and nerves stretched like wires about to snap, awaiting the right moment.

There was no right moment now. Just an awareness that something very wrong in this town was threatening Kylie or children or both. How the two could be linked, he didn't know, but he was sure the police's focus would be on the fact that yet another child had been approached by a stranger.

A disguised stranger. Too much hair was possibly real, but sunglasses big enough for a clown? Little Mikey's description had painted deception all over the stranger.

But there was no way to know what the guy was after. He was sure doing a good job of creating emotional chaos, though. A great job. How much of it was distraction? And if any of it was distraction, which part? The kids or the message to Kylie?

Long practice made it easier for him to reach the nerve-tightening patience of awaiting the moment. Sure, he'd have liked to pound something, but he'd long since learned that that was wasted effort. He needed a clear head, and he needed to ratchet his tension down enough that it wouldn't interfere.

He kept watching Kylie, though, thinking how beautiful she was even in her distressed state. She wasn't ready to believe that the note was harmless, and neither was he, frankly. But why the hell involve the kid, except as a cover?

The thing with a stranger talking to a child had begun just before Kylie came home, so how could it be linked to her in any way? But he had a gut certainty that it was.

She spoke then, telling him her thoughts had run in the same direction. "I don't want a child to be hurt because of me."

Ah, hell. He felt his heart rip and could have groaned with the ache he felt for her. Hadn't this woman been through more than enough? "You shouldn't worry about that. There's no reason to believe that. It started before you came home, Kylie."

"It was no secret I was coming home. Glenda spent

two weeks packing me out of my old apartment. Why involve the kids? Why?"

"Diversion." It was the only answer to the question she asked. "But we don't know that. We don't know anything yet. This guy could be some creep who gets his jollies from getting everyone upset, that's all. He may not hurt anyone at all—may not want to. He's just enjoying the show."

"Then he's as sick as the guy who attacked me."

He couldn't argue with that. Finally he rose and without asking permission scooped her up out of her chair and planted her sideways on his lap on the couch, holding her close. She didn't struggle, but she didn't relax, either.

He stroked her silky hair with one hand while he kept the other arm wound tightly around her. "Just remember, you're not alone. I won't leave you alone for a minute, okay?"

"You can't promise me that. You came to see Connie and her kids. You have every right to do that and I'd hate myself if I prevented it."

"And while I go visit them, Glenda will be with you. Okay? For heaven's sake, don't be worrying about how I spend my time. I'm pretty sure Connie would be on my side, anyway. You've been friends for a long time. You think she isn't as worried about you as she is about anyone else?"

A small sound escaped her. "She's got enough to worry about."

"And you're as important as everyone else. Why wouldn't you think so? A lot of people actually care about you, Kylie. A lot."

"I should have just stayed in Denver," she said tautly. "I feel like I brought the horror here with me."

"You can't possibly hold yourself responsible for that. What were you supposed to do, Kylie? You'd suffered severe injuries and amnesia. Glenda said you can't even work yet. So what would have happened? You'd have wound up on the street. Sure, that's the answer."

After a minute, he felt her begin to relax into his embrace, and then a small laugh escaped her. "You're right. Are you always so logical?"

"Not always," he admitted. "Right now I'd like to wring someone's neck, but the problem is I don't know whose. So here we are, blind and blindsided by some jerk who may just be getting his laughs for all we know."

She sighed and snuggled a little closer. His body leaped in immediate response and he hoped like hell she didn't feel it. He didn't want to be a source for more worries.

"If he wants me, I just wish he'd leave the children out of it. But another thing worries me."

"Yes?"

"I could be the diversion. If everyone thinks he really wants me and lets their guard down about the children…"

He hadn't thought of that, and was astonished by his own oversight. He was usually quicker than that. But one thing he knew with certainty. "Folks aren't going to let their guard down about the kids. Trust me. They're everyone's primary concern."

"I hope so."

"You know Connie better than I do. What do you think?"

She graced him with another small laugh. "She'd never let that happen."

"Exactly. And from what she's told me, the whole dang sheriff's department isn't going to get lax, either. At most they'll spare a little time for keeping an eye out in your direction. But no one is going to stop worrying about the children until they catch the guy."

"You're right."

"So we'll skip the part about you feeling guilty for coming home?"

She twisted until her head lay in the crook of his arm and she could look up at him. "Hey, Gunny?"

"Yo?"

"I bet your men feel secure with you."

Surprise washed through him. "Why would you say that?"

"Because you're clearheaded and focused on what matters. Me, lately I've been scattered all over the place, thoughts flying like crazy birds in every direction. When I talk to you, you ground me again. I bet they appreciate that as much as I do."

Instead of accepting the compliment, he found himself looking at his hands and thinking of all the horrible things they'd done. She wouldn't even want them holding her if she knew. Yeah, it was war. But war carried a price that got burned into the soul, the same as terror had been branded on her. But that was something he wasn't prepared to share with an innocent.

"Just don't put me on a pedestal," he said finally. "I'm an ordinary guy with plenty of flaws."

"I'm sure you are. Well, I'm not sure about the ordinary part, anyway…"

He laughed. "Cut it out."

She smiled, still cradled in his arms, and he saw that the shadows had withdrawn a little. Not completely, but she was pushing them into the background. Remarkable resilience, he thought. After all she'd been through, he wouldn't blame her for having the screaming meemies tonight. A kid shows up at the door with an envelope for her from a stranger? He wouldn't have blamed anyone for freaking out.

"Why did you call Connie?" she asked again.

"Because it all felt wrong. A kid at the door with an envelope for you from a stranger? It was hardly a leap of brilliance not to take the envelope and close the door."

"I guess not." She chewed her lower lip and her fingers worried a button on the front of his flannel shirt. Oh, man, the places that made his thoughts run. He yanked them back into line like an out-of-step squad. Not that it helped much with this woman's soft curves filling his arms and lap, and her scents filling his senses.

Ah, he hoped before all was said and done they could make love. Yeah, he had to go back to the corps, but if she'd tolerate it, that didn't have to be a farewell.

A frightened, traumatized woman was actually making him consider something he'd never allowed into his thoughts before: a future. Oops. Time to cool it.

But he didn't let go of her or move her. She seemed comfortable and she was relaxing, and he didn't care what it cost him to make her feel that way. He'd dealt with harder things than ignoring his male urges.

She shifted, and he could have sworn she was snuggling closer. "I wonder what Glenda's going to think about this."

"I couldn't guess. I don't know your sister that well yet. But she seems pretty levelheaded."

"She's a nurse. Of course she's levelheaded. I was once, too."

That refreshed the ache he felt for her. "I'm sure you still are."

"Not when I'm afraid of every shadow."

"That'll pass," he said with more certainty than he felt.

"God, I hope so. I was so close to finishing my master's

and testing to be a physician's assistant. So close. And now I've forgotten all of that. I'm not competent to be a nurse any longer because no one is sure what I might have forgotten, and it's like…that man stole my life from me, Coop, even if he didn't kill me."

He tightened his hold on her and wished he had some comfort to offer. He didn't have the expertise, and regardless, she wouldn't believe the platitudes right now. She was wrestling with something every bit as big as the terror she'd been left with. He hadn't really thought about that. "Isn't there anything that can be done?"

"When I'm better, Glenda suggested I double up with her on shifts, kind of an internship to see how well I do. So maybe I could be trusted again with patient care, but that'll take a long time, and it can't happen for a while. Right now they're still a little worried about the brain injury and how it will finish healing. But no matter what happens, unless I suddenly remember those three years, I'd have to start my master's program again."

"Damn."

"Yeah." She shook her head a little. "I can't tell you how that daunts me right now. It looks overwhelming."

He understood. "Maybe it'll look less daunting after you've had more time to heal."

"Maybe. I hope so." She paused. "So you decided not to be a lifer?"

"I used to think I'd go for thirty. Now, like I told you, I think about just finishing my twenty. Leaving time to do something else. I just haven't figured out what."

"The whole world would be open to you."

He shook his head a little. "My experience is a bit specialized. No, I'd need to go back to school and pick up some new tricks. But that would be okay."

"You're certainly young enough."

By what measure, he wondered wryly, but gave her one simple fact. "I'm thirty-five."

"Twenty-nine," she answered. "We're both a long way from old."

Again, that depended on the measuring stick, but at least she was looking forward, and he was glad for her. As he knew all too well, looking forward could often be a very difficult thing to do. Sometimes the road ahead appeared to be a series of high brick walls. Sometimes you could swear no doorway had ever been invented.

"Well, we'll figure it out. I may not know Glenda well, but if you want to get back into nursing, I'd bet on her finding a way to get you there. She seems determined. You know, like you."

Kylie gave a little negative shake of her head. "I haven't been very determined lately. Look at me."

"I'm looking and I like what I see. You'll get it all back one way or another," he said firmly. "You're not the type to quit. If you were, you'd have already done it."

"Like I've been in control of much."

He hesitated, then said, "You were in control of whether you lived or died. Don't question me about that—I've seen too much death. There's a point where it could go either way for some people, and there's a choice. Why do you think you were trained to tell dying patients to stay with you?"

She drew a shaky breath. "You're right."

"We have even more brutal ways, which I won't share, of making sure guys don't give up. Trust me, you had a choice and you made it."

He held her, enjoying the way she snuggled a tiny bit closer, while she thought about that. "You know," she said presently, "I like that. The idea that I actually made the choice to live. Now admittedly, I could still argue that maybe that wasn't wise, given what's going on, but I like thinking it was my choice."

"It was," he said firmly. He'd seen too many men return from the brink of death by being reminded of life, however painfully that reminder was delivered. He'd seen enough to know that choosing death was too often far easier than choosing life.

"You know," she said a while later, "when I decided to become a physician's assistant, I also thought about going to medical school instead. I would have liked becoming a doctor, but I wasn't ready to make the investment in time and money."

"Then do it," he said. "You've got plenty of opportunity and reason to make a change now."

"Maybe I do." She paused. "But have you thought about anything else at all? For later?"

As if he had a whole lot of time between missions to sit around daydreaming about a future. When he wasn't in the field, he was training constantly. Time off meant a weekend with some buddies, a little side trip to a casino or to go fishing. He didn't leave a whole lot of room for thinking unless he went to a meeting with other combat vets, and then he was mostly focused on the past. He supposed he could have made time, but empty time left too much room for thinking.

He sighed finally, rubbing his palm down her arm. "I guess I ought to give it some thought. Things have flitted across my mind from time to time but nothing that really grabbed me."

"Well, you're pretty much engaged in a job right now. I didn't think about doing much but medicine from the time I settled on nursing school."

"But now possibilities are open."

"I guess they are, once I can trust my brain again."

Conversation flagged then, and he felt the last of the tension seep out of her. Good. He'd hold her like this all night if it made her feel safe. Unfortunately, the silence was filled with his desire for her and the unwanted awareness that if he lived he needed to start thinking about a future.

That was the part that he didn't think about often, and certainly wouldn't share with her, but the assignments he received…well, his life expectancy wasn't great. He tended to look at the future, when he did, through a very short lens. Immediacy. A week from now might never happen. That didn't encourage much long-range planning.

Not that he lived with the constant fear of dying. In fact, he didn't think about his personal safety very often. He had other men to be concerned about, and he put himself in the background emotionally. Just something he didn't worry about.

He guessed he was kind of fatalistic. When his time came, it would come, and he had no way of knowing when that might be. All he could do was be sensible.

But Kylie had asked him, and the idea of retiring in another couple of years had been occurring to him already. So maybe he needed to put some of his fatalism aside and ponder possibilities.

Kylie dozed finally, and the night grew amazingly peaceful. Despite everything that life threw at people, there were still good moments. There was still peace.

He was a man with the experience to savor it whenever he could.

Peace vanished when Glenda came home from her shift at a little past seven. She sailed in the door with a bag of pastries and bagels from the bakery and immediately wanted to know, "What the hell happened last night? Everyone's buzzing."

Kylie, her eyes still full of sleep, was making coffee. Coop had been checking the fridge for eggs. The bakery bag put an end to the search.

"Nothing really," he said at the same moment Kylie said, "Not much."

"Oh, cut it out," Glenda said irritably, banging plates as she pulled some out of the cupboard. "Coop, grab some butter and some knives."

"Yes, ma'am."

Soon they were seated at the table with a mound of food and fresh mugs of coffee. Glenda attacked a bagel, buttering it carelessly, clearly annoyed. "Something happened here last night, and I want to know what it was. Quit stalling. Cops in front of my house? Something about a child?"

Kylie and Coop exchanged glances. Cops in front of this house? Kylie thought. Yeah, that would hit the grapevine fast.

"A little boy came here," Coop said. "Mikey, maybe five. A stranger had given him a letter to deliver to Kylie."

Glenda dropped her butter knife with a clatter, her eyes leaping from her sister to Coop. "What? What was in the envelope?"

"Connie took it. We don't know. She promised to let us know today."

Glenda looked at her sister. "You must have been scared out of your mind."

"Coop was here." Which was shading the truth, but Kylie was getting awfully tired of talking about how afraid she was at times. She felt like a broken loop, around and around, even if she couldn't help it.

"Coop was here." It almost sounded like a groan. Breakfast forgotten, Glenda put her chin in her hand and simply stared at her sister. "Any ideas?"

"None," Kylie said. "Coop and I talked about it. We don't know what's going on. Are the kids a diversion? Am I a diversion from the threat to the kids? What do you think?"

"I think I'm grateful as hell Coop was here last night," Glenda groused. "Grateful as hell you weren't alone. What kind of sicko do we have running around this town?"

No one had an answer, of course. Finally Glenda went back to buttering her bagel. "Sorry, I forgot the cream cheese. I was upset."

"I'm surprised you went to the bakery," Kylie said. "Being worried and all."

"I needed food. It was a long night. Two traffic accidents and some boy found his daddy's gun and shot himself in the leg. Everyone will survive, but we were pretty busy."

Food and milk began to settle her down. She eyed Kylie again. "You're sure you're okay?"

"As okay as I can be." Which was the truth. Nothing had been okay since she woke up from that coma, but she was firmly settled in her new normal at the moment.

Except for wondering what had been in that envelope. Half of her wanted to know, and half of her hoped she never had to. Something or nothing…either one wouldn't matter. Its arrival had been threatening, and she couldn't escape that.

"Don't lie to me," Glenda said. "You must have been scared out of your mind."

"I was for a while. But I wasn't alone. I slept. Coop watched over me, and this morning I'm okay, all right?"

Suddenly Glenda smiled. "It's nice to see you getting some of your spunk back. So we're waiting on Connie?"

"At the moment."

Breakfast went better after that, calmer. Coop had a faint smile hovering around his mouth, as if something had amused him, but it was a gentle smile so Kylie didn't ask what was so funny. Let him enjoy it. Any humor would probably leave this day suddenly and quickly when Connie showed up.

"Okay," Glenda said when she'd finished her bagel, "what's the plan for the day, Coop? You going over to see Connie's kids? When? I need to schedule my sleep."

"How about you go to sleep right now? The kids have school, anyway. I can spend some time with them this afternoon."

Glenda reached across the table and patted his forearm. "You have no idea how grateful I am to you."

He smiled. "No need. Once I knew the situation, wild horses couldn't have kept me away."

"Probably not. Marine, through and through."

"Semper Fi," he replied.

Semper Fi. Kylie thought about that shortened phrasing of *semper fidelis*—always faithful. She'd heard it used a few times, almost like a verbal handshake between a couple of people, usually men. It had slid past her awareness then, but now she thought about it in light of knowing Coop. She didn't know the entire marine corps, of course, but she'd seen enough of this one man to know that the words held real meaning for him. They weren't just a verbal tic.

Being a marine had probably been seared into his identity the way being a nurse had been part of her. She knew what she'd lost when she lost nursing, and she wondered if Coop would ever be able to leave the corps behind. He said he was thinking about it, but it wasn't a decision he needed to make yet. He might not be able to do it.

If not, she would certainly understand why. Medicine had meant everything to her. Everything. And some criminal had stolen it from her. Why would Coop relinquish his identity by choice? Unless he found something else that meant as much to him, it wasn't likely.

Nor was it anything she needed to be wondering about except that it wasn't her own situation, which she'd have gladly thrown out the window never to be thought of again.

And what he'd said last night, about how she'd made the choice to survive…well, sometimes she wondered why.

Whatever, she told herself before gloom could overtake her. She must still have something left to do in this life. The problem would be figuring it out.

After extracting a promise that Kylie would wake her if Connie brought any news, Glenda went up to bed. Coop insisted on cleaning up the breakfast mess, and Kylie sat watching him, enjoying the view. He moved so fluidly, he was so perfectly built and today's clothes of a gray polo shirt and jeans only seemed to emphasize his manliness. A hunk. For the first time she truly let herself wallow in appreciation.

Before that awareness had kind of skimmed through her mind, as if she wasn't ready for the full impact of this man. Drooling, she told herself with a quiver of amusement, would be unbecoming indeed. However, she didn't at all mind the tingling heat at her center. It made her feel good to be alive.

But before she could fully enjoy a few minutes of

being just an ordinary woman, the anxiety returned, as if it refused to give her much relief.

"Oh, heck." She sighed, almost under her breath.

Coop's attention turned immediately to her. "What?"

"The anxiety. It comes at me out of the blue. I just wish it would go away."

"It'll lessen with time." He dried his hands on a towel and joined her at the table. "I know what you're going through. This isn't my first rodeo, you know."

"I suppose not," she said. Impulsively she reached across the table and seized his hand. He immediately turned it over and grasped her fingers with his. His skin was warm, slightly roughened, and the pressure he returned comforted her.

"Listen," he said. "I've been in and out of war since the invasion of Afghanistan. It changes me, when I'm over there. I have to think about things in a whole new way, live with a threat that isn't always visible, but is very present. So when I come home, all that comes with me. The tension. The extreme awareness that anything could be a threat. There's danger around every corner, and relaxing is damn near impossible. It's gotten easier with time to make the transition, but I still have to make it. I'm still not completely settled from my last tour, so don't be surprised if I overreact sometimes, especially to unexpected movements or sounds. But I *do* relax eventually, Kylie. Trust me, you will, too."

"So sure," she said, trying to smile even though she felt as if a sword would fall on her at any moment.

"Positive. Part of the problem you're facing here, if you don't mind my penny-ante psychology, is that you have no memory of what happened. You have nothing to process, which I admit would be miserable, but at least you'd have something to work through. Instead you're dealing with a big blank that left a whole lot of fear but nothing else. The anxiety is understandable, but you can't deal with what you can't remember."

He might have a point, she thought, staring at their linked hands. Awful as the experience of the attack must have been, at least she'd have something to grasp, to think about, to face. All she had now was a big blank and a lot of lingering terror.

"I have nightmares," he said. "Not all the time, but I have them. Once in a while I even have them when I'm awake. They pop into my head and all of a sudden I'm back in the middle of something that happened over there. But I know what I'm dealing with. I can work on it. I can look at it. You... What are you supposed to process? Intellectually you know what happened, but the rest of it is gone, leaving only the fear."

"It would have been nice to have forgotten the fear part."

"Yeah, it would. But that didn't happen. So you don't have a face, a place, a situation to pin it on. Nothing you can grieve, or rage at. You just know what the outcome was. Eventually you'll work through the fear. I don't know about the rest."

She tightened her hold on his hand. "Sometimes I desperately want to remember. I want all of those three years back. Then, other times, it scares me as much as anything. I keep trying to tell myself it's a blessing I can't remember the attack."

"But if you could remember his face, at least you'd know you didn't have to be afraid of nearly everyone."

She drew a sharp breath. "I hadn't thought of that. I'm not afraid of people I know. I'm not afraid of you, but..."

"But anyone you don't immediately recognize is a different story, am I right?"

She nodded slowly. "Very different. And I'm afraid to be in a crowd."

"Because you have to pick through all those faces for familiar ones. That's not easy to do."

"I hated the grocery store. Everyone wanted to speak with me."

"I get it. Everyone needs to be evaluated. If you had a mental picture of the guy, you'd feel safer."

"Maybe so." She closed her eyes, and once more searched her empty memory. Almost immediately, a headache tried to grip her, so she stopped. Not ready for that yet. But she wondered about the link between trying to recover her memory and getting a headache. Next time she saw the neurologist, she needed to ask. Was that some kind of mental warning? *Don't look.* She could almost believe it.

But she realized he was right. The first time she saw each person, even those she knew from her life here, her first instinct was to tense in expectation of attack. It didn't last long, but it happened on every first meeting.

She was constantly on guard, constantly alert for threat. No wonder she couldn't relax much or often. Damn!

She raised her gaze to his face and realized he was dealing with much the same thing. His only advantage was that he didn't have to perceive every new face in this town as a threat. Or did he?

"Coop?"

"Yeah?"

"When you meet people for the first time here, do you tense up?"

"Sometimes. It's inevitable. You can't walk out of the valley of death and not bring some ghosts along with you. It's getting easier to make the transition the more often I do it, but…" He stopped.

"But what?"

"The nightmares aren't getting any better," he said quietly. "The more times I have to go back over there, the more ghosts I bring back with me. I deal with it better, but the crowd keeps growing."

"God." For the first time in weeks she honestly hurt for someone besides herself. "I'm so sorry."

"That's part of what war does to you. Pretty soon you're carrying around a graveyard of ghosts. Somehow you have to make peace with them."

"But how?"

He shook his head a little. "You remember them. You do them the honor of remembering them. Every single one of them. Give them their due. Then they kind of recede, although they're never gone."

"But I can't do that."

"Not yet," he agreed. "I don't exactly know how to explain it. But those faces, as much as they haunt me, all they need is to be remembered. To not be forgotten. But my situation isn't like yours. You didn't do anything to draw this attack. If ever there was an innocent victim…" He sighed. "Kylie, you're the face I'd never want to have to remember. The one I wouldn't want in my personal cemetery."

"Do you have faces like that?"

"It was war."

He closed his jaw in a way that warned her he felt he'd revealed enough. Maybe more than enough.

But apparently he had another thought, because he spoke again. "One of the things that really bugs me about your attacker was that he wanted to add an innocent to his ghosts. He *wanted* it. He deserves no forgiveness, and his face deserves to be forgotten forever."

"I seem to have done that." And hadn't he just said that was part of her problem in dealing with this? That she couldn't remember? He was confusing her.

He sighed. "I'm not making sense. It would help you to remember him, but once you do, forget him. Whatever it takes. He doesn't deserve another single second of your thoughts or caring once you've banished him. That's what I mean."

Now she understood and decided he might be right. But thinking about Coop's "cemetery," she wished there was something, anything, she could do to help this man leave his ghosts behind. She believed she understood what he meant but, good Lord, what a burden to have to carry.

She hated even imagining it. Closing her eyes, she could almost see the gray figures surrounding him, some of them with love, some with hate, some with fear, and all of them part of him now.

Two wars and all those years in the marine corps had given him that. While she appreciated the military, gave thanks for their sacrifices and the security they provided, she'd never really thought before about the lifelong burden the job imposed on them. Oh, sure, she knew about the disabilities, but she'd never thought about it in the way he had described it.

"Kylie? You okay?"

"I was thinking about your ghosts." She opened her eyes and met his blue gaze.

"Don't. They're mine. Nobody else needs to carry them. Let's talk about something else."

She was agreeable, if it would make him more comfortable. "You said you grew a beard to blend?"

"Yep."

"So how do those blue eyes blend?"

He laughed, visibly relaxing. "You'd be surprised how many blue-eyed people there are over there. Everyone thinks dark hair, dark eyes, but blue eyes are common enough."

"I never would have guessed."

"One of our medics commented on it once. She said they have some of the most beautiful blue eyes she's ever seen. You have to remember Afghanistan was a part of the Silk Road. Caravans passed through there all the time. It's a beautiful mix of genetics."

"And what a storied place it must be."

"Yeah. It's a damn shame people couldn't just leave it alone."

Kylie smiled. "I think you could say that about most of the world."

He laughed. "True that."

Then the doorbell rang, and Kylie's fear came crashing back.

Coop rose immediately to answer it. He waved Kylie to stay at the table, but she didn't listen and he wasn't surprised. After last night she had a real struggle going on, and while she was dealing well with it, it was still there and she wasn't about to wait for the news secondhand.

If it was news.

He opened the door to see his cousin, Connie, standing there in uniform. "Hey, Cuz. Come on in."

"Kylie here?"

From right behind him came her voice. "Where else would I be? Is it bad?"

"I don't know." Connie stepped inside. "Got any coffee?"

Kylie led the way back to the kitchen, and Coop poured her a cup. Connie adjusted herself on a chair, getting a belt full of equipment out of the way, and wrapped her hands around the mug. "How you doing?" she asked Kylie.

"Trying not to sit on the edge of my seat. Just cut to the chase, Connie."

"Not much of a chase," Connie said. "Mikey's description of the man was useless. Can't even identify the car except it was really old. As for the envelope, no prints inside or out. Anyone could have sent it."

Kylie apparently had had enough of dragging this out. "But it was sent to me. What the hell was in it?"

Connie frowned and rested her elbows on the table. "A pressed, dead black rose."

Coop caught Kylie before she fell out of the chair.

She came to lying on the couch with two concerned faces hovering over her. "I'm okay," she managed, and even sounded a bit querulous.

"Right," said Coop, and backed up.

Connie remained squatting beside her. "You're the nurse. You don't need me to tell you to sit up slowly."

Kylie took the advice, the same advice she would have given, and pushed herself carefully upright. The world no longer spun or tried to turn black. "I'm fine. Really. Did you say a dead black rose?"

"Unfortunately," Connie answered. Straightening, she sat beside Kylie on the couch. Coop paced to the front window, folding his arms and staring out. Kylie wondered which of his hells he was visiting. She knew the one she was teetering in.

"So what do you think is going on?" Kylie asked her friend.

"We're still discussing it, but you've risen to the top of our list, right alongside the kids. Nobody thinks this was just a sick joke."

No, nobody thought that, and if they had, Kylie wouldn't have believed it. "Do you think this guy is just using the kids? Are they the distraction or am I?"

"Or do we have two creeps in town?" Connie offered. "No answers, kiddo. None. But, Coop?"

Slowly he turned from the window. His face was as set as stone, and he didn't unfold his arms.

"We need you," Connie said. "Forget everything else. We need you with Kylie all the time. You've just been deputized. Unless you object."

"I don't object." His voice had turned steely. "I just want more information."

"Don't we all. We're shorthanded. We've got too many schools and playgrounds and kids to watch, plus our regular duties, and now Kylie. It may all be one creep, but it could be two and we can't take the risk. You need a weapon?"

Coop unfolded his arms then and looked at his hands, clenching them. Something in Kylie shivered. "These are all I really need, but given we have an unpredictable situation, I'll take you up on a Taser and a Glock 43."

"You'll have it as soon as I go out to my car, along with a badge and radio."

"What about a knife?"

"None standard issue, but I don't think anyone will complain if you carry one."

Kylie felt a tear seep out of the corner of one eye. "Coop, I'm sorry."

He arched a brow. "For what?"

"I've sent you back to war."

Connie left a few minutes later, after getting Coop equipment plus armor, telling him they were working on the black rose angle, since they might be able to find out where one could be bought, and possibly who had bought it. Other than that, they had nothing to work with.

When she was gone, Coop said, "You promised to wake Glenda."

"Let her sleep. She needs it and she has a shift tonight. When she wakes is soon enough. Besides, it's not like we learned anything useful. No point waking her so she can wonder about a black rose."

Coop nodded and sat beside her on the couch. "Talk about clear messaging."

"Seems pretty clear, doesn't it? But we can still run in circles. I know I am. Are the kids really the ones at risk? Was the rose sent by someone who heard what happened to me but had nothing at all to do with it? Was it just a way to stir up more anxiety, especially about the children?"

"I'm more concerned about *you*," he said. "How are you feeling? Even more anxious?"

Surprised, she paused a moment. "Oddly, no. It kind of went away. Maybe I just needed to faint."

That brought an odd smile to his lips. "Right. Truth is, you've got something concrete to think about, even if it's ugly. That often helps."

She leaned back on the couch and drummed her fingers on her thighs. "You're right. A black rose is weird. I don't suppose they're impossible to buy, but it's still weird. Was it dead for a reason or by accident?

It seems like a threat, but maybe it's not. Yeah, that's easier to think about than the big blank in my head."

Then it really struck her and she turned to him. "You were right. Having something I can actually deal with makes it easier somehow."

He nodded. "A face would be better but yeah. You've got something solid now."

She cast her gaze down, letting her thoughts roam. A black rose. A definite message of some kind. But something else was niggling at her. She just wished she could figure out what it was.

A black rose…

Suddenly she lifted her head. "Coop? Could you give Connie a call? Ask her to find out if there was anything in the Denver police report about a black rose?"

"About your attack, you mean? What is it?"

"I don't know," she admitted, hating the emptiness in her mind. "Just a feeling. I don't know what good it could be but…"

"It might be a link," he said firmly. Without wasting time, he pulled out his cell phone and called his cousin. Swiftly he outlined what Kylie was thinking and ended with, "Thanks." He faced Kylie. "She's going to check into it. She sounded excited, if you can believe it."

Kylie tried to smile. "We'll see. But, Coop, what I said before about sending you back to war? I'm so very sorry."

He slipped his arm around her and tucked her into his side. "I'm not. I'm designed for this and you need me. You know, that means a whole lot to me."

It meant a whole lot to her, too, to have him beside her, ready to protect her. She leaned her cheek on his shoulder and gave thanks for Evan Cooper. Without the anxiety plaguing her, the strength of his arms felt better than anything she'd felt in a long time.

Sexy, even. She let herself enjoy the feeling. God knew, it probably wouldn't last long.

Chapter 7

Glenda came downstairs at three and found the two of them playing Parcheesi on a card table in the living room. "Well, isn't this cozy?" she said brightly.

"It passes the time," Kylie answered. "Now, don't be mad at me, but Connie came by. I couldn't see any reason to wake you up because it wasn't informative. The envelope provided no information. All they found was a dead black rose."

Glenda's cheer vanished instantly. She sank onto the arm of the couch. "You didn't think it was important for me to know that?"

"Not unless you know where to buy black roses around here," Kylie answered. "I told Coop that waking you up to wonder about it would be a waste of your sleep. So there you have it. No real news, really."

"But a black rose!" Glenda was clearly disturbed. "What an ugly thing."

"Ugly, but maybe meaningless," Kylie answered. "Somebody with a sick sense of humor. Oh, and Coop has been deputized to be my bodyguard, so you can relax about everything."

Glenda looked at Coop. "Enjoying yourself?"

"Enjoying Kylie's company, yes."

"Some leave," Glenda said. "You came for some R and R and wind up on sentry duty."

"I don't mind one little bit. What I'd mind is being told to go away with all this happening. That just doesn't suit my nature at all." He rolled the dice and moved a couple of pieces. "Kylie's too good at this game. I keep trying to talk her into chess."

"Not a chance," Kylie answered.

"She always did prefer to win," Glenda said wryly. "God, a black rose. I guess I'm glad you didn't wake me because I'd have been pacing up and down worrying about the threat. How can you be so calm, Kylie?"

"Because now I actually have something in my head to focus on besides a big blank. And Coop was kind enough to ask Connie to check into something for me."

Glenda stiffened. "Which was?"

"Whether there were any black roses involved in the attack on me."

Glenda swore, unusual for her. "Damn, next time you promise to wake me, would you for heaven's sake please do it?"

"We haven't heard anything. Why shouldn't you sleep?" Kylie pushed back from the card table and hugged her sister. She felt as if the big block of terrified ice that had been encasing her was melting. First she had feelings for what all this must be putting Coop through, and now she ached for her sister's distress. At long last she was rediscovering feelings for someone besides herself. It hurt, but it was the start of healing. At last, a giant forward leap.

"Glenda, I love you. Nothing's happened that you can do anything about. And I'm feeling better because now we actually have something to work on. So cheer up for my sake."

Glenda looked up at Kylie. "Cheer up? Really?" Then she shook her head. "You're going to promise me something and this time you're going to keep your promise. If Connie calls about roses, you're going to call me, even at work. I mean it."

"I promise I will."

Glenda looked at Coop. "I'm counting on you to make sure she does. Sheesh!" She threw up her hands. "What's for dinner? I didn't even think about that. It's got to be fast."

"It's got to be already in the oven," Kylie said. "I made some mac and cheese."

Glenda sagged a little. "Why am I suddenly feeling useless?"

Kylie hugged her again. "You're not. You saved me. You got me home. You're not useless at all, sis. I love you. I need you. But I don't need to be totally useless, either."

Glenda nodded finally. "Okay, then. Dinner's cooking. You guys got room for another player?"

After Glenda left for work, the house felt terribly silent for a while. Coop apparently didn't have much to say, but he paced the perimeter of the house from time to time, like a sentry. He paused and listened and then walked some more.

Finally he said to Kylie, "How are you doing? If this waiting doesn't make you anxious, I'd be surprised."

"What I'm doing is feeling better."

He faced her. "Better? How?"

Shame danced across her face. "Since I woke up in the hospital, I haven't thought about a thing except myself. Today I started thinking about other people again. You. Glenda. I'm so glad I haven't forgotten how."

"I don't think you ever forgot," he said. "Other matters just overwhelmed you."

"Maybe. But I was being truly selfish, and that's not the kind of person I ever want to be. So…" She ventured a smile. "I'm sorry I'm putting you through this, I'm sorry Glenda's worried and I wish I could do more to help."

"You don't need to help me," he protested. "Like I said, I'm designed for this. Second nature. As for the entire situation…Kylie, you didn't bring this on yourself. You were attacked. You have no responsibility to any of us except to heal and stay safe."

Lord, she liked this man. Wherever he'd been, whatever he'd done, he had a heart of gold. His warmth, she realized, had touched her heart. Like a hot fire on an icy day, it was helping thaw her out.

Given the times he'd been in combat and all the hardening it must cause, that made him pretty damn special.

Connie called at eight that evening to talk with Kylie. "I don't know what you remembered," she said, "but the police report says there was a black rose on your chest when they found you. God, Kylie, what that man did to you. I'm so glad you're still alive."

Kylie had some idea of the injuries she had suffered, of course, but didn't want to discuss them. They didn't matter right now. Ice coursed through her veins as

Connie's words penetrated. A black rose on her chest. A signature.

A warning.

She nearly dropped the phone back into the cradle and was grateful to feel Coop's arms wind around her from behind. Tight, they pulled her hard against his chest, feeling like steel bands of protection.

"What?" he demanded.

"There was a black rose on me when the cops found me."

He swore then, vile words she would never speak herself, but somehow they made her feel a little better, as if his anger was driving back the ice.

"Are you okay?" he asked.

"I feel frozen," she said, her lips stiff. "Frozen."

"God, I can imagine why. Let me call Glenda for you."

"But…" But what? Glenda would be upset, but she'd be even more upset if she broke her promise again. And Coop had promised, too.

But the darkness was swimming close, the demons seemed to be emerging from hiding, laughing in glee as shock and terror warred inside her. A black rose. There could be no doubt now.

She sank onto the couch and put her head between her knees while Coop called Glenda. The worst of all possible nightmares had happened.

The killer had found her and, what was worse, he clearly wasn't finished with her.

Todd never really left town. He drove away toward Saint Louis, but returned that night, concealing his car in the old barn he rarely used. Having a few lights on at night was something that he always did when he was away, so unless he made himself visible in some way or changed something, everyone would assume he was gone.

But he wasn't. The only thing that maddened him was that he'd never know the reaction to the black rose. From a distance he gathered that the cops were still busy worrying about the kids, but he had no idea if they were paying additional attention to Kylie.

Not that he really cared. He had time, and he enjoyed thinking of her fright dragging out day after day. He had no doubt that she'd learn soon he'd left a black rose with her after he was done in Denver. They'd figure that one out, and they'd tell her.

But they were stretched so thin watching the children that he figured they wouldn't have much left over for her. Which left Cooper. What a bad time for that guy to be hanging around Glenda's house.

He knew plenty of people, though, and it was easy enough to pretend to be calling from Saint Louis when he phoned a friend or two. They were only too eager to update him on the latest stranger contact with a child, and to tell him the cops were all over it. As for Kylie…well, no one knew a thing about that situation. He wondered if a call to one of her friends might seem out of line.

Or if he could call Kylie himself to see how she was doing.

He wanted to savor her terror, and it killed him that he couldn't be close enough to taste it and watch it. But he was also smart and realistic. The time would come when he'd get her alone again, and then he was going to finish the job.

God, he had finally come to hate that woman and to hate himself for pursuing her. She'd treated him like crap in high school, and it hadn't improved much over the years. So pretty, so sweet, liked by nearly everyone.

Only *he* could see how ugly she really was inside, where it counted. Only *he* knew how little she cared for the feelings of others.

But he knew it intimately. *I just don't feel like we're connecting, Todd. I'm sorry.* Why not? No answer to that question. She just didn't want to date him. Then she'd turned him down for the prom and stayed home rather than go with him. Selfish bitch.

Oh, when he ran into her in Denver, just once despite what he'd said to confuse the issue, she'd agreed to have coffee with him, but he could feel her reluctance. Well, there was nothing wrong with him, so there had to be something wrong with her. And he was so tired of her snubs, of her barely concealed dislike of him. She could smile so sweetly, then stab him in the back.

That coffee meeting in Denver had been the last straw. He'd asked her to take in a movie with him—how much more innocent could you get?—but she'd turned him down. Too much work, she said. Too much work to spare a couple of hours? He wasn't buying it, especially since he'd started following her and discovered she had time to go out occasionally with her friends.

No, it was him she objected to, and for no good reason. He'd had enough. Her rejections had stung for years, and then she'd added another one.

Now here she was, almost in his grasp again, and all he had to do was separate her from her watchdogs long enough to take her away with him. He now knew he wasn't going to get over what she'd done to him until she never drew another breath.

It was the only way to erase the slate.

Eventually Coop settled on the couch. The night had deepened, and whatever had made him so edgy seemed to have let go. That made Kylie feel better. She wondered how many of his ghosts and bad memories this situation was reawakening, but she wasn't sure she should ask.

He tucked her against him, as if it were the way he expected them to sit, and she didn't object at all. Everything about him appealed to her. Everything. His scent, his strength, his appearance, but mostly his good, brave heart. A lot of men would have wanted no part of her in her damaged state, and even fewer considering the trouble she brought with her. At every single turn he had treated her with kindness and patience.

"You're a good man, Coop."

"Sometimes."

She wanted to argue with him about that, but figured she couldn't. He had memories he'd never share with her, memories that clearly troubled him. She just hoped that someday he would once again believe that he was a good man. Because he was.

He ran his palm lightly up and down her arm, from shoulder to elbow. Tingles of pleasure began to run through her, warming cold and hollow places inside her. Because of her amnesia, she didn't know how long it had been for her, but she knew how desperately she needed this feeling now. Good, normal feelings. Nice feelings. As naturally as breathing, she turned into him and smiled up at him. "I like that."

His gaze jumped to her upturned face, then a slow smile was born. "Dangerous words, lady. And a dangerous time to have them."

But despite his warning, he bent his head a bit so he could brush a kiss on her lips. Sparklers ignited inside her. Just that light, soft touch, and she was sizzling.

"Wrong time," he murmured.

"Is there ever a right one?"

"Actually, yeah. Trust me, when you're waiting for the enemy, you don't want to be distracted the way you'd distract me."

Her heart sank, but she knew he was right. It was nice to know, however, that he was responding to her. Now she not only had something on which to focus her anxiety, but she had something truly pleasurable to think about. Coop. She imagined that if she let him, he'd fill her whole world, at least for a while.

He dropped another kiss on her lips, caressing her cheek lightly with his thumb, then hugged her a little closer. "Now behave yourself. Never let it be said that a marine was caught with his drawers down."

A little giggle escaped her, leavening her heart again, filling the house with a much-needed happy sound.

"Does anyone call you Evan?" she asked.

"Not much anymore. Coop to friends, or Gunny. I'm not sure I'd answer if anyone called for Evan."

"I've never been anything but Kylie. Well, except for a few people in Denver who called me Nurse Brewer. But mostly it's Kylie, or Nurse Kylie. We're very casual at the hospital here in town. The docs go by first name even with the patients. Dr. Ted, Dr. Joe, that kind of thing."

"It's certainly friendlier."

"Evidently we think so here." And that finished that topic. Funny how hard it had become for her to make casual conversation since she lost her memory. Losing three years shouldn't have meant losing every ordinary skill she had.

But maybe other things had gone wrong with her, and she was going to discover them one by one. Like her occasional tendency to blurt things she once wouldn't have said. God, what a depressing thought.

She dragged herself away from that mire. It was likely

to suck her in without offering a single answer. Some matters were just going to have to await the experience of time.

Easier said than done, of course, but Coop's continuing hug, and the gentle stroking of his hand, helped. Soon she was able to let go of her fears and sink back into the present moment. There was no escaping the fact that the future would come, but it didn't do a lick of good to worry about things she didn't know yet.

There was something much more immediate on her horizon, and she didn't want to think about that, either.

"What I need," she said, "is someone to read me a story. I'm like a kid who can't settle for the night."

A quiet sound of amusement escaped him. "I know that feeling. Let me think a moment. Maybe I can find a story to share."

She hoped he would because it would be nice to learn something more about him. He was fairly closemouthed about himself, probably with good reason, but surely during all those years in the marines he'd had experiences he could share.

"Well, there was the time we were in formation with fixed bayonets, and the idiot behind me sliced my scalp pretty good."

"Oh, no! What happened?"

"I stayed in formation and finished my evolutions with blood pouring down the back of my uniform."

"They didn't pull you out?"

"Why would they? If I couldn't handle that, I couldn't handle the rest of what was in store. Anyway, ten staples fixed me up, and the idiot did a lot of punishment detail. I was fine."

She couldn't imagine it. "If I'd been there, I would have stopped everything."

"Of course. You're a nurse. Big difference."

Obviously. She sighed and let her head once again return to the comfort of his shoulder. "That's just amazing to me."

"Well, not everything that happened involved bleeding. It was just the first memory that popped to mind."

After his own personal self-censorship, she surmised, but didn't say so.

"Then there's the ghost story."

"Ghost story? For real?"

His hand squeezed her arm gently. "For real. A lot of them come out of war zones, believe it or not. People can get really skittish, even experienced veterans, when they're stationed in a place where there's been a fight and people have died. Hell, to be fair, I can get uneasy myself. It's like something stains the ground or the air. I don't know a better way to describe it."

She nodded slowly. "I guess I can see that. Why wouldn't some awful tragedy leave a mark behind, a mark that might reach through time?"

"Maybe so. I could never explain it. Just a feeling I did my best to ignore. Anyway, a squad was stationed at one forward base, maybe ten of them. They weren't the first ones to occupy it, but apparently it had a history stretching back to Alexander the Great. One fort built on top of another, creating kind of a huge hill. The second night they were there, they had a guy up on the roof as a sentry. He got so scared up there he came running down and demanded that someone stand watch with him. So one of the other guys agreed to go up with him."

She waited while he paused, watched him shake his head a little. "Then there were more shook-up marines. They swore a black figure was standing watch with them. After that, they always put two men on watch up there.

One guy refused completely and nutted out enough that they thought it best to send him back to the main base. He said he heard a voice whisper in his ear. I guess a number of them saw strange lights in the nightscopes that they couldn't see with the naked eye, or heard screams. Anyway, the black figure may have been too much for that one guy."

"Wow. A black figure?"

"That's how they described it. Anyway, I'm not sure how much the story got embellished over time, but I've had some feelings myself from time to time, so I won't dismiss them."

She shivered a little as she thought about it.

"I'm sorry, did I frighten you with that?"

"No...no. I was just thinking about the black figure. He, it, was standing watch, too. It doesn't matter if he was one of ours or someone else's. Russian, Afghani, Roman...what disturbs me is thinking that he's dead and stuck there doing his duty."

"Still standing post," he murmured. "You're right, that is sad."

"Were there other stories?"

"Ghosts, you mean? A few. It didn't happen to everyone and didn't happen everywhere. But every so often I'd hear about another one."

"I wouldn't be surprised if battlefields were haunted."

"Frankly, neither would I."

She said nothing more, trying to give him space to back out of his war experiences if that was what he wanted to do. Some things deserved the respect of silence.

"Anyway," he said presently, moving them away from Afghanistan, "when I was younger my dad used to like to take trips to Civil War battlefields. Everyone swears

Gettysburg is haunted, but I didn't feel it. To me it feels incredibly peaceful there. But Antietam was a different story. That was the first time I ever felt like the ground was crying out. I shook it off, but I still remember the way I felt at first. As if the very earth had been scarred."

"Oh, man," she whispered.

"And I don't suppose you were looking for ghost stories to help you sleep."

She managed to tip her head and give him a faint smile. "I needed a distraction. I got it."

"I need to think of something more cheerful to tell you about."

A thought occurred to her. "Do you have that dress blue uniform? Does everyone?"

"We only get them if we need them for an assignment unless we buy them ourselves. But yeah, I had an assignment once that required it when I was in DC, and yes, I have the uniform."

"I'd love to see you in it."

"Everyone loves those uniforms," he said lightly. Then he shifted a little and pulled out his wallet from his hip pocket. Flipping it open with one hand, he passed it to her so she could see the photo of him in dress blues.

"You can tell I'm not so young anymore."

"You look fantastic," she said sincerely. "And you don't look that much older, either. What were you doing?"

"I was selected for the unit that does the Friday night parade at the barracks in DC. And that ramrod straightness owes a lot to duct tape."

"What?" The word came out on a laugh.

"Seriously. When you need to be perfectly straight and still for hours on end, you apply a little help. Duct tape to the torso."

"I never would have guessed."

"Good." He laughed. "Inside secret. The human back doesn't take kindly to that treatment for long."

She giggled. "I'm glad you told me. I used to think it was superhuman."

"Nothing superhuman about it."

Suddenly he grew still. "Shh." He waited a moment, then leaned toward her. "I think I heard something. Stay here."

Her chest tightened instantly and her heart began to race until she felt she couldn't suck in enough air. Probably nothing, she told herself. Probably nothing at all. She was safe here with Coop.

Then why didn't she believe it?

Todd drove one of his old cars to town and parked it a couple of blocks away from the Brewer house. Standing on the sidewalk, he could see through the sheers that covered the front window. Those two were looking entirely too cozy, he thought. Kylie had never let him put his arm around her like that. Never.

But this guy she hardly knew? It must be the marine thing. She was being sucked in by a freaking uniform.

The burn deep within him that seldom quit anymore grew stronger. Infuriated, he looked down at the ground and found a pebble.

When he straightened, he watched Kylie laugh up into that guy's face.

Fury gripped him. Without another thought, he threw that pebble against the side of the house. At once the Coop guy froze.

Good.

But then he stood up to walk around. Todd shrank back into the shadows and hid behind a bush a few houses down.

Maybe he'd add Coop to the list he wanted to take care of. But no, Kylie first.

He'd been waiting a long time to teach her a lesson.

Coop had been seriously uneasy since the news about the black rose. Not that he'd been totally sanguine about Kylie's fears before, but that rose... She was being stalked.

And while he might put on a casual face to keep her calm about all of this, it remained that he was on high alert, and wasn't about to relax it.

He heard something hit the side of the house. Maybe nothing. He hated those sheers on the living room window and was going to have to do something about them. It was like living in a cloudy fishbowl.

As he left Kylie to walk around the house, he knew the sound had come from outside. But first he was going to make sure every single door and window was properly secured. Then he could walk the perimeter outdoors.

Once he was certain they were buttoned up, he returned to the living room. Kylie had paled again, her hazel eyes too big for her face. "Everything's locked up tighter than a drum," he assured her. "No one is inside."

She managed a jerky nod.

"Now I need to check the outside."

At once he saw terror pass over her face. She croaked his name.

He squatted in front of her. "I'm going to go out there and you're going to lock the door behind me. Can you do that?"

Another nod as she gnawed her lip.

"And if there's any way to cover the front window of this place, find it. Those sheers don't give enough privacy. Can you work on that?"

Again she nodded.

Then he took her hands and gave them a quick squeeze. "Come with me. Lock the door behind me."

God, he hated to do this to her, but he *had* to check outside. If there was a lurker, he might have left some sign of his presence. He'd be derelict if he failed to look.

"I won't be long," he promised before he stepped out the door. He heard the dead bolt thud home as she locked up.

The night was quiet, only the usual sounds of cars on other streets, an open window that released the sounds of someone's TV. Nobody walking about.

But someone was watching. That preternatural instinct warned him. He wanted to search the whole street, but figured if the guy saw him coming he'd just pull away farther. So for now, just around this house and yard.

His skin crawled with awareness of the eyes on him. The stalker was nearby. The sound? He didn't know what that had been, but it had sounded as if it had hit the front of the house. The siding. Maybe he could find out what it was.

But first he had to make sure no one was hiding in the yard anywhere. He scanned the front near the house, then started around the corner. Immediately the sense of being watched disappeared.

Well, that gave him a direction for the stalker, but he didn't dare risk there being some kind of threat out here. A bomb, a booby trap, something. He scanned carefully, moving as quickly as he could, determined to get back to the front of the house and see if he could localize whoever was watching.

He saw nothing on the ground, now slightly damp with dew, that betrayed the passage of anything except a dog. The animal's paw prints appeared dark where they had wiped away the dew. Around to the far side, approach the street but not too quickly. And unfortunately, the dew hadn't fallen nearer to the warmer street. None in the front yard or on the pavement.

He felt just an instant, one instant, of those eyes on him again, and then they vanished. Someone had been watching the front of the house, but now had turned away. Possibly meaningless, but he wasn't going to trust in that.

As he reached the porch, he paused. Was that a pebble?

He searched his memory rapidly and couldn't remember anything like that on the porch. Glenda swept it every time she cleaned. Hell, he'd swept it for her just a couple of days ago because of some leaves leftover from autumn.

So the pebble was probably what had hit the house. No accident. He looked toward the sidewalk. The watching eyes were still gone, but he could easily imagine a man standing out there watching.

Slowly he approached the sidewalk and turned to face the house. Entirely too much was visible through those sheers. Like watching a fuzzy TV. Glancing down he could see the grass had been partially flattened. No dew to suggest a direction to look.

Hating it, but knowing there was no more he could do tonight without leaving Kylie alone, he climbed the porch steps, leaving the pebble in place and knocked. "Kylie, it's me."

The door opened swiftly and he stepped inside. God, she looked rattled. As soon as the door was closed behind him and once again locked, he pulled her into his arms and hugged her tightly as if he could squeeze the fear from her.

What he would have liked to have done was wring someone's throat.

But instead he held this lovely, frightened woman and wished he could make her feel safe again. Whoever had sent that rose was cruel beyond belief. Taunting his victim, terrifying her, keeping the nightmare alive.

Yeah, he could have strangled the guy with his bare hands.

He stroked Kylie's hair, feeling a shudder run through her as he held her. "It's okay," he said.

"Nobody?"

"Not now, anyway. We have to deal with that front window, though. Anybody walking by can see in. Did you think about that?"

Lame way to try to pull her back from the precipice of her fears, but sometimes thinking about a problem could be the only way.

"Yeah. There are heavy curtains for the winter. The rod is still up. We just need to hang them."

"Then as soon as you feel ready, we're going to do exactly that."

Then she amazed him. She seemed to shake herself a little, and leaned back within his embrace. "I'm sorry. I didn't use to be such a wimp. And I'm not going to be a wimp now. I think I know where Glenda keeps the curtains."

She was dealing with the immediate problem, an excellent sign. He followed her down the hallway to the linen closet and held out his arms to receive the heavy folded curtains she passed to him.

"They'll have creases in them," she remarked.

"I don't care as long as they shutter the fishbowl."

She paused as she pulled out the last stack. "Is that what it feels like to you?"

"Right now it does."

Her movements slowed just a bit. "I never really thought about it."

"No reason you should have. These streets are usually safe for you, aren't they?"

"They used to be."

He thought that acknowledgment sounded terribly sad, and he made up his mind he was going to make those streets safe for her again.

As he carried the armload of curtains out to the living room, she asked, "Should we call the police?"

"They wouldn't find any more than I did, and it wasn't much. Someone threw a pebble against the side of the house. I couldn't track him. He's probably long gone by now."

"Throwing a pebble seems like a childish thing to do."

He agreed, but he wasn't going to tell her the other interpretations he could put on it. Such as that the guy had seen her laughing and had been angry, striking out in the only way he could when she wasn't alone. Childish or not, he'd had the sense to stay on the sidewalk, out of the grass that might have made him trackable. Definitely not an idiot.

He helped her unfold the heavyweight blue curtains. Fortunately, they had ring hooks that clamped around the rod, and while she held the bottom to take most of the weight off, he strung all the panels. An easy job, and fifteen minutes later, after a little arranging, the living room was no longer visible from the street.

His arms had tightened a little after being over his head too long, but it didn't take much effort to shake them out.

"That's not going to make Glenda happy," Kylie remarked as she stood back and surveyed their work.

"Why not?"

"Because she loves it when it gets warm enough to take them down and let the light in."

He slipped his arm around her shoulders, loving the way she melted into his side. "I think Glenda will understand."

"I'm sure." Kylie sighed and retreated to the sofa. "I'm beginning to feel like a prisoner. It was bad enough when I was just afraid and couldn't remember so much of my life, but now I feel trapped in a cage."

Well, he couldn't deny that she was. Out there on those once-safe streets was a killer who still wanted her. That was certainly one definition of prison. Covering the windows, staying with her every second as a guard… that was another definition.

He paced for a while, wondering how he could ease her mind even a little. In some ways, she was a lot like the young guys he took into their first truly dangerous situations, but in her case she didn't have any training to prepare her or stand by her in the clutch.

God, she must feel at sea with a big hole in her memory and a shadowy figure stalking her. He wouldn't blame her if she freaked out.

But she hadn't yet. Somehow she always found the internal strength and resilience to take each new blow. He admired the hell out of her.

But all this stress was clearly exhausting her, and sleeping on the couch night after night couldn't be truly restful for her.

"Kylie?"

"Yeah?"

"Why don't you go to bed? Your real bed. You need some decent sleep."

For an instant her face froze, and her eyes darted as if expecting something to leap at her from almost any direction. Then she visibly shook herself. She'd slept alone before, after all. Reaching for her independence. But it had been *her* idea then. "You must be awfully tired of me."

"I'm not tired of you at all!" His protest was vehement. "Whatever gave you that idea? That I think you need a good night's sleep? I know it isn't easy with all that's going on. I'll be right there, I swear. And you don't have to worry about me dozing off because I've trained myself to wake at the slightest sound. Survival. So just go get ready for bed."

"Really? You can wake?"

"My ears are better than any alarm clock. I put cats to shame, okay?"

That at least brought a small smile to her face. "Cats, huh?"

"Believe it. Now go get ready for bed. I'll tuck you in, if you want."

He watched her climb the stairs, feeling his insides swelling with emotions he didn't want to deal with right then. He could afford only one thing: watching that woman and keeping her safe. Afterward…well, afterward might be a long time away.

So he could get Cooper away from the woman. Todd headed back to the old car, thinking about that chink. Cooper had been outside for nearly ten minutes looking for whoever had thrown that pebble. That meant that given a proper excuse, he could separate the two of them.

He just had to think of a way. And he would. Of that he was very certain.

Chapter 8

Kylie washed up, changed into a fresh cotton nightshirt and climbed beneath the sheets. She had to admit Coop was right about going to bed. It felt a whole lot more comfortable than the couch. She had a feeling she might indeed sleep better, as long as he was there. As she'd discovered the one night she'd tried this alone, she still woke with panic attacks. But that hadn't happened once when he was there.

She could do this, but not alone.

"Coop?"

A minute later he appeared in the doorway. "Now that's a nice sight, you in a real bed." He smiled.

"Stay with me?"

He hesitated, eyeing the rocker in one corner, then seemed to shake himself.

"Sure," he said.

She was so relieved when he chose to lie down beside

her on top of the covers. Fully clothed, still wearing his boots, but right beside her, big, strong, warm and safe.

"Thank you," she whispered.

"Just behave."

She surprised herself by emitting a small giggle. "No marines caught with their drawers down, huh?"

"Never." Then he rolled onto his side. The only light in the room came from the lamp on the end table behind him, leaving him in shadows as he propped his head in one hand. "Now, it could be that I'd like nothing better. In fact, I'm quite sure I'd love to make love to you until exhaustion overwhelmed us. But you don't need me to explain why the timing stinks."

"Not after the rose," she admitted. She hated it, though. She hated it that some sick man had destroyed her life once and was trying to destroy it again. "You know, Coop, I've devoted my life to helping people, to saving lives. But right now I think I'm capable of murder. Hasn't he stolen enough from me?"

He sighed. "Not by his lights evidently." He reached out his other hand and brushed her hair back from her face before cupping her cheek. "We'll get through this, Kylie. I'll keep you safe and we'll get this guy."

"Nobody can promise that."

"I'm not nobody, okay?"

She believed him. He'd been to war, he'd led men into battle…she couldn't have asked for a better protector. But even marines failed sometimes. There were enough of them in Arlington National Cemetery to prove it.

She closed her eyes, enjoying his touch, wishing she could have so much more. "Promise me," she said.

"What?"

"That when this is over we'll make love. Wild, wonderful love."

"Oh, hey, lady, I can promise that for certain. You drive me to the edge. I can't look at you without wanting you. We will have our day. Maybe lots of days, okay?"

"Okay," she whispered.

She felt his lips touch her forehead lightly and he whispered back, "You can't imagine the ways I want to love you. I want to know every square inch of you. I want to make you so hot you glow."

A shiver ran through her, one of pure delight, and in an instant she flamed with desire. "You're killing me," she murmured.

"Sorry. I'll keep the sexy talk for another time."

"Yeah, before you find out that nurses can go on the attack, too."

A soft laugh escaped him. "I'm looking forward to that. Now sleep, darlin'. Please sleep."

So she closed her eyes, hoping her fluttering nerves would settle enough to let her. His gentle stroking of her hair was soothing, and finally she felt sleep creeping up on her. Wonderful, soothing sleep.

Then in her mind something flashed and she sat bolt upright, a scream escaping her.

Coop hit instant readiness, leaping from the bed fully alert. Nothing had changed; he was sure he hadn't dozed, and not a single unusual sound had broken the quiet of the night.

But there was Kylie sitting bolt upright, staring at something only she could see. Part of him wanted to pull the knife he kept tucked in his boot, but his training warned him against it. Nothing had actually happened, so why scare Kylie?

But something had scared her and he had the definite feeling it had happened inside her.

Afraid of disturbing her when she was caught in some terror, probably a form of the PTSD he knew all too well, he remained standing by the bed.

"Kylie," he said gently. When she didn't respond he made his voice a bit sharper. "Kylie! Do you hear me?"

After what seemed forever, she turned her head a bit and croaked, "I remembered something."

He gathered it wasn't a good memory. "Tell me?"

"A knife," she murmured. "A knife. It flashed as it came down on me. I can feel the blow…"

Thank God he hadn't pulled out his own knife. Under these circumstances the fallout from that could have been thermonuclear. "Can I sit beside you?"

"Yes." Barely audible.

He eased down beside her, trying not to startle her in the least little way. "Did you see anything else?"

"Just the knife." Then she turned into him, burying her face in his shoulder as if she wanted to crawl inside of him.

He wrapped his arms around her, hugging her as tightly as he dared. "I'm here. That was just a memory. Come back to me, Kylie. Please."

She came back, all right. The sobs racked her entire body and her tears soaked his shirt. Gently he rocked her, trying to soothe her. Of all the things to remember, he thought bitterly. Not a useful face, just the flash of the knife that had tormented her. The memory of pain.

"I'm sorry," she hiccuped a few minutes later.

"No need," he said sincerely. "I know what it's like. Cry it out, Kylie."

"Do you cry?"

"I get angry."

She sniffled and another wave of sobs ripped through her. "I'd rather be angry."

He was certain she'd get there eventually. How could she not? She hadn't been exaggerating in the least when she said this guy had stolen everything from her. Her future, her sense of security, her memory. That was a helluva list, and didn't even begin to address the physical suffering she had endured. He honestly hoped she remembered no more of it. The guy's face would be the only useful thing to remember about that attack.

The rest of her memory…that would be a good thing to get back, but he'd bet at this point she'd always wonder what was still missing and whether she could trust herself.

Another terrible thing to do to someone. Sure, memory was flexible and was always being rewritten, but to lose it all and then face having to trust it as it came back in dribs and drabs? He doubted she'd even be able to pick up her schooling where she'd been forced to leave off simply because she'd never be certain of her knowledge.

Anger thrummed in him, tamped down because he didn't want her to sense it, but he felt growing inside himself more than a need to protect this woman. He wanted to avenge her.

That wasn't good. He'd always felt vengeance was wrong, the worst of all possible motivations, but he couldn't escape the fact that he wanted vengeance right now.

Gradually Kylie's sobs eased, and she sagged into his embrace, exhausted by the storm that had just ripped through her. Holding her close, he stroked her back and hair and wished he could do something more. But this was it, to just be here. It didn't feel like anywhere near enough.

"I soaked you," she said eventually, her voice hoarse.

"I've been wet before." He gave her a squeeze. "I'll be right back."

It was almost painful to let go of her, but he made himself do it. First he went to the bathroom and got a warm, damp washcloth. Perching beside her, he gently wiped the tears from her face. Her eyes remained puffy and red, but at least he could get rid of the salty tears.

Her gown was damp, too. "Got a fresh nightie or something?"

"Yeah. Top drawer."

He rose, headed for the bathroom to dump the washcloth, then returned to the dimly lighted bedroom. She was off the bed, already pulling her damp nightshirt over her head.

He froze. In the lamplight she looked almost bronze, perfect in every line as she stretched her arms over her head. He'd seen plenty of naked women, but this one appeared more perfect to him than all the rest. High, small breasts, a tiny waist, long willowy legs.

And scars. Even in the dim light he could see where the attacker's knife had slashed her as if he wanted to ruin her beauty. Amazing he hadn't gone for her face, but he'd sure tried to ruin all the rest.

Catching himself, realizing Kylie might be upset if she caught him gawking, he stepped back quickly and went to his own room to change into a blue sweatshirt. The night held a spring chill now.

When he got back to her room, she was covered by a flannel nightshirt and rubbing her arms. "When did it get so cold?" she asked.

Probably about the time she remembered the knife, he thought, but avoided saying. "It's still spring," he said as cheerfully as he could. "Now get under those blankets."

He wished he could get under them with her. The

memory of her sexy body was seared into his brain and still flaming. Bad timing. He knew all about bad timing and how catastrophic it could become.

She slid under the covers and wiped her arm over her face. "Sorry about all the tears."

"I told you, no need." He sat on the edge of the bed, looking down at her.

"So you get angry?"

"I think it's a guy thing. Tears might be more productive."

"Do you smash things?"

"I try very hard not to do that. I usually succeed."

One corner of her mouth tugged down. "What do you get mad about? Your cemetery?"

That slammed him. It shouldn't have because he'd told her about it. But then he added a piece of the truth he rarely shared, because somehow it seemed important that she know this before she decided what kind of man he was. "My cemetery," he agreed. "And the people who must be standing weeping beside all those graves."

She sat up quickly and threw her arms around him. "Oh, Coop, I'm so sorry."

Hesitantly he put his arms around her. "War has a price, Kylie. We all pay it—everyone who gets involved, civilian or military. Different people pay different prices because none of us are the same, but we all pay in some way. It's inescapable."

"How do you deal?"

"The same way you're dealing. One foot in front of another, day by day. We can't change the past. What matters is what we do with the next moment, and the next. I'm no pacifist. I believe in what I do. I'm trying to do the right thing. Sometimes I wonder if I am, but I have to keep moving forward and do the best I can."

YOUR PARTICIPATION IS REQUESTED!

Dear Reader,

Since you are a lover of our books – we would like to get to know you!

Inside you will find a short Reader's Survey. Sharing your answers with us will help our editorial staff understand who you are and what activities you enjoy.

To thank you for your participation, we would like to send you 2 books and 2 gifts – **ABSOLUTELY FREE!**

Enjoy your gifts with our appreciation,

Pam Powers

SEE INSIDE FOR READER'S SURVEY

For Your Reading Pleasure...

We'll send you 2 books and 2 gifts
ABSOLUTELY FREE
just for completing our Reader's Survey!

YOUR READER'S SURVEY
"THANK YOU" FREE GIFTS INCLUDE:
- ▶ **2 FREE books**
- ▶ **2 lovely surprise gifts**

PLEASE **FILL IN THE CIRCLES COMPLETELY TO RESPOND**

1) What type of fiction books do you enjoy reading? (Check all that apply)
- ○ Suspense/Thrillers ○ Action/Adventure ○ Modern-day Romances
- ○ Historical Romance ○ Humor ○ Paranormal Romance

2) What attracted you most to the last fiction book you purchased on impulse?
- ○ The Title ○ The Cover ○ The Author ○ The Story

3) What is usually the greatest influencer when you <u>plan</u> to buy a book?
- ○ Advertising ○ Referral ○ Book Review

4) How often do you access the internet?
- ○ Daily ○ Weekly ○ Monthly ○ Rarely or never.

5) How many NEW paperback fiction novels have you purchased in the past 3 months?
- ○ 0 - 2 ○ 3 - 6 ○ 7 or more

YES! I have completed the Reader's Survey. Please send me the 2 FREE books and 2 FREE gifts (gifts are worth about $10) for which I qualify. I understand that I am under no obligation to purchase any books, as explained on the back of this card.

240/340 HDL GLDC

FIRST NAME	LAST NAME

ADDRESS

APT.#	CITY

STATE/ PROV.	ZIP/ POSTAL CODE

© 2016 ENTERPRISES LIMITED
® and ™ are trademarks owned and used by the trademark owner and/or its licensee. Printed in the U.S.A.

RS-816-SFF15

Accepting your 2 free Harlequin® Romantic Suspense books and 2 free gifts (gifts valued at approximately $10.00) places you under no obligation to buy anything. You may keep the books and gifts and return the shipping statement marked "cancel." If you do not cancel, about a month later we'll send you 4 additional books and bill you just $4.74 each in the U.S. or $5.49 each in Canada. That is a savings of at least 12% off the cover price. It's quite a bargain! Shipping and handling is just 50¢ per book in the U.S. and 75¢ per book in Canada.* You may cancel at any time, but if you choose to continue, every month we'll send you 4 more books, which you may either purchase at the discount price or return to us and cancel your subscription. *Terms and prices subject to change without notice. Prices do not include applicable taxes. Sales tax applicable in N.Y. Canadian residents will be charged applicable taxes. Offer not valid in Quebec. Books received may not be as shown. All orders subject to approval. Credit or debit balances in a customer's account(s) may be offset by any other outstanding balance owed by or to the customer. Please allow 4 to 6 weeks for delivery. Offer available while quantities last.

▼ If offer card is missing write to: Reader Service, P.O. Box 1867, Buffalo, NY 14240-1867 or visit www.ReaderService.com ▼

BUSINESS REPLY MAIL
FIRST-CLASS MAIL   PERMIT NO. 717   BUFFALO, NY

POSTAGE WILL BE PAID BY ADDRESSEE

READER SERVICE
PO BOX 1867
BUFFALO NY 14240-9952

NO POSTAGE
NECESSARY
IF MAILED
IN THE
UNITED STATES

She rested against him gently, almost as comforting as a blanket. "That's what I need to do, too. Keep moving, even though this creep is out there still."

"Well," Coop admitted, "he's a hell of a wrinkle. But everyone's on the lookout for you, especially me and Glenda. So maybe instead of worrying about him every minute, you should be thinking about all the tomorrows still to come. Like maybe medical school?"

She sighed, and he felt her soften even more. Apparently her moments of terror had receded into the background, and he was thankful for that.

"Medical school is a pipe dream," she said finally. "I know it. First of all, I have this amnesia problem, but even without that, I figured I couldn't afford it. Not even with loans. I mean, any way I looked at it, I'd need a job at the same time, it would take four years and then I'd need to intern and…well, I could maybe be looking for a job in my midthirties. That's a big commitment, and I am kind of worried I might not be able to do it alone. I started hearing about medical students who get married just to have a spouse to pay the living expenses. I wouldn't want to use someone that way. It turned me off."

"I can see why." He certainly could. But if it was really her dream… Well, not his place. Apparently she'd been happily working toward being a physician's assistant. "So do you think you'll resume your degree program?"

"My master's? I don't know. Every time I think about my amnesia I get queasy. How much have I forgotten? I don't even know if I'd be fit to go back to regular nursing now. Maybe I'll feel differently later, but right now I'm uncertain about everything."

"Time will help with that, I think." He sure hoped so.

He couldn't begin to imagine what it must be like to be going through life with such a huge hole in your memory, unable to trust almost everything about yourself.

Most people went through life thinking of themselves as a seamless flow into the distant past. This woman's life had been interrupted. No seamless flow for her. Yeah, that would make her uncertain about most things. And even if her memory came back, like she said, would she entirely trust it? Probably not.

She spoke again. "Thank you for being so patient with me."

"Patient?" The word surprised him. "I'm not being patient."

"Sure you are. I've wrecked your entire vacation and you didn't even know me until my sister dragged you into this. You could be off having a good time instead of babysitting me."

The word shook him. He took her by the shoulders and held her a few inches away so he could look into her face. "I don't feel like a babysitter. I'm not being patient. In fact, I should probably thank you for giving me a chance to try to protect you. It feels good, damn it."

"Really?" She searched his face, then the corners of her mouth tipped up. "You're an awfully good man, Evan Cooper. Thank you for watching over me."

He couldn't imagine anyone who wouldn't want to. Well, except for one sicko, anyway. "My pleasure and my honor," he answered. "Now…do you think you can sleep?"

He wasn't surprised by her answer.

"I'm afraid to close my eyes again."

Well, he could hardly blame her for that now. "Wanna try for the couch again?"

She hesitated. "Maybe so. I haven't had any trouble sleeping with my head on your lap."

Small comforts. He was glad to offer his lap, but he wished he could really help this woman, help her escape her terror.

But he'd wished for a lot of things in his life, and few enough of them had come his way.

A short while later, Kylie lay on her side on the sofa, her head cradled on Coop's thigh. It was a powerful thigh, hard, too hard to be called a pillow, but somehow more comfortable and reassuring than a real, soft pillow. She felt that strength, that power beneath her cheek and she felt secure. Even his masculine scents, stronger when she was this close, reached out and enveloped her in a more pleasant reality. The possibility of an exciting one.

She wondered if he made everyone feel that way. His effect on her was undeniable. She wanted him sexually. The burning need of it never quieted anymore. It strengthened at times, then settled, then resurged. Only a couple of times had it completely vanished: when the rose had been delivered and she learned there had been one in Denver, and then tonight when she remembered that flashing blade. It had caught light from somewhere, but that had only allowed her to see her own blood on it.

She didn't want to close her eyes again. She stared at the curtains they'd hung, glanced around the softly lit room, but barely dared to blink.

She didn't want to see that image again as vividly as she had seen it earlier. Now it had entered the realm of memory, but then it had been very real and very much in the now when it had popped into her head. As if she'd been thrown back in time.

She felt Coop rest his hand on her shoulder. Heavy, strong, comforting. Amazing man. Not once had he told her to stiffen her spine or quit wallowing. No, she was the one who told herself that from time to time.

Life happened. Once it did there was no choice but to keep going. One foot in front of the other, as Coop said. Memory or no memory, she still had to do that. Life wouldn't let her opt out.

But the idea that her attacker was stalking her made the future seem awfully hazy. Even with Coop and the entire Conard County Sheriff's Department on alert for strangers, she couldn't quite believe the guy wouldn't find a way to get her.

Because he had gotten her before.

She didn't even realize she had sighed until Coop spoke quietly.

"Heavy sigh," he said. "Penny?"

"Nothing really. Part of me is mad at myself for letting this guy get to me this way, and part of me is scared to death. I'm kinda tired of being frightened."

"I know. But this is one roller coaster you're just going to have to ride, Kylie. The bumps will start to level out eventually."

"Not if we don't catch this guy. Shouldn't it be possible to find out where someone bought a black rose? And who bought it?"

"I don't know how many places sell them. And if he bought one with cash… I don't know, Kylie. I'd be very surprised if the police haven't looked into it, though. They sure didn't overlook it."

"You're right. How else could Connie have gotten that information?"

"Exactly." He rubbed her shoulder. "I can't imagine sending anyone black roses, but given the world I suppose it's probably easy enough to do. People do all kinds of things I'd never think of if I didn't run into them."

"They could make an interesting gag gift."

He laughed quietly. "Yeah. Or they might be the way to the heart of a woman who adores black. Not my cup of tea, but I'm sure there are lots of people who feel differently."

"Probably. That's one thing nursing taught me. The limits of *my* imagination aren't necessarily the limits of someone else's."

"Hah. Don't tell me. I've already seen enough that I couldn't have imagined."

She bet he had. She rubbed her cheek against his thigh and felt him squeeze her shoulder. Beyond these walls, the night held a threat, a huge threat, for her, but within, close to Coop, she felt as if she were protected by a magic bubble.

She wished she knew some way to express that without embarrassing him. He seemed to consider what he was doing as perfectly normal, and the few times that she had said he was special, he'd dismissed it.

Maybe because of his personal cemetery. Maybe bodies buried there haunted him in ways she could scarcely imagine. Maybe because he said he honored them by remembering them. That was an awful burden to carry in his heart, but to her that merely spoke of what a truly good man he was. He said he believed in what he did, yet apparently he also felt the weight of it, for good or ill.

And she thought she'd had a rough time of it? She probably had no idea how rough life could really get. None at all.

At least she didn't remember. Maybe she should stop thinking of that as a loss and start thinking of it as a mercy, even if it had changed her entire life in ways she was just beginning to understand.

He spoke. "Maybe you ought to give medical school another look."

"Why?"

"Because you've had this great big interruption. Instead of trying to pick up things where you left off, maybe you should go for what you really want. Start at the beginning of the big adventure. And don't use money as an excuse. People go to medical school somehow, and when they get done they manage to pay their loans back. Maybe you need to take a fresh look at it."

"Maybe," she said slowly. A little kernel of excitement awoke in her, and she realized that she *still* wanted to be a physician. A doctor. Nothing had cut that out of her. And nothing had blocked her except herself.

As the idea turned in her mind, she thought of all the obstacles. She'd have to bone up for the MCAT so she could get admitted. She'd have to make sure the finances would work. But why not take another look at it? Her entire life had been run through a shredder. Maybe it was time to go for it.

Maybe she was being given a second chance.

For the first time it occurred to her that something positive could come out of all of this.

"You're special, Coop." She blurted the words. "And don't argue with me, okay? I'm not asking for your opinion—I'm giving you mine. You're special."

His hand paused as it stroked her shoulder, then resumed. "Thank you," he said finally. As if it hurt to accept the compliment.

What in the world did this man believe about himself? she wondered. That he just did his job and no more? That he could have been replaced by any of a billion men?

She wondered if she'd ever met a man with so little ego. He was clearly capable and competent in many ways. He accepted that, but as if it were just average. Maybe for a marine it was, but somehow she doubted it. Maybe the standard he measured himself against was impossibly high.

Whatever, it was not something she could bring up. As much time as they had spent together, they hadn't reached that kind of intimacy.

Thinking about Coop took her out of herself. So much so that she finally fell asleep without realizing it.

Never knowing that the man who held her watched her sleep and smiled.

Todd's father had never gotten rid of an old car when he replaced it. The man had quit farming when *his* father had died and instead had become a financial planner. A trade he taught to Todd.

But the cars remained in the unused barn, an excuse for working on engines on a Saturday or Sunday. Todd had always hated it, but his dad had loved it, so he'd put up with it. Which meant that there were three old cars in the barn, rusting and aging, but as tuned up as race cars. Most of the time they sat on blocks. Once in a while Todd picked up some retread tires for one or another of them. And when he needed anonymity he had it.

None of the cars were registered any longer, so every year he stole useful license plates from other states, just in case he needed to drive one. Cops weren't interested in stolen plates at all, not unless they stopped you and one was on your car. Since he only drove his own vehicle on road trips, he had nothing to fear.

Lately he'd been using the old Biscayne, but maybe it

was time to switch to the Olds. He didn't want to become recognizable around town, not at all.

So tomorrow he'd move the tires from the Biscayne to the Olds, and the Illinois license plate, as well. Or maybe he should switch to the Missouri plate, in case someone had noted the Illinois plate.

He'd think about that tomorrow.

At least he'd gotten away from Cooper. Thank goodness he hadn't driven close to the Brewer house. No trail. He had to keep that in mind, because now he was dealing with a marine, and he hadn't the faintest doubt that Cooper could track well.

Stay off the grass; use a car no one would identify—not the one he'd been using to talk to the kids. Not when he went for Kylie.

In fact, he told himself to stop sending her warnings. The black rose had been irresistible, but that was enough. Any more and he might make a mistake he couldn't afford.

But as soon as he lectured himself, he started dreaming about other ways to scare her. He was discovering that he enjoyed playing with his prey.

Maybe when he was done with Kylie, he'd look for someone else to taunt and torment. It was just too delicious.

He couldn't believe he hadn't done this before.

Coop allowed himself to doze on the couch with Kylie's head safely in his lap. He wasn't kidding when he said he was as good as a cat at waking up. Years in extreme danger had turned him into the ultimate light sleeper. He could doze off at the drop of a hat at any moment when he felt safe, and wake even more quickly at any unusual sound, however quiet.

But Kylie's sudden gasp was hardly quiet. Instantly

awake, instantly alert, he looked down at her and saw that her eyes were wide open, staring. She felt as rigid as steel.

"Kylie?" He waited, hoping she might just go back to sleep. She might not really be awake. But then her voice reached him.

"I...remembered more."

Aw, hell. Without a word, he scooped her stiff body onto his lap and wrapped her in whatever security his arms could provide. "So it's coming back."

"I'm afraid so." She whispered the words, and her hand clutched the front of his sweatshirt in a death grip.

"His face?" Coop asked.

"No. Just more of...the knife. It's almost like a fixation."

"Hardly surprising." He meant it. The horror of what had happened to her had probably focused on the instrument that had struck at her more than her attacker. Her eyes would have fixated on it, as well as her mind.

"Useless," she muttered.

He hesitated, then said, "Hardly. You're getting your memory back. That's probably a good thing."

She didn't dissolve into terrified sobs this time. In fact, the tension eased out of her remarkably quickly. As if she were making some internal adjustment to her memory. Progress? He hoped so.

When at last she seemed comfortable against him he said, "Why don't you try to see if you've recovered any other memories? Ordinary ones, like school, and your job. Maybe more is returning—it's just not grabbing your attention."

"That's possible," she admitted. "But how could I be sure I'm not just making it up?"

"I guess that's the whole problem with memory."

Her hand loosened on his shirt and she absently began to brush it smooth again. The gentle touches quickly lit the bonfire of his desire and he had to close his eyes, trying to dampen it. But no matter how much self-control he needed, he didn't want her to stop touching him.

He forced his attention to a more important matter. "Is there someone around here you could talk to about it? A professional?"

"I'm sure. But they can't fill in the blanks, and I'll probably never be sure that I've filled in the blanks correctly. Will I?"

He absolutely didn't know how to answer that. "Kylie, I'm not a professional. My gut says you should just trust yourself. What else can you do? We all have to trust our memories, and how often have you heard two people disagree on exactly what happened even yesterday?"

"I guess you're right. Maybe I should dig out my textbooks and find out what's familiar to me."

"That's an idea."

Then she sighed and leaned into him even more. "You're so reassuring. But honestly, Coop, that knife… I wish I could stop seeing it. You must have memories like that. How do you deal?"

Deal? Good question. You couldn't fight them; you just had to live with them until age deprived them of their power over you. Some of those memories had an awfully long lifespan. "I live with it," he said finally. "There's no other way. In time, it usually gets better. The brain kind of burns out and it grows more distant. It has less impact. This is fresh, so hang on."

He felt her head bob a little against his shoulder. "Medical school?" she said questioningly.

"What about it?"

"Should I really look into it again? I mean…"

"I can't answer that. It just seems to me it was a dream of yours once upon a time. Maybe you can turn this mess into something positive by finding a way to do it. Or not. What do I know?"

She sighed and continued rubbing his chest. "You feel good."

He didn't know how to take that. "Meaning?"

"You just feel good. I like touching you. Sorry if that bothers you. It's just... I like it."

Well, he sure liked it, too. "It doesn't bother me at all." At least not in a negative way, because it was sure bothering him in other ways. "Don't stop," he said, hoping his voice didn't sound as thick as it felt.

"I don't want to," she said.

Then, moments later, she put an instant end to the haze of desire that had been enveloping him.

"Why," she asked, "would someone do this to me? How could I have made someone this angry?"

Shock drew him up short. She was blaming herself? For what some sicko had done? Chances were she'd never seen the guy before he attacked her.

"I mean...he must have been furious," she said.

"How about any fury was all in his own head? Maybe he never set eyes on you before the attack. For the love of God, Kylie, don't blame yourself for what *he* did."

"But there had to be a *reason*! And why *me*?"

"The only reason had to exist somewhere inside his head. It probably had nothing to do with you. And even if you did make him mad... Kylie, how many times in your life have you gotten angry? Did you ever want to kill someone?"

"No," she said quietly.

"Then there you go. Don't you dare blame yourself for what that creep did. He's twisted, and his reasons will never justify what he did, nor should you take any responsibility for it."

"It's hard not to," she admitted. "We always think things happen for a reason. I know it's not true. I mean, I've treated little kids for cancer. What did they ever do to deserve that? What does anyone do? But I can't shake it. I must have done something."

"If you did, like I said, it doesn't justify what he did to you. Nothing can or will. Just please don't blame yourself while you wonder why this happened. I can understand wanting a reason for it. That's normal. But accepting the blame, any part of it, for what he did? Don't you do that."

He hugged her as tightly as he dared, suddenly very worried about how she might process this. He had plenty to blame himself for, and plenty that he knew wasn't his fault. The idea that she might accept guilt for what had been done to her seemed like a huge deal, something that had to be prevented.

Maybe he should mention this to Glenda in the morning. She might have some ideas about how to help.

He closed his eyes again, letting his ears do the work while Kylie rested securely in his arms.

He knew men like the one who had attacked her. He'd met a few of them in the military. They never suffered a pang; they damn well enjoyed the brutality. They were few and far between, and for some it was a coping mechanism that vanished as soon as they were out of combat. But for others…for others it satisfied some deep need, and he could only hope that those guys were never let out on the streets again. Unfortunately, some of them probably were, but maybe many who were had enough self-control to realize they could no longer indulge their personal cruelty, at least not in big ways.

But the brutality too often came home. To wives and

kids. The military had entire programs to deal with spousal and child abuse. Men like that were the minority, of course, but they existed.

And somehow it flowed seamlessly into a society where such things were all too common. Nobody remarked on it. Tongues clucked; people were sent for diversion, for therapy; relationships ended… Yeah, it was a background to life everywhere.

So the worst creeps might find an outlet that didn't land them in a maximum security prison.

Which left people like the man who had attacked Kylie. People who couldn't control their sadistic urges. He would never understand them.

What he *did* understand was that they were responsible for their own actions. Blaming the victim had never been in his nature. It just plain hurt to hear Kylie trying to blame herself. He understood her need for a reason, but that was exactly the wrong direction to go.

Somehow she needed to be convinced of that because he was certain her nightmare was about to deepen. The man was still stalking her, and her memory was beginning to return.

He didn't pray often, but he prayed now that Kylie would start to recall happier memories. Anything that would make her smile and remember the joy of being alive.

Because that creep had all but destroyed her.

Chapter 9

In the morning, while Coop made eggs and Kylie started buttering toast, Glenda returned home, entering the house with a single word: "Coffee."

Behind her, to Kylie's surprise, came Connie in her uniform. "News?" she asked instantly.

Connie shook her head. "Sorry, no. Nothing since the rose, and nobody has any idea yet where it was purchased. The crime lab is looking into it. Apparently black roses can be as individual as fingerprints, revealing where they were grown, or if they were dyed a certain way. They might be able to track it, might even be able to locate the buyer. God, I hope so, but evidently it's going to take time. It's not like there's a national database on them."

She sat at the table while Kylie poured her and Glenda mugs of coffee. "What about the kids?" Kylie asked.

"Nothing more has happened. What about you?"

Kylie hesitated. She looked at Coop, surprised at how reluctant she was to talk about her two flashes of memory. Last night they'd preoccupied her. Now she was almost afraid to mention them, feeling an unreasonable superstition about it. Don't mention it and it wouldn't happen. Really?

"Kylie's getting her memory back," Coop said, evidently deciding he wasn't going to let her withhold that. "Just two little snatches. She remembers the knife, and some of the pain, but nothing else."

"Well, doesn't that stink," Glenda said, joining Connie at the table. Her scrubs looked rumpled from the long night, and strands of her hair had escaped her bun in a few places. "Of all the things to come back."

"We were talking," Coop continued, "about how she may have also begun to remember other things. They wouldn't just leap out at her the way that did. She suggested reviewing her textbooks."

"I've got a better idea," Glenda said, looking at her sister. "Come to work with me tonight. Just for a couple of hours. See how familiar it feels. See what you remember about treatment."

"But that was from before."

"That was also one of the things you were worrying about. That you might have lost more than just three years. So let's test it. Maybe being back in the hospital setting will help you remember more."

"I'll think about it." For some odd reason, Kylie felt reluctant to take the kind offer. Perhaps she was afraid she wouldn't remember anything. Maybe she'd find out that she'd lost more than three years. Or maybe…what exactly? Was she afraid to leave Coop's protection? Even at a busy hospital?

Oh, man, that was dependency, and certainly one she

couldn't afford. Coop had a career to get back to soon. What was she going to do when he left? Hide in a closet?

Coop served everyone eggs, including Connie, then scrambled a couple more for himself. Kylie popped two more slices of rye bread into the toaster.

"You know, this whole setup is weird," Connie remarked as she ate. "First a stranger approaching a kid, a stranger who does nothing except talk. Sure that's scary. But then Kylie comes home and another kid is approached, this time to bring her a message. This doesn't sound like your average child predator."

"No," Coop agreed instantly. "It doesn't."

Connie asked, "But why should this have anything to do with Kylie? It started before she came home. The rose might not even be related to the person who made the first approach. What's more, it isn't like it was all over the media that she was coming back here. I don't think it made a blip in the paper or on TV in Denver. All the interest died once it was known that she didn't remember anything. She faded into the wall as far as news was concerned."

"It definitely wasn't in the press," Glenda said. "I know because I was looking out for it. Connie's right about the interest vanishing, at least in Denver. Not so much here, of course, because Kylie is known to most people hereabouts."

"So very weird," said Connie. "The stuff with the kids may be separate incidents. I'm not sure how many people around here knew when Kylie was coming back. All I know is this case is giving me a mental case of the hives."

Coop spoke. "It sure doesn't feel right."

"No, it doesn't." Connie frowned at her plate, then bit into a slice of toast. After she swallowed, she said, "We're all troubled by it in the department. Either we've got two actors involved, or we've got one actor who is doing it all, and that doesn't make sense. I mean, the rose could be a diversion from something with the kids, but it doesn't work the other way around. It certainly doesn't divert us from keeping an eye on Kylie. Quite the opposite."

Kylie felt as if something cold slithered down her spine. "The kids," she said. "It would be a great distraction from the kids, dividing your attention. Don't let that happen, Connie. I'd just die if something happened to a child because you were using too many resources to look out for me."

"Nothing's going to happen because of you," Connie said.

"Thank you," Coop muttered.

"What?" Glenda asked.

Kylie looked down. She didn't know if she wanted this discussed, but she didn't see how she could silence Coop. Her stomach began to sink.

"Kylie is beginning to wonder if she did something to make this guy attack her."

Glenda drew a sharp breath. Connie responded. "I've seen a lot of victims do that. Just stop right there, Kylie. Nobody makes someone do something like that. No one forces someone to harm a child. You couldn't have done anything in your life to justify the kind of attack you endured. Nothing."

Kylie managed a nod. Intellectually she knew they were right. Emotionally it felt very different. Part of her kept wondering what she had done to bring this on herself. That need for a reason could be poisonous, she realized. Even so, she still wanted one, as if she could ever understand.

"So," said Glenda, still frowning but clearly trying

to be more cheerful. "Want to come to work with me tonight?"

Kylie's answer was instantaneous. "No. I'm not ready." Somewhere deep inside she knew that. "Maybe next week, Glenda. I appreciate it, but I just don't feel ready yet."

"Well, that's understandable. You haven't been out of the hospital that long yourself. Just let me know when you want to give it a try. I'm sure everyone at the hospital would be glad to see you." Then she let it go, much to Kylie's relief.

But the conversation left her wondering just how damaged she was. Would she ever be able to walk into a hospital again? Or was she afraid of being away from Coop's protection? But what safer place could there be than in a hospital surrounded by so many people who would watch out for her?

God, sometimes she felt as if she'd lost her mind along with her memory.

All she knew was that she wasn't ready to step back into her role as a nurse, even as an observer. Something deep within rebelled. Was she somehow associating that with the attack on her?

Later, after Connie had gone to work and Glenda had headed for bed, Kylie got a few of her textbooks from the box in her bedroom and carried them downstairs to sit at the kitchen table. Coop was right. She might remember something, or even a whole lot, if she scanned the texts.

"Kylie?"

She looked over her shoulder at Coop.

"I'll stay in the next room so you won't be disturbed by me, but…why were you so reluctant to take Glenda up on her offer?"

She almost blushed. She could hardly tell him she

didn't want to be away from the security he provided. But at the same time, it was more and she knew it. "I don't know for sure. I just felt everything inside me rise up and say no. I guess I'm not ready for that."

"I just wondered. I can't say I'm surprised. I'll be hanging out in the living room."

"You don't have to stay with me every moment," she said, trying to be brave. She'd discommoded this man more than she could believe. He hadn't left her side since she'd come home from Denver. That wasn't right.

"I have no desire to be anywhere else," he answered, as if that settled the whole issue.

She looked down at her books. Maybe it did. Because if there was one inescapable fact in all of this: someone was hunting her.

Coop was disturbed, too. For all he took a positive approach with Kylie, he knew too well that someone out there wanted to kill this woman, and unfortunately he knew how easy that could be. War had taught him that sometimes all the best security measures in the world weren't enough.

But he was also troubled by Connie's remark that the situations of the children and Kylie were giving her brain hives. An apt description, he thought. There was a burning in his head that wouldn't quit, the sense that something was going very wrong and that the direction wasn't fully identifiable.

That black rose, for example. The one notion no one had suggested, out of an excess of caution, was that it had simply been a cruel joke by someone who had heard about the black rose in Denver somehow. A person who had no desire to hurt Kylie. A stupid prankster who might not even be involved in the approach to that child.

Hell, there'd only been one child approached if you didn't count Mikey and his mission to deliver the rose.

At this point, it would be easy to say the kids were safe and Kylie was not, or that Kylie was probably safer than the children. Definitely brain hives.

But none of them could afford to overlook any potential threat.

One guy or two guys? Man, he'd love the answer to that. Two guys seemed like too much of a fluke, but as he'd learned too often coincidences appeared to be coincidental only until you knew what was behind them. Dang, the itch in his head wouldn't quit. He wanted answers. He wanted to be assured of Kylie's safety and the safety of the children in this town.

One guy or two? Misdirection? Damn, any way he looked at it, almost anything was possible now. He hated this. Despite all the uncertainty he'd had to face as a marine in hostile lands, he'd never learned to tolerate it well. Usually answers came in ugly packages, but they came.

Now here he was in this quiet little town facing a similar uncertainty and there wasn't a whole lot he could do about any of it.

Except protect Kylie. He had his mission. He just wished he knew where the threat might be coming from. How the pieces fit together, because fitting those pieces would give him insight into the enemy.

Right now he was flying blind, and he didn't like it at all.

He insisted they go to Maude's diner for lunch. They both needed to get out of this house. "You're going to start becoming agoraphobic if we keep this up."

She rewarded him with a smile. "Sounds good to me." She closed the book she'd been reading.

"Remember any of it?"

"Much to my surprise, quite a bit." She was still smiling as she ran to the bathroom to freshen up. He doubted he'd ever seen a woman who looked quite as good in jeans and a T-shirt. Not fancy, no makeup, just a fresh beauty all her own.

And she was remembering a lot of her textbook. He wondered where that would take her. Most likely not back to Denver to finish her program. But maybe another city.

Then he reined himself in. That had to be a long way down the road yet, and certainly until they found her attacker.

At least she was smiling.

Todd kept an eye on them from the security of the old Oldsmobile. He had a ball cap pulled down over his forehead, and a messy red wig and beard to conceal his identity. He hadn't spared any money on these wigs and beards once he'd decided he needed a disguise. They looked as natural as if they'd grown on him…as long as no one got within six inches, and he wasn't planning on allowing that until he had Kylie again.

So they went to the diner for lunch. He'd brought his own sandwich and a soft drink and drove farther down the street so he wouldn't appear suspicious.

Time, he thought, to do something else. Time to scare another kid's family. He didn't much care if the little kid got nervous; they'd get over it. But he wanted the parents in an uproar, demanding a stronger police presence.

He wanted the attention of everyone to move away from Kylie.

The real problem was that Cooper guy. Apparently he was joined at the hip with Kylie. Except for the night he'd slipped outside to look around, he hadn't been more than a foot or two from her.

So he needed to do more than create another uproar about someone stalking kids. He had to find a way to get that damn marine away from Kylie. He didn't need long. Ten or fifteen minutes so he could take Kylie elsewhere.

Just a short break in the surveillance. There had to be a way to accomplish that, and since Todd was pretty bright he had no doubt he'd figure it out.

He glanced at his watch. Elementary school was letting out in forty-five minutes. Then he'd unleash a new uproar.

Yeah. Pretty soon most everybody would forget Kylie.

"Did you feel watched?" Kylie asked Coop as they settled at a booth in the diner. She noticed he seated himself so he could see the door. Habit or caution?

"Yeah," he said after a moment. "But look how many people are out and about."

She wondered if he was dismissing her, then decided he wasn't the kind of man to do that. There'd been plenty of times when he could have waved away the things she said, but instead he'd listened and tried to be reassuring. He was probably trying to reassure her now, to judge by the way his eyes never stopped moving. He surveyed the street and the diners around them ceaselessly.

Okay, he'd felt it, too, and didn't think it was simply someone curious glancing at them. Suddenly she wished her back wasn't to the door, and craned her neck to look out at the street.

Maude brought her back with a slam of coffee mugs on the table. "What'll it be?"

Kylie didn't answer immediately, strangely fascinated by the coffee that was pouring into the mugs.

"Kylie?" Coop said, yanking her back yet again.

"Chef salad," Kylie said. The coffee had stopped pouring and she felt as if she'd been freed from the edge of a nightmare. Why? What was she trying to remember. "A little extra turkey if that's okay, Maude?"

"Fine," the woman grumped, then took Coop's order.

Silence fell over their table, while people around them continued to talk.

"Kylie?"

She turned her gaze to Coop. "Yeah?"

"You feeling spooked?"

"I was for a moment."

He frowned faintly. "Then what happened? You were fixated there."

"I don't know," she admitted. "I was watching the coffee pour, and it was like…like I was on the cliff edge of remembering something. But I can't imagine what. Maybe just some other time when coffee poured into cups."

"Maybe so." But he continued to look faintly troubled as he scanned their surroundings.

Coffee pouring into a mug. Now that was a weird thing to get hung up on, she thought. But she couldn't let go of it. It clung to her mind like cold, wet leaves, unwilling to just vanish. But how many times in her life had she watched coffee pour? A million?

The image of the dark brown liquid pouring into the cup remained throughout lunch, and when Maude refilled their mugs she watched again, but her reaction was nowhere near as strong. It remained, but didn't seem subtly threatening. Interesting.

During lunch they talked casually about Connie,

Ethan and their kids, about what she remembered from her textbooks and how she felt about it.

"It was good," she admitted. "I definitely didn't feel as if I were looking at them for the first time. Familiarity, and some I remembered clearly. I guess I didn't lose it all."

He smiled. "That's great news."

"Maybe. And perhaps I should continue reading them. The neurologist said I'd start rebuilding connections with time. Maybe that'll help."

He nodded. "I'd vote for that."

She smiled. "It won't rebuild the trust, though."

His expression sobered a bit. "You know what I think about that. We trust our memories entirely too much to begin with. We can pack a lot of factual information in, and given the right stimulus, I suppose we can recall a lot of it. You depend on that as a nurse, right?"

"A lot," she admitted.

"I depend on it a lot, too. But then there's this other thing called muscle memory. You'd have no way of parsing it, but I bet you do a lot of things as a nurse that your body simply remembers how to do and doesn't have to appeal to your memory at all."

That gave her some food for thought. Of course a lot of what she did had to be automatic. She didn't have to think about it every time she gave an injection or applied a dressing. That would have been crazily time-consuming. Which made her wonder how much of that kind of memory was still available to her. How often had she looked at something and known exactly what to do about it without pausing to think? Plenty. Pressure to a wound, a tourniquet, the time she'd had to perform a tracheotomy in an emergency... It was like CPR. If you

had to think too much about it, you might not do it right.
Or you'd waste too much time.

"Thanks, Coop. I hadn't thought about that before."

He shrugged one shoulder. "Autopilot is often a great
thing."

They were just finishing up, pushing their plates to
the side, Coop asking if she wanted a dessert, when the
coffee hit her again as Maude refilled them.

Coffee pouring into mugs. A white plastic tabletop.
Someone sitting across from her. Not here. There.

Then.

Coop saw her face go cold as stone, as if her soul had
just abandoned her body. He recognized the signs, and
he knew he had to get her out of there now. He waved
for Maude. She stopped over and he handed her a couple
of bills. "Kylie needs to go."

For once Maude didn't grump or argue. "Then git,"
was all she said, taking the bills.

Coop slid out of the booth and urged Kylie to slide
out, too. She was stiff, almost as if rigor had seized her.
People were staring, but he didn't care. He had to get her
to some place where she'd feel safe.

With an arm around her waist, he practically dragged
her to the car and stuffed her in.

"Kylie."

She didn't answer. Cussing under his breath, he headed
back to her and Glenda's place, hoping the familiarity of
home would help pull her out of the hell she was visiting.

At least he didn't have that sensation of being watched.
Whatever had caused it had moved on. Good. He had
enough to handle right now, trying to bring Kylie back
to the present.

What had she remembered?

And when it was over, would she make up her mind that she was too crippled to return to her career? God, he hoped not. This woman had lost enough.

Glenda was still soundly sleeping, so he led Kylie into the living room. When he gently urged her to sit on the couch, she didn't resist. She was coming back. He just hoped she could tell him from what.

He sat beside her, cradling her, wishing he could carry her to bed and shelter her entire body in his, but that could be a big mistake, not knowing what she remembered. The last thing he wanted to do was push her farther over the edge.

It probably wouldn't take much right now.

The kids were getting out of school and the area all around was crawling with city cops and sheriff deputies. Plenty of parents had arrived to pick up their own children.

So all the resources were directed around the schools. Too bad Kylie wasn't alone.

But Todd had another goal in mind and Kylie could wait for now. First he needed to stir the pot of a fear that might soon start to wane.

And he knew exactly how to do it.

For all the cops were so smart, and for all the caring parents who were now afraid to let their kids walk home alone, there were always some strays.

Some had parents who were tied to jobs and trusted the police. Some had parents who didn't care. And some kids, for whatever reasons, preferred not to be watched and shepherded by police, usually because Daddy or Mommy had had some trouble with the law.

So if Todd circled far enough out from the immediate zone of threat, he knew he'd find his target. It took nearly a half hour. The cordon was beginning to loosen as kids disappeared from the streets without any alarm being raised.

Then he saw her just ahead of him. Walking alone, a ragamuffin of a child with a battered backpack, pausing occasionally to kick at a stone on the broken sidewalk. Every town had neighborhoods like this where the forgotten and poor lived as best they could. A plantation of potential victims, he sometimes thought. Problem was, none of them had anything worth taking. But they had something worth scaring.

The streets were deserted. The child was probably going home to an empty house. The only question was how far he wanted to take this. He had no particular interest in children except as tools. This little redhead with her dirty Orphan Annie curls would be a perfect tool.

He swung the car around and came back across the street before stopping.

Immediately he could tell she had heard the warnings in school. As soon as he braked, she moved to the far side of the walk and began to move faster.

"Say, little girl," he called from the far side of the street. She hesitated. "I just want to ask you a question."

When she didn't move, he took the opportunity to swing around and come closer, this time with the driver's side near the sidewalk. Her eyes grew huge and she backed up, watching him warily, clearly ready to run. "I just want to know which way to the grocery store." He smiled. "I'm new here." He leaned over, holding a candy bar out the window. "You can have this if you'll tell me…"

The candy bar did it. *Never take candy from strangers.* The girl's hesitation vanished, and she took off down the street and across the grass, screaming.

Todd hit the gas and cleared the street before any doors started flying open.

Job well done. Distraction accomplished.

Now to figure out how to separate Kylie from that damn marine. Or take him out so Todd could get to Kylie. Either one would work.

Whistling, Todd drove out of town, past his own place, planning to come back after dark when no one would be likely to see him park in his barn.

A plan. He was one step away from success. He just needed the final plan.

Kylie came back slowly, but she came back. He felt the softening in her body, then a ripple of tremors.

"Sorry," she whispered.

"What triggered it?"

"Pouring coffee."

Pouring coffee? That sounded weird, all right, but not beyond the realm of what he'd seen grab some of his comrades. "What about it?"

"I don't know. It's not like I haven't seen coffee poured a gazillion times."

He gave her a little squeeze and risked dropping a kiss on the top of her head. He didn't know if she was completely back yet, and everything he did chanced sending her back to that place.

"How are you feeling now?"

"I don't know," she admitted. "Strange. But I'm not locked in it anymore."

"One memory or more?"

"First it was just the coffee. That was so strange I managed to push it aside, mostly. But then I remembered more. A tabletop. Someone sitting across from me. Coffee being poured."

"Could you see who was there? Or where it was?"

"Not really. I think it was a cheap restaurant near the hospital. I remember a white plastic tabletop. And that someone else was there. Not a medical person."

"How can you know that?"

"No scrubs," she answered simply.

"A friend, maybe," he suggested tentatively.

"I don't know!" The words burst out of her. An instant later she'd left his embrace and started pacing. "Coffee. Just some damn coffee and an ordinary table and absolutely no reason to react that way! None. God, it just froze me up inside. Not when I first saw Maude pour the coffee, although that grabbed me. But when it happened again. The second memory. That was real, Coop. *Real!*"

"I believe you." Much as he wanted to rise and give her a huge comforting hug, he feared that touching her right now might be more than she could stand. Let her pace, let her deal, make sure that nothing upset her more. Damn, he hated being helpless to do anything. It grated on him; it always had, and this time seemed worse because it was Kylie, a woman who'd been totally victimized for no reason at all. Or maybe because it was Kylie and she had become important to him.

The thought drew him up short. He was well aware that for many years now he'd been very careful where he committed his emotions. Caring was dangerous. He'd cared about too many people in the early days of his service only to lose them. Situations like that made it reasonable to harden the heart. Everything about what he did had made that a sensible choice.

Reaching out to Connie after all this time had been a risky move. A few letters, a few phone calls—they didn't create strong emotional ties. But then something had started pushing at him until finally he'd decided to deepen his connection with his cousin and her family.

Which had brought him here, and now he found an injured woman worming her way past all his defenses. Something bad could happen to Kylie. That was obvious since the rose, but he was breaking his own self-imposed protective measures with each passing moment. Taking the biggest risk of all: giving a damn.

None of this was wise. Kylie was leaning on him because she was afraid. He was caring about her in defiance of everything he'd learned. Bad situation for both of them.

He didn't want to hurt her. But what if that self-protective carapace slammed into place again? She'd feel it. And what if he allowed himself to care about a woman who wouldn't need him at all once they caught her attacker?

He could smell trouble from kilometers away, days away, and he smelled trouble now.

The hell of it was, he had no idea what to do about any of it. He couldn't just walk away, not in this situation. He couldn't protect Kylie if he wasn't here, and if he stayed, apparently he couldn't protect himself.

Great job, Coop, he thought sourly. *Great job.*

Then he gave up his internal argument and looked at the agitated woman pacing the living room. She was all that mattered. Whatever the cost, he had to keep her safe.

Period.

* * *

As she paced, Kylie battered at her memory, trying to add detail to the memory of the coffee and table. Useless. How could she trust herself if she filled in parts of the picture? Coop was absolutely right about the malleability of memory. In the end, all she did was give herself another headache.

And a serious case of frustration. A knife. Coffee. Not nearly enough to figure out who was after her. Useless bits. Why couldn't something useful have struck her?

Instead she'd reacted all out of proportion to the sight of coffee being poured.

"You must think I'm crazy," she said tautly.

"Who, me? I don't think you're crazy at all," Coop said.

"Really? A woman who panics because someone pours coffee?"

"The coffee wasn't the reason for your panic. Whatever it's associated with was."

She stopped pacing, planted her feet and stared at him. "How are you always so calm? Don't you have memories like this?"

"Of course I do." Now he wished he could stand up and pace, too, but given his size and the smallness of the room he figured he might intimidate her, and he didn't want to do that. "I've got plenty of those memories."

"Then how do you handle them?"

"I told you. And with time…" He hesitated. "Finally you get to the point where you just plain don't let yourself care anymore. But that's me, that's my situation, and yours is very different."

Her expression changed subtly. "What do you mean you don't care anymore?"

He hesitated. "That's not exactly what I mean. I try

to avoid forging strong bonds with people I might lose. That's all. Doesn't exactly always work."

"Your cemetery."

"Exactly."

No, it didn't always work. He'd tried to deaden himself, but he knew all the times he'd failed. Just as he was failing with Kylie.

She left the room. He followed.

"Just a headache," she said, opening the kitchen cabinet. "Every single time I push my memory, my head starts throbbing." This was more than some broken neural connections, she thought. This was a whole big mental block. Whatever memories she might actually have lost through the injury to her head, she seemed to have lost a whole lot more to her mind's unwillingness to remember.

She popped a couple of pills, swallowing them with water. Then she turned, leaning back against the counter, folding her arms. Coop was there. Coop was always there. His presence made her feel safe.

But she also wondered about something else. "How can you stand spending so much time with me, Coop? I'm a mess. I'm weirding out at odd times… Wouldn't you rather be with your nieces and nephew?"

He shoved his fingers into his jeans pockets, then canted his hips to one side, staring steadily at her. "I like Connie's kids. They're adorable. But I hardly know them yet, and besides, they don't need me."

"But I do?"

"For the moment."

She shook her head. She didn't like that answer at all. In fact, the longer this situation went on, the less she liked needing a bodyguard around the clock. She couldn't imagine why he would even do it. She wasn't fun, not anymore. Interesting? Hardly, with only one thing on her mind. She bored herself to tears, or would have if she weren't living with constant, creeping terror.

"Relax," he said presently. "I told you, I think, that I'm exactly where I want to be. Maybe now would be a good time for you to try thinking about something else, rather than giving yourself a headache. Like when you grew up here, or something. I'm open."

She gazed back at him, wondering if he was bucking for sainthood. Or if he felt he was paying some karmic debt. Because frankly, if she could escape her own head, she would. Lickety-split. He was *choosing* to stay.

"God, you're amazing," she said. "I'd be long since done with me."

He gave a quiet laugh. "Good thing you're not the one making the decision. So, childhood?"

"I don't want to talk about that. Other than growing up with my grandparents, it was all very ordinary for Glenda and me. We had a nice life."

"At least stop thinking about the coffee," he suggested. "Giving yourself a headache isn't going to help anything."

"Actually, it might have."

"How so?"

She chewed her lower lip a moment, then said, "I'm starting to wonder how much of this amnesia is psychological, not physical."

He stepped closer, keeping his hands in his pockets. "Meaning?"

"If this were neurological damage alone… I don't understand why I get headaches when I try to remember. I'm wondering if I'm stopping myself from remembering."

His eyebrows lifted a bit. "I could sure understand that."

"So can I. I'm not sure what's going on. I could be all wet. But the headaches… That feels more like pushback."

"Wow," he murmured. His gaze trailed away from her, and for a minute he stared into space. "I know it can happen. I've seen it happen. The brain has some pretty good built-in protection. I've seen it build walls that some guys could never get past." His eyes shifted back to her. "So the headaches got you wondering?"

"That and the fact that so much in my textbooks seemed so familiar." She sighed, folding her arms even tighter. "But it doesn't add up. Why would I lose so much of three years to block one incident?"

"I don't know," he admitted.

"The neurologist said my brain would start building new connections and that I might get big parts of my memory back. I suppose that could be happening. I mean, why else would I lose three years? That seems so weird."

"How long were you in Denver training?"

She felt the color drain from her face and reached out a hand to steady herself. "Three years," she whispered. "Oh, God, do you suppose I wiped out everything to do with Denver to cover one memory?"

"You're asking the wrong guy here. But it seems possible to me. Wipe out Denver, and you wipe out any need to stay there or go back there. Or maybe you just make one supremely important blank seem like part of a larger blank. But you need a professional for this, not me."

"Yeah, I guess I do. But you just gave me a lot to think about." Strength began to return to her, and she let go of the counter, pointing at the stack of textbooks still on the table. "They were so familiar as I was looking through them. I remembered studying them. I could remember a lot of what was in them."

Then she raised worried eyes to his. "What if I've done this to myself?"

Chapter 10

"Did what to yourself?" Glenda asked. She entered the kitchen clad in light cotton pajamas covered with prints of small cats. Yawning, she headed straight for the coffeepot.

"The amnesia," Kylie said tautly. "What if it's not the brain damage that did it?"

"Then booyah," Glenda said around another yawn. "A lot of amnesia is purely traumatic, and if I had my druthers, that would be the best kind. Come on, Kylie, I'm sure you remember this much. If it's traumatic, the chances are good most everything you've forgotten will come back to you. That's what you want, isn't it?"

She plopped at the table and drank half her cup of coffee before eyeing the two of them. "Neither of you looks really happy. What's been going on while I was asleep?"

When Kylie hesitated, Coop didn't step in. She realized

he believed this was her story to tell. Unfortunately, that would spare her none of the ugliness or the questions. Man, she was turning into a major coward. She was just talking to her sister, for crying out loud.

"I had a memory," she said finally, sitting near Glenda because it was suddenly hard to trust her legs. "It seems so meaningless—coffee being poured into cups on a white plastic table. Someone else was there but I couldn't see who. Just the coffee mostly."

Glenda glanced up and gave Coop a smile as he refilled her coffee cup. "Okay, you had a memory. I take it that it didn't exactly strike you as meaningless."

"She lost touch for a while," Coop said flatly.

Glenda closed her eyes for a long moment, and drew a deep, slow breath. "So, okay, somehow related to the attack. Except for the effect on you, I'd say this was good. You're starting to recall. Why do I think you'd rather not?"

"Why would I want to, Glenda? That business with the knife, and the pain I felt… Why would I want to know any more?"

Glenda's expression turned suddenly fierce. "So we can catch the bastard who hurt you!" She jumped up from the table. "I'm going to get ready and go into work early. I want to talk to some people about this. The neurologist. The psychiatrist. Maybe they'll have some ideas…"

She was gone. Kylie sat staring at the air Glenda had recently occupied and felt her stomach twist into knots. She'd never seen her sister look quite like that. And worse, she didn't want to upset Glenda like this, although how she could avoid it…

"I shouldn't have told her," she said.

"You did exactly the right thing. And if you'd skated around it, I wouldn't have. This is too important, Kylie."

She shook her head a little, then felt Coop's hand come to rest on her shoulder. He gave it a squeeze.

"I didn't want to make her feel worse, Coop."

"I think that's pretty much impossible since the rose arrived. She just hides it well."

Maybe so, Kylie thought. Whatever demon pursued her, now it was affecting everyone around her. She wished with all her might that she had some way to put a stop to this. To spare everyone.

Coop tried to distract Kylie with a card game after Glenda left, but he knew her heart wasn't in it. Finally he said, "Kylie, you've got to give yourself a break. You can't focus on this all the time."

"That's easy to say when you don't have someone out there hunting you like this. When you aren't worried about the safety of everyone you know."

As soon as she spoke, she knew she'd said the wrong thing. His face darkened and he pushed back from the table, leaving the room.

Oh, man, she'd put her foot in it big-time. He didn't talk about it much, but this man had been in combat. He must have spent countless hours knowing he was being hunted, worrying about the men he was with. To imply he didn't understand…

She felt about two inches tall and wished she could find a way to take those words back. She'd have given nearly everything for a hole to just swallow her up.

But a few minutes later, he reappeared, his face calm again. "I know it's hard," he said. "I remember how hard it was, especially at first. All we could do, Kylie, was distract ourselves as much as possible. We played cards and other games when we weren't standing post. We wrote letters home. Anything to take a break from the tension. You've got to find a way to do that before you snap."

"I'm sorry for what I said. But I think I'm already snapping."

"You're not anywhere near snapping. You've had a couple of memories, and as far as I can see you've done a damn good job of handling them. Trust me on this. If cards won't distract you, we'll find something else. Anything that'll work that won't put you in more danger."

She acknowledged the justice of what he said. "I don't know how to do this."

"None of us do at first. But the harder you beat your head on this, the more likely you are to wear yourself out or stymie the very memories that could put an end to this. Let your subconscious do the work and find a way to relax a little."

Easier said than done, she thought. Ever since waking in the hospital, one thing had been first and foremost on her mind: the attack. The memory loss.

The loss of her future.

But even as she had these familiar thoughts, thoughts that had been running in her head like a hamster on a wheel for weeks now, something else crept in. Anger. Real anger. Was she going to let that creep keep stealing every single moment of her life from her? Was she going to wallow in the grave he'd tried to dig for her?

Or was she going to take charge of something? Anything. Just a small part of herself. Glenda had offered her an opportunity to shadow her at the hospital but she'd turned it down out of fear. What if she went with Glenda and realized she hadn't forgotten how to be a nurse?

Was she afraid of that, too?

"You're right," she said, her voice surprisingly firm. "I'm terrifying myself more than that guy ever could. I'm letting him run every waking moment of my life. Enough."

"Enough?"

"Enough. Whatever the future holds, there won't be much of one if I keep cowering like this. It stops now."

"How do you want to stop it?" he asked.

She looked at him standing there, probably the most attractive man she'd ever seen, or at least noticed, and decided to take a huge risk. She could no longer try to ignore those broad shoulders and narrow hips, the easy way he moved as if he were at home in his body. She couldn't ignore the attraction any longer.

Rising from the table, she crossed the kitchen and took his warm hand.

He didn't say anything, but let her lead him to the living room couch. With a gentle push, she urged him to sit, then she curled up beside him and leaned into him.

"I think," she said, only the faintest tremor in her voice, "that it would be safe for a marine to drop his drawers sometimes."

He caught his breath, then laughed. But he didn't argue. Twisting, he caught her face with one hand and found her mouth with a kiss that seared its way past all her barriers, finding the icy places inside her and heating them until they blazed. Just a kiss. No kiss had made her feel like steel melting into a puddle of glowing heat. His did.

She raised her arms, wrapping them around his neck, wanting him as close as she could get him. The world receded quickly, leaving nothing but the two of them in a growing blaze of desire.

His tongue plundered her, learning every contour of her mouth, and each movement sent another spear of longing through her. She could hardly wait for more, and nearly held her breath in anticipation.

Then his hand began to slide down her shoulder, slowly. Too slowly. She wanted to hurry him up, but didn't want to risk destroying the moment. Lower it slid until at last it found her breast.

She nearly arched as he squeezed her, her head tipping back from his kiss as she gasped for air.

"Too much?" he whispered.

"Not enough," she managed. It would never be enough, not until they joined in a tangle of sheets.

His hand traveled lower, slipping under her T-shirt. He trailed his fingers across her naked midriff, drawing gasp after gasp of delight from her. She loosened one arm, seeking the buttons of his shirt, wanting so badly to feel his bare chest beneath her palms. But then his hand slipped up and under her bra, finding bare skin and her nipple all at once. He squeezed the nub, and a soft cry of pleasure escaped her.

Yesss!

Then the doorbell rang.

"Hell." Coop's cuss punctuated the sudden silence. The two of them separated, startled.

"We could ignore it," Kylie said almost wistfully.

But then the bell was replaced by a hammering.

Coop looked at her ruefully. "That sounds official."

It did. She looked down at herself, quickly rearranging her shirt and bra.

"Dang," he said. "I didn't even have enough time to give you a beard burn."

The remark was so unexpected that a giggle escaped

her. Desire thrummed hotly inside her, but it was slowly giving way to the demands of the moment.

"I'll get it," Coop said. "You look fine."

Kylie just hoped embarrassment wasn't written all over her face. She wondered if it was Ashley. School should have let out a little while ago. Or maybe Julie, who'd just recently married that guy Trace Archer. Funny, she remembered that, vaguely remembered going to their wedding. So maybe the last three years weren't all gone.

But it was Connie Parish, looking as serious as a funeral. "Thanks," she said in answer to Coop's offer of coffee. "I could sure use some."

Adjusting her belt a bit, she sat in the armchair and studied Kylie. "Heard you had a bad time at Maude's earlier."

"Did that get all over town?"

"Is there anything that doesn't?"

Kylie wanted to sink. She'd grown up with local gossip and had gotten used to it. Still, this was something she didn't want all over the place. Although how she could hide it, she didn't know. Everyone probably knew what had happened to her and about her memory loss. Why shouldn't they know she'd become upset in the diner? She was drawing ridiculous lines. "What are folks saying?"

"Only that you looked sick and Coop had to help you to the car. Were you, or was it something else?"

If there was anyone else on this planet who deserved an honest answer to that question, it was Connie. "I had a memory. A useless one, but somehow terrifying. It's like I slammed back in time."

Connie nodded, accepting the coffee from Coop with a nod. "I'm sorry. It probably won't be the last one."

"So did you just want to check up on me?"

"Partly. One of these days soon I'd love to have a purely social get-together with you and the girls. Ashley sends her best, but she won't be stopping by today."

At once Kylie stiffened. She didn't miss the subtext. "What happened?"

"Despite our best efforts, the creep approached the little Halburn girl. You remember her at all? Red curly hair?"

"I remember the Halburns. They're not doing so well. The daughter…Katie?"

"That's her. Anyway, she was nearly home when the guy called out to her. Said he wanted directions and offered her a candy bar. She took off screaming like a bat out of hell."

"Good for her!" Kylie's heart had begun to pound. Could it be the same guy who was coming after her? No, it sounded completely different.

"Not much of a description, I'm afraid. Red hair and red beard. Old car dabbed all over with that rust prevention paint, the orangey stuff. Hell, that points to a quarter of the cars in the county."

"Yeah." Her heart sank. What had she been hoping for? A miracle? "God, I hope you catch him."

"Unfortunately, he seems fairly bright." Connie sighed and sipped her coffee. "This whole town is on high alert, so maybe you can relax a bit. People are starting to look at their neighbors with suspicion. I don't like it."

Coop spoke for the first time. "That could be dangerous."

"Yeah, it could. Especially for strangers. We're letting it be known that you've been deputized but watch your back, anyway, Coop."

"I'm not leaving Kylie's side. If we go out, it's together."

"You're alibied, but sometime alibis come too late. Anyway, everyone knows you're my cousin. It's not like you came from nowhere. Just keep an eye out."

"I always do."

Kylie sat there hating this. Now Coop was at risk from some suspicious local? This was too much. "You should leave town," she said.

"Are you going with me?"

Startled, she looked at him, her mouth open.

"I didn't think so," he said. "I'm staying right here beside you."

But there was something in his gaze that made her heart slam hard. "Let me guess," she said. "Marines don't run from danger."

"Nope."

This, she decided, was a discussion for another time. Connie was looking entirely too amused. "How's Katie Halburn doing?"

"Scared, but okay. She did the right thing and ran. It didn't get bad enough to leave a permanent mark. At least I hope it didn't." Connie drummed her fingers on the arm of the chair, then lifted her mug again. "Katie is a symptom of something that's worrying me more."

"What's that?" Coop asked.

"Evidently some kids, for whatever reason, are trying to evade the police watchdogs. They know what's going on, they know we're watching out for them, but Katie isn't the first one to escape us. They can slip behind houses, and if no one sees it, they're off."

"But why?" Kylie asked. Connie was painting a scary picture. One of those little kids could wind up like her. The horror of it reached her very bones.

"As near as we can figure, some of those kids have family members who've had run-ins with the law. Maybe they don't trust us. Then there are those who are just too smart for their own good. Like this is a game."

She reached into her breast pocket. "Anyway, I'd like it if you'd put one of these in your front window. We're asking trustworthy people to do this. It lets the kids know it's a safe house."

"And we're here most of the time," Kylie said.

"Shoot for mornings before school and after school." She passed over the sticker.

"I'll put it up," Kylie said.

"Should have done something like this years ago," Connie remarked, rising. "Well, I'm off to hunt for a rusty old car driven by a bearded man. And if you believe that red hair and beard, I'll sell you a bridge."

"Well, that sure killed the mood," Coop said wryly after Connie left. "Probably for the best. I'll put that sticker up, if you want."

"Thanks." She handed it to him. While part of her was truly sorry that the passion they'd started to share had been interrupted, another part of her agreed it was for the best. She didn't want to use the man as a distraction. God, it would be so nice if everything would just go away so they could make love without any questions about why. Because once again she was questioning herself.

But those thoughts were squeezed out by the image of a terrified little girl running from a stranger in a car. Thank God the child had gotten away. She had a vague idea of what had been done to her, and the scars on her body to remind her. The thought of some little girl suffering that not only horrified her, it made her furious.

Coop stepped out front, apparently to decide where to place the sticker so it would be clear from the street.

When he came back in, he said, "All set. Very visible, too. They chose the colors well."

"Good. God, can you imagine the kind of man who'd be scaring kids like this? Totally sick. Sick!" Like the one who'd come after her. "Has the whole world gone crazy?"

"Sometimes I wonder." He sat beside her and took her hand, holding it snugly.

Before they could say anything else, the phone rang. Coop twisted and scanned the caller ID. "Glenda," he said, passing her the phone.

"Hi, sis," Kylie said.

"Hey, girl. Get Coop to bring you over to the hospital. The neurologist and psychiatrist want to see you."

Kylie was on pins and needles the whole short trip to the hospital. "Why so quickly?" she asked Coop, knowing he wouldn't have an answer any more than she did. "What's wrong?"

"Maybe nothing. Maybe it has to do with their schedules."

She hoped that was all it was, and tried to tell herself he was probably right. Except Glenda had sounded so adamant.

Glenda was waiting out front for them, chatting with a colleague. They parted ways and Glenda walked toward Kylie and Coop. "I hope I didn't scare you, but both doctors aren't in town every day. They won't be back again for a week, and I was lucky they agreed to see you before leaving today."

Relief washed through Kylie. She wasn't sure exactly what she had feared, because she wasn't supposed to go back to the doctor in Denver for three months, and even he'd said it was okay for her to find a doctor here, that he'd send the MRIs and other information.

Walking into the hospital hit her with familiarity. The sounds, but mostly the smells and scurrying people. It was like another homecoming, not so different from returning to the house she shared with Glenda.

"I belong here." The words popped out of her.

Glenda paused and smiled at her. "Yes, you do, Kylie. That's why I want you to come to work with me as soon as you feel you can. It's like home, isn't it?"

It was. A sense of belonging she'd almost forgotten flooded her. This was *her* turf, the focus of much of her life. She was glad, though, that they went nowhere near the emergency room. She didn't know if she was ready for those sounds. People in pain… No, she wasn't ready for that.

It felt good to have Coop at her side, and when they reached the doctor's office and he started to sit in the waiting room, she said, "No, I want Coop to hear it all. He's been dealing with it almost as much as I have."

Glenda studied her, then something in her gaze softened. "So it's like that," she murmured.

"What do you mean?"

"Nothing." She turned to the receptionist, who told them to go down the hall to the first room on the right. "There won't be a wait," the woman said. "They're expecting you."

"Are you sure about me hearing this?" Coop asked her.

"Absolutely. Sheesh, Coop, you dragged me out of the diner today. I think you have a right to know what we're dealing with."

Of that much, at least, she was certain. Everything else was up in the air, but if there was a reason for Coop to lose interest in her, she wanted it to happen now, before they got in any deeper. He deserved that much respect.

Dr. Nugent was a tall, thin man with slightly stooped shoulders, and his smile was automatic. The neurologist. Dr. Weathers, a dark-skinned woman, had a smile to light the night, filled with warmth. She was the psychiatrist. Surprise, Kylie thought. True to the stereotypes. If she hadn't been so nervous, she might have laughed.

"Where shall we begin?" Nugent asked.

"With you," Weathers answered. "Best to deal with the medical facts first."

"Fair enough." He rolled a chair over and faced Kylie. "You're the patient, Kylie Brewer."

Since they'd just been introduced, she blinked. "Yes, Doctor."

He nodded, a birdlike movement. "I've reviewed everything your doctor in Denver sent me. Your MRIs and other tests. It's really not bad news."

She felt her heart leap, and reached out with both hands. Glenda took one and Coop the other. "Not bad how? I had brain damage."

"Indeed you did. But at the time the last set of MRIs were taken, you showed a great deal of healing. If you want I can show you the images. You're a nurse, right? They might make sense to you."

He turned and clicked on a large screen on the wall. "Digital images," he said. "Highly defined. This is from your functional MRI, meaning your brain activity was being observed. You'll notice this small dark spot here." He pointed. "That's the damage. And compared to your earlier imaging, it's healing quite nicely."

She didn't know whether to be relieved or not. A long breath escaped her.

Dr. Nugent leaned forward, bobbing his head again.

"The thing is, Ms. Brewer, an injury of this sort would not simply have cut out three years of your memory with almost surgical precision. In fact, I'd wager to say the most it would do is affect your short-term memory for a while, and possibly cause you to be a bit impulsive. But it will heal. And yes, you may have lost parts of your memory, but only the most recent ones. Your brain is going to recover beautifully. With that, I'll turn you over to Dr. Weathers." He rose, bobbed his head again and walked out.

Kylie felt stunned. Totally stunned. "The other doctor..."

Glenda answered. "The other doctor was talking to you while you were still recovering. You heard Nugent. Problems with short-term memory. Can you really be certain who told you what?"

"But you asked, didn't you?"

Glenda nodded. "They said you'd recover from the trauma to your brain. I told you that. Nobody could explain all the amnesia. Remember?"

Kylie didn't remember. Her hands tightened until she was gripping Glenda and Coop so hard it was a wonder neither of them objected. "Then what's wrong with me?"

Dr. Weathers spoke, her voice warm and firm. "Absolutely nothing that time won't fix. Your amnesia is traumatic, Kylie. Definitely traumatic. But it's not from the injury. For some reason, probably a very good reason, your mind has blocked the last three years. Did something happen three years ago? A big life change?"

Kylie's mouth felt like sand. She licked her lips, and the doctor passed her an unopened water bottle. She drank a few sips, and finally answered, "I moved to Denver."

"Then that's where we'll begin," Dr. Weathers said. "I'm going to set up a weekly appointment with you, and we'll work on this until we chip away the block. Ms. Brewer, I think you forgot more than you needed to, but you probably had a very good reason for that. Once we figure that out, the puzzle pieces should start coming back together for you."

Kylie looked at her, liking her instinctively, and felt hope rising in her heart. "So I can be myself again?"

"Most likely. The question is when you'll be ready. But the news is pretty good, don't you think?"

As they were leaving, Dr. Weathers said, "Next week at three. And if you have trouble remembering what we discussed here, both your sister and Mr. Cooper can remind you."

Kylie nearly floated home with Coop. She was going to be normal again. She would eventually remember what she needed to. It wasn't a fault of brain damage.

But as soon as they reentered the house, darker thoughts tried to edge in. Why had she forgotten three whole years? She could understand having forgotten the attack and what led up to it, but three whole years? Ever since she went to Denver?

"You should be celebrating," Coop remarked, as if he sensed her change in mood.

"Now I'm wondering what's wrong with me that I forgot three whole years. Why not just the bad part at the end?"

"Obviously that's the reason for the therapy," he answered. "My guess is that Denver somehow got linked in your mind with the bad stuff. But you're going to have to figure that out, and that's one place I can't help you."

No one could, she supposed. She was about to embark on a journey of self-discovery, and she suspected not all of it would please her. But to get back her memory, or most of it? To be able to return to nursing? Maybe to even really think about medical school?

Coop was right—she should be celebrating. Finally she smiled at him, a bright, wide smile. "I think mostly I feel happy. There's hope. Lots of hope that I didn't think I had before."

Coop watched her twirl in delight, expressing a happiness he had hardly dared to hope to see in her. He smiled at the sight, but the ever-cautious part of him waited in anticipation of the crash. Too happy too fast seldom meant good things.

It happened in an instant. He watched her freeze and her expression changed. Waiting to see where she would take this, he was surprised when she spoke.

"Something to do with Denver," she said quietly. "Why else would I forget my entire time there? He must be someone I knew while I was there. I erased him."

"Possible," he said cautiously.

"What other reason could there be?" She threw up a hand. "Sorry. You can't answer these questions, and I guess I'm in for a whole lot of therapy to get the answers."

"But there will be answers."

She nodded, giving him a small smile. "Yes. There will be. And when it's done I'll be relieved, but I don't think it's going to be fun."

"Not likely."

"But I still feel better knowing it's not a wiring problem in my brain. Most of it, anyway. I'm kind of amazed that I forgot people told me that."

"Well, the doc did say you'd have some short-term memory problems. Probably less now than you did before. I haven't noticed any."

"I hope so." Her smile slowly brightened. "I guess there's no point in wondering what or who made me forget so much…because I've forgotten it."

Her joke took him unawares and drew a surprised laugh from him. He suspected he was getting a glimpse of the real Kylie, the woman she had been before fear had overtaken her life. He liked what he was seeing.

But he'd liked her all along. Yes, she'd been frightened, but he'd watched her struggle with it and try to maintain her balance. As he knew from experience, that was no easy thing to do. Of course it had preoccupied her. How could it not?

But now she had hope, and it was a beautiful thing. Quite a beautiful thing. He wanted so badly to reach for her and pull her into his arms, to join her circle of joy. But she hadn't invited him, so he just watched and waited as she absorbed the good news. Bless Glenda for not letting it lie.

Kylie had been given back her hope. Now he just had to make certain that some creep didn't steal it again.

It didn't take long for the word to reach Todd. He knew some people at the hospital—hell, he helped with their financial planning—and they thought they were sharing good news about his old friend Kylie Brewer.

Todd had great respect for gossip. He worked hard to generate none, unless there was something he wanted to make the rounds, but it was sure useful to keep tuned in to it.

He heard all about the fright he'd given that little redheaded girl, and savored the fact that nearly all the police resources were being directed toward protecting kids.

But then he picked up other whispers. Something had

happened to Kylie at the diner. Cooper had nearly had to carry her out. A memory? So it seemed when he learned she'd been to see the psychiatrist at the hospital.

The question was what she had remembered, but the danger lay in her remembering anything at all. He got seriously concerned when an orderly he'd grown up with said there was talk that Kylie's memory would come back, that it hadn't been the result of brain damage.

Good news? Not for him. And so much for keeping medical information confidential. Over the years he'd cultivated a few informants with loose lips because it was useful to his job. Now it was useful to his own life.

At any moment she might remember his face. Remember the number of times he had pressed her to have coffee with him until it became clear that she wanted nothing to do with him. That last time they'd had coffee together had set his course. She couldn't wait to get away from him, and barely managed to be polite.

What a way to treat an old friend. And no matter how many times he looked in a mirror, he couldn't figure out why she reacted to him that way. There sure as hell was nothing wrong with him. He was moderately successful; he presented well or he wouldn't be successful in his job. So why did Kylie keep trying to avoid him?

The resentment had built, and along with it a sense of humiliation. Who did Kylie Brewer think she was, anyway? No better than him, even if she acted like it. But one way or another, she kept treating him like something she wanted to scrape off her shoe.

Oh, not overtly. She was polite. But she kept evading his invitations, and finally when she felt it would be rude to do so any longer, they met for coffee. Just coffee. No dinner. No movie. No picnic, even though he'd suggested it. Coffee in a busy shop near the hospital was all she would give him.

Over time his thoughts toward her had grown more violent. A woman needed to know her place. His father had said so more than once when he hit his wife. Kylie needed to be disciplined. Taught a lesson. And then the idea of teaching her a lesson had blossomed into something much stronger. She was the source of his humiliation and there was only one way to put an end to it. He wondered how many other men she treated the way she treated him. He might be saving more than himself by getting rid of her for good.

There'd been a time, all too brief, when he'd wondered at himself, at his own ugly thoughts, but that time had passed quickly. The only answer to Kylie Brewer was to remove her. Never again would she humiliate him or anyone else.

He began to see himself as doing a huge service for the world. He even wondered, lately, how soon that Cooper guy would realize what Kylie really was. A man-hater. A tease who then tormented the men she had snared.

A woman like that needed more than discipline. She needed to be gone forever.

But time might be growing very short. He'd toyed with the idea that he could wait until Cooper went back to the marines, but if Kylie was beginning to remember… No, he had to find a way to get at her. Take out both of them if necessary, but he definitely had to get to Kylie.

It was time for all this to end. He was sick of wondering when she might remember, sick of the strain he was under. Sooner would be better, especially for him.

The question was how to accomplish it.

And he was just beginning to get some decent ideas.

Chapter 11

The next morning brought a beautiful spring day, warmer than the last week, warm enough that Kylie donned shorts and a sleeveless top before she went downstairs. She found Glenda looking exhausted from a long night, and Coop, as usual, making breakfast. This morning home fries perfumed the air along with bacon.

"Don't tell me how bad this food is for me," Glenda said by way of greeting. "Another night like last night and I may look for a new job. How are you feeling since you saw the doctors?"

"Much better," Kylie answered truthfully. "Can I help, Coop?"

"Yeah, get some coffee and sit. There's only room in this kitchen for one cook. Hungry?"

"Starved."

He flashed a smile and turned back to the stove.

"That was some pretty good news yesterday," Glenda

said. "But I have to admit I was surprised myself by how little you remembered of what you'd been told. Kylie, I never dreamed that you thought all your amnesia was due to brain damage."

"Well, somehow I came to that conclusion." She looked at Glenda just as Coop was spooning potatoes onto the plates in front of them. "Part of me is thrilled to realize that the memories aren't permanently gone. That with some work I might get them back."

"And go back to nursing," Glenda added.

"That, of course. But part of me is terrified, Glenda."

Her sister looked both sympathetic and concerned. "Of course you are. Terror is probably what gave you the amnesia in the first place. I'm familiar with the kind that happens directly because of a trauma. So are you. Like when car accident victims don't remember anything about the minutes before the crash or right after. But I have to admit, three years must be some kind of record. Count on you."

The way she said it lightened Kylie's mood and she laughed. "Yeah, count on me." Bacon joined the potatoes on the plate.

"And thus you have two major food groups," Coop said, joining them with his own full plate. "Three if you count the coffee, which I do. Dig in, ladies. Nothing worse than cold home fries."

"Delicious," Kylie pronounced at the first mouthful.

"Seconded," said Glenda.

"I'm really worried about the length of time I forgot," Kylie told her. "I was talking to Coop about it last night. Something or someone must have been there the whole time."

"Maybe," said Glenda. "Remember, that's why you're going to go to therapy. To learn the reasons. Speculation is pointless. Instead, enjoy knowing that you're not so damaged you'll never get your life back and start thinking about when you want to come to work with me."

"I will."

"And I have a suggestion for today," Coop offered. "Glenda needs her sleep, but you need to get out of this house. How about a long drive in the mountains? It's a perfect day for it."

Kylie's first impulse was to refuse. She felt safe within these walls with him, safer than she'd felt since the attack.

But as soon as the feeling chased through her, she realized how unfair she was being. She wasn't the only one in jail in this house. Coop was giving up his entire vacation, his chance to get to know his remaining family better, to watch over her. He must be desperate to get out and about.

"That sounds wonderful," she answered with a smile. And honestly, he was right. She needed to leave the safety of her cave once in a while. It wasn't as if she would be alone.

And the man who'd sent the rose wouldn't be likely to bother her when Coop was around, and certainly not while they were driving the mountain roads.

Shortly after Glenda went to bed, they packed a small cooler with a little ice and some bottled water, and made a few ham sandwiches. "I never travel without food," Coop explained. "We might be gone only an hour. Then again, you never know."

A valid point, she thought. She'd certainly seen enough of life to know the unexpected was part of it.

She was glad she brought a jacket, though. As the road wound higher into the mountains, the air grew a little chillier.

"I hear there's a ghost town up here," he remarked as they passed through the dappled shadows cast by the trees.

"Up this road another five miles. It's fenced off, though, because it's too dangerous. It was a gold-mining town and the mines started collapsing a number of years ago."

She twisted a little on the seat. "You heard about it from Connie?"

"Yeah. That's where her ex took Sophie when he kidnapped her all those years ago."

So it was natural he wanted to see it. "When I was younger we liked to come up here at night and get spooked. Boy, was it easy to get spooked."

"Who was 'we'?"

"Julie, Ashley, Connie, Glenda and some of the guys. The guys especially liked it because it was easy enough to make us scream."

"In the dark? I bet."

"And I'd bet teens are still doing it. They started with the orange plastic fencing and warning signs, but a couple of years ago they went to something a lot sturdier and hard to get past. The problem is, nobody knows how far those shafts extend out from the town. The ground for quite a distance around may not be safe at all."

"Then we'll be careful. I'm surprised nobody's looked into it, though."

"Jurisdiction," she answered. "Who owns it? It was once a town. Outside the county limits. Not inside the state or national forest. I suppose the state is responsible regardless, but they've got better things to spend money on."

"And why do I think that a certain number of foolish young men take the fences and warnings as a challenge?"

She laughed quietly. "You'd probably be right, but so far nobody's been killed in a cave-in."

"As far as you know," he said in horror movie tones.

That elicited a genuine laugh from her. It was such a beautiful day, and finally she was over her discomfort at being out. For the first time since the attack, she felt truly happy to be alive.

When they reached the ghost town, he pulled into the rutted turnout. "Wanna explore?"

"As long as we're careful."

"Careful is my middle name. That's why I'm still alive."

It was true, she thought as she stepped out of the car. Given what he did, recklessness would be a very dangerous thing, something to be used only when there was no other option. "So you commanded other men?" she asked, watching him pull out the cooler and a blanket that had somehow come to be in the backseat. The blanket reminded her of one of Connie's, she realized. So maybe it was.

"I prefer to think I led them." He shoved the door closed with his hip. "But yeah, sometimes I ordered."

He looked around, spied the ramshackle remnants of the old town through the trees. "Let's get a little closer, then sit for a while and soak it in. Places like this always fascinate me. I could spend hours making up stories about them."

"Then tell me some stories," she said, willing to enter the mood. Reality would return soon enough. Or maybe, she thought as they walked closer to the dilapidated town, this *was* reality.

Todd watched them drive out of town. He wished he could follow, but it was still too early in the year for a lot of traffic up there. He'd stick out like a sore thumb if he ran into them.

Then there was the house. He drove back to it, studying it briefly before moving on. He'd been inside it a few times in high school with a bunch of other kids and he supposed it probably hadn't changed much.

Back then he'd been part of "the gang." The group that did lots of things together on weekends. He thought Kylie had been the only one of the group who seemed to have a problem with him, and only after they dated—which meant there was something wrong with her, not him.

Maybe she was going to show Coop the old ghost town. They'd had a lot of fun times up there, scaring one another, but mostly the girls. Once he and Jim Reasoner had busted through the fence and given the girls a real scare. He could still hear them squealing warnings to be careful while he and Jim had used flashlights to explore as much as they could.

He would never have admitted it, but with each step he took on that unstable ground, he'd feared it would give way. He wasn't going to be a coward in front of Jim and all those girls, though.

So they'd poked around, and their flashlights made everything even eerier, until the moment when he and Jim could have sworn they saw a man standing in one of the doorways. Not solid, but awfully dark, like a slice of night. He knew that Jim had seen it, too, because of the looks they had exchanged.

Then Jim had given them the perfect way out. "I think we've scared the girls enough for one night."

Never had either of them spoken of what they'd seen. Instead they acted like nothing had happened. That was fine by Todd. He could just imagine what the others would have said about the two of them seeing a ghost.

Afterward, he and Jim had been more reluctant to go there after dark, and never again had they crossed the fence. It was almost a relief when it got replaced by a sturdier one. It might not keep anything in, but it sure as hell made it impossible for anyone to tease him into going in there again.

Then he pushed the old memories away, except for being part of the gang. The gang that included Kylie, who had scorned him. He'd made her squeal in Denver. He was going to find a way to separate her from Cooper and make her squeal again.

Even if it meant killing Cooper, an idea that was beginning to appeal to him.

Coop walked around the edge of the fence. Kylie noted that he lightened his step as he moved, making little noise and certainly not coming down hard on the ground. Kylie imitated him, walking behind him at his insistence.

"This is really cool," he said when they reached the halfway point. "Imagine the people who came all the way up here looking for riches and living in those little shacks." Like the pockmarked ground, many of those shacks had begun to collapse. Weathered gray, the small town looked exactly like a place that had been forgotten for a long time.

"There were sure never any mansions," she agreed. "And not much gold, I've heard. A few nuggets out of the river, some dust, but they never found a vein like they hoped. My science teacher in high school said the ground was all wrong for gold. If there's much up here, they were looking in the wrong place."

"Sad," Coop replied. "Very sad. And I guess a lot of these guys brought their families."

"What makes you say that?"

He pointed at a window with a shred of cloth stirring in the breeze. "Only a woman would put up curtains."

She laughed again, suspecting he was right. "What else can you tell me?"

"Hard life. Was Conard City here back then?"

"Yeah, just getting started to support the ranchers."

"Then I bet they bought their booze in town and brought it up here. It's not a hike or horseback ride you'd want to make every day."

She was surprised that he'd thought of booze, but he was probably right. "I heard there were a few gunfights, but not big ones. Two guys quarreling usually."

"Booze would certainly help that along."

"Do you suppose they brought children, too?"

He nodded. "Most likely. Probably a lot of them were single guys, but in those days if you had a wife and kid, you couldn't leave them behind. How would they survive without the breadwinner? Besides, kids would be useful in the mining, the same way they were on farms."

Child labor. Of course. "The things I never thought about."

"Life was different back then, at least here. It's still like that in large parts of the world, though."

She looked at him, realizing he'd probably seen it in a lot of the places he went. "So in Afghanistan, the kids work?"

"From a pretty early age, whether it's in shops or on farms. Some are lucky and get to stay in school till they're ten or twelve. Some even longer if their parents can afford it. But mostly they're needed to help support their families."

He smiled at her. "It used to be that way here, too. And I bet you still see some of it on family-owned ranches."

Then he looked around. "I suggest we sit under a sturdy tree. If it hasn't tipped over, the ground beneath is stable enough to hold it."

Something that never would have occurred to her. They spread the blanket beneath the tree, but the shadows made the air even chillier, and soon Coop pulled it up so it was wrapped around their shoulders. "That iced water in the chest doesn't sound real good right now."

She laughed. "I'd forgotten it gets chillier up here."

"I shouldn't have." But he was smiling. "This is a wonderful place."

"It's fascinating. But you see those piles of dirt where nothing is growing?"

"Yeah."

"Over a hundred years and the stuff they pulled out of the ground is still poisonous with heavy metals. There's been occasional talk of cleaning it up, but it never seemed like a big enough problem. It's far enough away from water supplies here that I imagine most of it just seeps back into the ground where it belongs."

He nodded, scanning the area. "I never thought about that."

"Nobody's exactly worrying. It's so far out of the way. But what amazes me is the amount of labor that went into digging it out. Men with shovels, buckets, picks…and if they were lucky a mule to help haul it. It's a wonder they didn't die from overwork."

"Or something else, considering what they were digging. Imagine inhaling that stuff. Probably swallowing it."

Birds, that had evidently quieted at their arrival, began to call here and there. It was still early enough in the spring that the migratory birds hadn't all returned, but the sound of birdsong, even just a little, helped make the moment relaxing. Kylie felt herself letting go of a major amount of tension, some of it she hadn't even been aware she was holding. It was so easy now to lean into Coop and let every bit of her unwind. When his arm wrapped around her waist, she realized she hadn't felt this much peace since she awoke in the hospital.

She didn't want to go home. She wanted to stay here forever, wrapped in this man's strength and warmth, and let everything blow away on the breeze that ruffled the very tops of the trees.

Life could still be good. It could still be almost perfect. She let that realization sink into her battered heart and soul, let stirrings of happiness replace it.

Then Coop shifted, turning her toward him within their cocoon of blankets. He smiled into her eyes as he cupped her chilly cheek with a warm hand and stroked it gently with his thumb.

"You are one beautiful woman, Kylie Brewer. You make me crazy with wanting you."

She caught her breath, staring at him in amazement. She'd sensed his desire, even tasted a bit of it, but driving him crazy with it? It felt like an injection of power through her entire body.

"You know I have to leave," he said, still holding her gaze, still caressing her cheek. "Uncle Sam will call and I'll have to go."

Her happiness in the moment teetered, in danger of falling.

"I don't make promises I can't keep," he said. "I need you to understand that. I'll have to go, and even if you wanted to come with me, you couldn't come to some of those places. I want to make love with you, but I need you to understand my limitations. I already made a promise to the government and the United States Marines."

"I understand." She did, too, except she wondered why he thought these caveats were suddenly so important. She'd understood from the outset that he would only be here until his leave was over. That one of these days all too soon he'd have to go back. It made her sad to even think about it, but she'd already accepted it. It had been built-in from day one.

He moved his hand, brushing hair back behind her ear. "I like looking at you," he said. "You're a feast for my eyes. And if we weren't up here on this mountainside, I'd be so tempted to love you. Thank goodness it's too dang cold."

She didn't know how to take that. "You're grateful it's too cold? What does that mean?"

He dropped a chilly kiss on her lips. "Only that you know my intentions and now you'll have time to think about them. I don't want to take anything from you that you aren't willing to give."

So he thought he'd be taking and giving nothing in return? She didn't feel that way at all. At this point in her life, a long-term relationship was the last thing she felt comfortable thinking about. But a fling with this gorgeous man? She suspected it would give her the kind of memories she'd recall in old age to warm her on chilly nights.

Assuming, of course, that she didn't forget the whole thing. But the thought surprised her by amusing her. Making love would involve a heck of a lot more than her short-term memory. She suspected Coop would imprint himself so deeply on her that she'd remember nearly every touch.

And, oh, how she wanted those touches. Part of her felt as if they would help bring her back to life, moving her away from the precipice she had felt was so close since the attack. Reminding her of all the good things she had to look forward to, rather than the bad things she'd forgotten.

A journey of discovery, an opening door when for weeks now she'd felt as if every door was closed.

If a brief fling was all he could give her, what could be wrong with taking it? Since she'd learned her memory loss wasn't physical, after all, but rather something that would be corrected by therapy and time, she'd felt an increasing thirst for life, and Coop was part of the thirst she was feeling.

God, she just wanted to be a woman again, to put aside all her worries for a little while. Including the maniac who still seemed to be after her. If she let him, he'd just keep leaching every possible moment of joy from her life.

Was she scared? Of course she was. But she was also extremely tired of being held in thrall by that fear, by some man she couldn't even remember. It was as if he controlled her life by remote, impressing fear on her until she sacrificed everything but her terror of him.

She could feel a shift coming inside her, as if a dungeon door were opening and letting in the light. If she had only another day or two, then let them be good days.

She snuggled closer and was pleased when his arm tightened around her. "Can I be honest?"

"Please. I prefer it."

"Then…I want you, too. However little or much you can give me. I know it might only be a few days. But I might only have a few days."

She felt him stiffen, and for a long time he didn't say anything. Then, "Kylie?"

"What?"

"I'm better than that."

"Better than what?"

"If that guy comes near you, I'll take him out. But apart from that...I don't want to take advantage of you because you think you have only a short time left."

She was stunned. "I didn't mean it that way at all!"

He twisted until they were face-to-face. The chilly mountain air crept under the blanket, but she barely felt it and he didn't seem to notice at all.

"Then what did you mean?"

"Only that I know you have to leave! Time is short no matter which measure I use. Him or you. I get it. I still want to live as much of that short time as I can. I'm tired of moping around and feeling as if everything is pointless. I'm tired of being afraid. I want to grab the goodness that life offers with both hands for however long I can have it. I want *you*."

He wrapped both arms around her then, holding her so tightly his muscles felt almost like steel. "I live on the edge so much of the time that I grasp what you're trying to say. All I want is for you to be as sure as you can. I don't want to leave any regrets behind me."

Boy, that sounded pretty final. No prettied-up suggestions that he might ever return or want anything more from her.

Squeezed in his embrace, she nodded, although she knew she still had some thinking to do. Maybe she'd been harboring some furtive hope that he'd say he'd come back. He'd just made it clear that wasn't in his plan.

So did she want this fling or not? That question suddenly loomed as large as the threat against her.

Todd was beginning to go a bit crazy. Kylie was within reach yet out of reach. That damn Cooper was always there, and on the rare occasions he stepped out, Glenda was home.

How was he going to separate that herd? The pressure to finish Kylie off was growing like a disease in his system, raising his emotional temperature to the boiling point. He no longer questioned his desire to get rid of her. That was lost in the mists of time.

She had scorned him once too often, and then she hadn't died when she should have. Defiant bitch. He needed to finish teaching her the lesson he hadn't finished in Denver. Afterward...

Well, afterward he might find another woman to teach. He'd found his thoughts drifting that way more and more often since he'd finally worked up the nerve to take Kylie down. Had discovered he'd enjoyed the screams, enjoyed knocking her senseless, enjoyed watching the blood flow from the knife wounds. God, he'd felt so powerful, her life in his hands.

Yeah, doing it again would be fun. But first he had to take care of number one, the woman who had first gotten under his skin in high school and had ever since been like a burr under his saddle, irritating, maddening, rubbing him raw. It wasn't as if he hadn't given her a chance. He'd given her more than one chance over the years, including several in Denver.

But she always left him feeling as if she wished he were a thousand miles away. Nothing she exactly said or did, but something in the way she hurried away, slipped to the side to avoid even the merest of touches.

Then, in the midst of the seething cauldron of his lust for vengeance, came the idea. How to separate the herd?

Connie Parish had three children. The oldest had been taken once before, but he ruled her out mostly because she was old enough to be a problem.

But she had two younger children. The six-year-old boy would be the best. The hard part was going to be getting anywhere near that kid. He was being watched like a hawk. But he'd manage. Just make him disappear for a short while. Everyone would be looking for him, most especially his uncle Coop. Oh, yeah, with his cousin's child missing, Coop would put the search on the front burner and Kylie on the back. He'd leave her somewhere he considered safe enough, like the house, and he'd go looking for the child.

All Todd needed to do was grab the kid and hide him somewhere, causing a panic everywhere. Hell, even Kylie might go out looking.

But first he had to watch the Parish kids and figure out when he'd have an opportunity to take the boy. The minute he saw it, he'd jump.

And then when everyone was in an uproar, he'd find an opportunity to snatch Kylie.

It wasn't the most careful plan in the world, but he'd finally realized one thing for certain: he was going to have to take any chance that presented itself, or he was never going to get Kylie.

And if she happened to remember him first…well, he plain couldn't take that risk.

Kylie and Coop stopped at the grocery after they came back from the mountains. Glenda would be starting to wake for another night at work, and they wanted to make her a dinner before she left.

Kylie found the market easier to bear this time. Either people were staring at her less, or she was getting more comfortable with it. Staring less, she decided. She was no longer the most recent event and people were probably used to her being home by now.

Given that time was relatively short, they skipped over time-consuming ideas for dinner. Coop finally settled on some steaks, a salad and baked potatoes, which sounded really good to Kylie, too. Easy to make, as well, and Glenda had a small gas grill behind the house.

When they arrived home, they found Glenda draped over the kitchen table with the local newspaper and her first cup of coffee.

"The news about the kids is getting big headlines," she said as soon as they entered the door carrying bags. "God, I hope they catch this creep soon."

Kylie looked down at the paper and realized she'd never seen a bigger headline on it. At least not that she could remember. With the masthead, it took up most of the top half of the page.

"It's horrible," she said. "Just horrible. I hate to think of how scared the children must be getting."

"Not to mention their parents," Glenda remarked. She shoved the paper aside. "What have you been up to?"

"Oh, we took a nice drive in the mountains, then stopped at the grocery. Coop bought us a wonderful dinner."

"Oh?" Glenda lifted a brow.

Coop had dropped the bags on the counter, but he now pulled out the foam flat bearing three strip steaks. "Look good?"

"Like I'm in heaven," Glenda replied, smiling at last.

"You just relax," Kylie said. "I'm making the salad and potatoes. Coop is going to grill the steaks."

"Grill?" Glenda perked up even more. "You have no idea how rarely I do that just for myself."

"There's a lot I don't cook just for myself, either," Kylie remarked. "It gets boring, but who wants to spend the time?"

Coop laughed. "When I'm not in the field, I'll spend all the time it takes to cook a good meal."

A totally different perspective, Kylie thought as she began to rinse greens for the salad. Completely.

While the greens dried on paper towels, she prepared the baking potatoes and put them in the oven. With about an hour to bake the potatoes there was no rush. But there was time to spend with her sister.

Coop was about to leave the room, apparently to give them some time alone together, but Glenda waved him back in. "You're family now, Coop, so unless you want to be somewhere else, join us."

He smiled and sat next to Kylie. He still carried the scent of fresh air and woods about him, a pleasantly enticing scent. Kylie felt herself stirring with the pleasant heat he awoke in her so easily. Fling? Oh, yes, she wanted the fling. Whatever the price, she was willing to pay it.

When he inadvertently brushed her arm, she tingled all the way to her center. Any minute now she'd be panting and Glenda would know exactly what was going on. Not good. She drew a steadying breath and reluctantly edged away from Coop. Just a tiny bit.

He glanced at her, and something in the way the corners of his eyes creased told her he knew why she'd done it. Oh, heavens, she hoped her face didn't flame.

Under the table, his hand captured hers, and she had the strangest reaction. Instead of pushing her excitement to higher levels, it seemed to fill her with a soothing calm. Inside she felt everything go soft and warm. The last of the tension seeped out of her and she was able to relax.

Glenda leaned back, rolling her shoulders. "I'm really upset about this person stalking kids. But I'm even more worried about Kylie."

"Why?" Kylie asked.

"Because so far the stalker hasn't harmed a single child. Not even made any attempt to. But you getting a dead black rose? That makes my skin crawl."

Everything inside Kylie clenched as her fear returned. She'd successfully avoided thinking about it all day, concentrating instead on being with Coop, but as Glenda spoke she knew it had all been just a diversion. She was still terrified of the man who had tried to kill her, a man who apparently hadn't given up.

Coop squeezed her hand, as if to offer reassurance. But there was no real reassurance as she looked past her sister to the late-spring afternoon outside. None. Not unless she could remember who had attacked her. That was the only way she could free herself of the fear, to put that man away.

For now she just had to do her best to live with it.

She tightened her hand around Coop's, wondering if she was hanging on to him for dear life.

"I guess I said exactly the wrong thing," Glenda said. "Hell, I'm sorry, Kylie."

"You didn't say anything wrong," Kylie reassured her, trying to feel a bravery that kept eluding her. "It's true. That man is still out there. I can't afford to forget that for very long." And that was true, too. A short vacation from fear was all she could hope for at this point.

The doorbell rang and Glenda went to answer it. She spoke to someone and Kylie recognized the answering voice immediately. "Todd," she muttered to Coop, then sighed.

"What's wrong with him?" Coop asked.

"I couldn't tell you. For some reason it didn't work between us years ago. He's only a friend. I guess I just don't feel like seeing anyone right now."

But that was ridiculous. She had to start picking up the reins of life again, one way or another. She drew her hand from Coop's and pushed back from the table. It wouldn't kill her to be pleasant for a little while.

Todd was standing inside the foyer. He smiled warmly when he saw Kylie. "You're looking a lot better. I got back from Saint Louis today and I wanted to see how you were doing."

"Loads better," Kylie answered with a smile. "Except for my memory, anyway. That's still gone." She had no desire to tell anyone else about those brief flashes she'd had.

Todd's smile faded. "That's got to be awful, Kylie."

"Maybe it's for the best," she answered, trying to sound bright. "I'm sure there are things I'd rather not ever remember. We're getting close to dinner, but would you like to have some coffee with us?"

She was surprised to see that he appeared taken aback. Kind of an odd reaction to a simple gesture she'd have offered to anyone she knew.

"Uh...I really can't. I just wanted to see how you were doing and to give you something. I don't know if you still like this stuff, but I brought you a little statue of the arch." He stuffed his hand into his pocket and brought out a four-inch piece of metal shaped like the Gateway Arch.

She accepted it and smiled. "What a sweet thought!"

"Maybe you don't do it anymore, but I remember you had a collection of things like that."

"She did," said Glenda. "Up in the attic since she went to Denver, but maybe we'll bring that out again. Sure you don't want coffee, Todd?"

"Maybe another time. It's been a long drive and I just

want to get home." He smiled at both women in turn and promised to see them in a few days. Then he was gone.

Coop spoke from the kitchen door. "Why don't I like that guy?"

"I don't know," Glenda answered. "He's all right. Not exciting, but okay."

Kylie, however, was looking at the arch in her hand. He'd bought this for her? Something inside her squeezed. It couldn't be new.

It was tarnished.

Chapter 12

"It's tarnished?" Coop repeated after Glenda left for the night. Kylie hadn't mentioned it earlier, and she felt weird for mentioning it now.

"I know," she said. "I'm being ungrateful. Maybe he just didn't notice."

"Let me see," he said, holding out his hand.

She passed him the arch, watching him carry it over to a lamp in the hallway to study it in brighter light. "Well," he said after a bit, "it's certainly not new. Maybe he picked it up in some antiques shop or something."

"Maybe. It was a nice gesture. I don't know why it bothered me."

He looked up from the trinket that nearly vanished in his large hand. "Well, you didn't like him very much in high school. Hardly strange that you wouldn't want gifts from him now." He straightened and put the arch on the table beneath the lamp. "I'll grant you it's odd, but no big deal. Maybe it just caught his eye and he remembered that collection he mentioned."

"Maybe." That was a valid point. The fist that had been gripping her began to ease.

He glanced down at it again. "And maybe he didn't want to seem like he was overdoing it. I'll give him credit for that much."

"Overdoing it how?"

"Well, you barely got home before he was here with flowers. His reception was not exactly, um..."

She laughed. "Okay, I was a little cold to him. Not very nice of me, was it?"

"I don't know. Sometimes we just don't like people. Nothing we can help. And he was a little quick on the draw given what had happened. Why do I get the feeling that back in your school days he was the guy who always went a little too far?"

Kylie sat on the couch. "Maybe so. Tried too hard? I don't know. He was part of our group, but it was more like he was on the fringe. It's hard to explain, but it wasn't that no one liked him. For a while I was interested enough that I dated him a couple of times, but then something just didn't feel right. I don't know what. Anyway, I dated him, so he couldn't be all weird, right?"

Coop laughed heartily. "Goes without saying. He still likes *you*, however. To wit, one trinket and a mess of grocery store flowers earlier."

She giggled. "Oh, don't pick on him about the flowers. We don't have a florist in town."

"Okay, I'll be fair." He winked, then crossed the room to sit beside her. At once he snaked out an arm and wrapped her in it, drawing her close. Smiling, she leaned her face against his shoulder. He made it so easy to forget everything except him. And unlike Glenda, he didn't do a thing to remind her of all that should be scaring her.

Of course, Glenda was merely expressing sisterly concern. She'd been a rock through all of this, never losing her cool. She was certainly entitled to admit how worried she was.

Feeling oddly content and happy, a rare mood for her since the attack, she didn't want to lose a moment of the good feeling. In fact, she wanted more.

The words emerged with a boldness that surprised her. One of the changes since her brain injury. "Make love to me, Coop."

She heard him draw a sharp breath. "I told you about marines and drawers."

A quiet laugh escaped her. "Somehow I think you'd be able to protect me just as well stark naked. And I kind of like the image."

His arm tightened around her, and she heard his heart accelerate beneath her ear. "I gave you the caveats."

"Yup. You were completely honest. Leaving soon, going places no woman can follow. I didn't miss any of it."

He turned suddenly and took her by the shoulders. "You've been through a lot, Kylie," he said, his blue eyes boring into her. "I don't want to be something else you have to survive."

Her mood began to sink. How many kind excuses was he going to give her? Clearly he didn't really want her. She'd mistaken the looks, the kiss, the little gestures. "It's okay. You don't have to do anything you don't want to." She tried to pull away, but his grip on her upper arms tightened.

"Aww, hell," he said. Then, almost faster than she could believe, she was lying back on the couch, him half over her, his mouth taking hers in a penetrating, demanding kiss. He caught her head between his hands, giving her no opportunity to escape, making her feel instantly possessed by him.

It was like striking a match deep inside her. The simmering longings burst into full life, the entire world went away and she cared about nothing except the mouth plundering hers, the man's weight on her torso. She reached up with both arms, hanging on to his shoulders, wanting to make sure he couldn't escape, either.

Even as passion rose in her, something else seemed to be settling, as if somewhere deep inside she had been waiting for this man, this moment, forever.

He shifted over her, until his hips rested between her legs, and began a gentle rocking movement that lifted her even higher. Her own hips responded instinctively, moving in time to his tongue's incursions into her mouth. She felt he had entered her from head to foot, as if he had taken possession of her entire being.

An ache blossomed between her legs, hot and heavy, and she tried to lift her legs to bring him closer to her throbbing center. The weight of him, the pressure…all of it was perfect.

He released her mouth and she gasped for air, digging her nails into his shoulders as their bodies followed the timeless rocking that carried them closer and closer to the pinnacle.

Another gasp escaped her as he pulled up her shirt and lowered his head, sucking one nipple through her lacy bra. An arc of heat shot through, so hot she was surprised she didn't turn into a cinder. With each tug of his mouth on her nipple, another arc of fire shot through her, leaving her utterly mindless, in thrall to sensation and pleasure.

Her thighs tightened around his narrow hips, feeling his movements against her in every way possible. Wanting more, so much more.

She felt so heavy at her center, but so light everywhere else. The throbbing had spread until it became a drumbeat in her ears as well as her core. Pounding, aching, needing, hovering on the very edge of anticipation, the very edge of satisfaction. She quivered with hunger throughout every cell of her body.

"Oh, Coop," she breathed as if the sigh could hurry him up.

He knew what she wanted. He wanted it, too. But he enjoyed the buildup as much as he enjoyed the climax, and he was in no rush to reach the end of this story. Her sweet scents filled his head, giving him a rush. The writhing of her body beneath his drove him to the edge of madness. His entire being seemed to be centered between his legs, except for the splinter that was nursing her lovely breasts, first one and then the other.

But as much as he wanted to delay, to hang on to each of these exquisite moments, he knew he couldn't do it. Delaying too long might push her to a point where she started to tumble without satisfaction. He didn't want to do that to her, stretch her so tightly only to have her snap the wrong way.

But damn, there was no finesse in this, he thought vaguely, then gave up. Later. There'd be time later.

Pumping harder, hating the material that separated them, he lifted them both to the lip of the chasm. When he heard her gasp and felt the shudder run through her, causing her to buck against him, then heard the cry, he knew she had arrived. Moments later he followed her into the abyss of perfect pleasure, each jet of his body sending a racking shudder through him.

When he collapsed on her, it was to feel her arms grab him and hold him as if she feared she might fall forever. The rictus of satisfaction eased into a soft smile as he buried his face in her hair. He felt drained to his very soul.

Kylie never wanted to move again. She felt as if the sun and the moon and the stars had exploded inside her, leaving her so drained and so satisfied that there was nothing left of her. She was drifting like a feather on a sense of completion she never wanted to lose.

But finally reality began to return. Coop eased off her and fell to the floor beside the couch with a groan. She turned her head as much as she could without disturbing her sense of utter relaxation. "You okay?" she whispered.

"Better than," he answered huskily. "Um, wow?"

If she'd had the energy, she might have laughed. She felt the same way. No words would suffice. When her hand slipped from the couch and dangled, he caught her fingers gently and held them.

Minutes passed in contented silence. But at last Coop stirred and sat up. "I need to clean up. Then maybe a reprise."

Her eyes opened wider and she found his face only inches from her own, covered with a soft smile. "I'm all for that," she said softly.

"Count on it," he said, and dropped a kiss on her lips. "Give me a few."

As she watched him rise and walk out of the living room, her sense of humor decided to get involved. "Hey, marine?"

He turned. "Yeah?"

"You never dropped your drawers."

She lay there grinning happily as his hearty laugh filled the house and followed him down the hall. "I can remedy that," he called back.

She bet he could.

Since he'd gone upstairs to freshen up, she used the powder room downstairs to take care of her own needs. It was little more than a small closet beneath the stairway, but their grandmother had decorated it for guests. The wallpaper and pictures on the wall had long since passed outdated into some version of old-fashioned charm.

She smiled at her reflection in the old mirror and noted that this time he had indeed given her some beard burn. A washcloth with cool water helped quiet it down. When she heard his steps on the stairs, she hurried up to join him. Now he wore a clean blue T-shirt with the Marine Corps logo on it and gray sweatpants. The thing she didn't miss, though, was that he wore his laced-up boots.

She felt her mood waver. "Boots?"

"Habit," he said. "I need something to eat and drink before I explore your charms further. Join me?"

Habit? Maybe. But more like preparedness. Maybe it wasn't just his drawers he wouldn't drop.

Feeling a little sad, a whole lot happy and just generally mixed up, she followed him into the kitchen. No, they couldn't afford to forget that some sicko was after her, but still…this night should be unsullied. Honesty told her that wasn't possible, but she didn't have to be happy about it.

After he pulled some cold cuts and mayonnaise from the fridge and brought bread, plates and utensils to the table, he suddenly squatted beside her. With his forefinger he touched her chin and urged her to look at him. "What happened?"

"Reality," she admitted. "The boots. I just don't want to face it."

Still squatting, he wrapped her in his arms and drew her close until she was leaning against his chest and his warm breath stirred the hair on top of her head. "We can't entirely forget," he said. "But I sure understand how you feel. You want me to take the boots off?"

She shook her head a little. "You wouldn't feel good about it. I get it. You're supposed to be protecting me. We had a nice interlude, but in case something happens…"

At that he turned her chin upward so she looked at him. "That wasn't an interlude. Don't ever think that."

Then he kissed her so deeply that she lost her breath. She felt almost dazed when he released her and calmly set about making sandwiches.

As he passed her a plate, his eyes smiled at her. "We may have to be careful, but we don't have to give up everything. You'll see."

The warmth flooded her again, driving her demons into the background. She knew they wouldn't go away until the creep was caught, but that didn't mean she had to turn over her entire life to him. No, she was entitled to some minutes all her own.

The ever-brilliant Todd, as he occasionally liked to think of himself, although he avoided doing it too often, had solved the problem of how to kidnap the little Parish boy. It still seemed like the best way to separate Cooper from Kylie. He couldn't imagine Cooper not hunting for his cousin's child. What's more, he'd probably leave Kylie locked in the house thinking she'd be safe on her own for a few hours.

So he had to make sure the hue and cry went up shortly after Glenda reported for work at the hospital, at a time when the evening would start to dim the light and all attention would be focused on the missing child.

If somehow Cooper didn't leave Kylie on her own for a while, he'd find another way, of that he was certain. As for the kid, he wouldn't have to take him very far. He could ensure he'd be found in a matter of hours, or sooner. Safe and sound. He didn't have anything against the kid. Hell, if it came to that, maybe he could make himself the hero.

But he'd noticed Connie Parish's older daughter, Sophie, was more interested in gabbing with her friends on the phone than watching her two younger siblings. Ethan got home late from the ranch where he was helping his dad; the oldest girl was left in charge, and the little ones often went into the backyard to play. The youngest daughter often returned inside after only a few short minutes, but the boy loved to spend long periods playing with his miniature cars in the sandbox.

Easy to get, then. All the way at the back corner of the yard, near the alley. The wooden privacy fence offered a barrier, but not much. The gate was right beside the sandbox, so all the wood fences lining the alley would help him more than they'd help the boy. He could snatch him, cover him with a heavy blanket to muffle his cries and carry him off quickly.

Then he could leave him bound and gagged in one of the abandoned houses that had been empty since the semiconductor plant closed. There were a lot of them, so he devoted some time to choosing one that wouldn't be obvious but that would allow the child to eventually be found.

After all, he didn't need long to grab Kylie, and once

he had her, they might look all over, but it would never occur to anyone to check his place. No, they'd be looking for some stranger who had come from elsewhere. Nor would it take him very long to deal with Kylie. Then he could search for her along with everyone else.

He realized he needed to clarify his planning a bit more, but he had all night and most of tomorrow. Because he couldn't wait any longer. He was scared himself, too. Scared that Kylie would remember him.

In his barn, he pushed one of the old cars to the far end and began to dig the hole. Soon Kylie would occupy it. The thought made him hum as he dug.

After the sandwiches, Coop wasted no time in pulling Kylie upstairs to the bedroom. Her heart began to beat wildly even as a smile grew on her face. She been almost afraid to hope that he would take her all the way with him. Afraid to hope that he'd lower his barriers that much. The couch had been nice, but incomplete.

Now she could have all of him.

Except his feet, it seemed.

Standing beside the bed, he pulled her T-shirt over her head. The air felt contradictorily chilly and warm— chill from the spring night, heated by his gaze traveling over her. Her insides quivered in anticipation, and it felt as if the oxygen was leaving the room.

"So beautiful," he said, as if she had no scars. She knew those scars, all four of them on her torso. She almost blushed as he released her bra and pulled it away. One of the ugliest gashes was on her left breast, but Coop merely bent to kiss it. "So brave," he murmured.

Trailing his mouth downward, he slid to his knees and reached for the button of her jeans. She closed her eyes as she felt it release and listened to the sound of the zipper being lowered. Feeling dizzy with need and weak with hunger, she reached out, steadying herself on his shoulders.

Then, inch by inch, his mouth tracing the trip, her panties and jeans lowered, leaving her almost completely bare to his gaze.

She couldn't have opened her eyes to save her life. Everything inside her except passion had shut down, leaving her tangled in yearnings so strong they nearly collapsed her.

Hands gripped her waist and put her on the bed. Oh, man, she wanted to see him, but then he began to stroke her from head to foot. Somewhere her sneakers and socks went away. She knew she was utterly naked, but his caressing hands held her in thrall; her core throbbed so strongly she nearly cried out.

She heard something and managed to open her eyes a crack. He was pulling off his shirt. Satisfied that he would come to her, she opened her arms wide to receive him.

But he had a different idea. He stroked her inner thighs with those magic hands of his, deepening the pulsations inside her until she was gasping like a runner near the end of a race.

"Coop…"

"Shh…"

She parted her legs in invitation, feeling her hips rise trying to find his. Then at long last he settled between her legs. She could feel his hardness against her dewy center. His arms slipped beneath her waist, and the next thing she knew, he had rolled them over.

She was lying atop him. Startled, her eyes opened.

"Ride me, darlin'," he said thickly. "Ride me."

She looked down, saw the point where their bodies

would join, then raised her gaze to see his sleepy smile. Man, he was gorgeous, that broad chest of his begging for her touch.

Rearing up, cradling his condom-covered hardness between her thighs, she smiled lazily down at him and began to run her hands over his chest. Those small pointed nipples of his were as sensitive as her own, she discovered as she heard him gasp and felt him buck a little.

But then he retaliated, swallowing her breasts with his large hands, caressing her nipples with his thumbs. Then he gave her a pinch that made her cry out and arch.

"Ride me," he said again, and this time there was no mistaking what he wanted. His hands gripped her waist, lifting her a little, until the exquisite moment when he entered her, piercing her, answering the ache deep within her with what she needed most in the world.

Then he slowly guided her movements until her body took over. Propping herself on his shoulders she rocked, desperation growing apace with need. His big hands steadied her, but she could hear from the pace of his breathing that he was coming with her.

Thought flew away. Her body controlled everything now, and it was pushing, pushing, needing, reaching for satisfaction as it never had before. Life summoned her and she answered.

"Now," he growled. "Now!"

As if she could have held back. She rocked a couple more times, then felt the shattering begin. She became one big, almost-painful ache from head to toe, stiffened, and a moment later she rode the tsunami to the other side. An instant later, she felt him jerk inside her, which unleashed another astonishing wave of completion inside her.

A million stars exploded in her head. It was a long time before she moved again.

Eons later, or so it felt, she rolled off him. He turned with her, cuddling her close. "I got some business I need to attend."

She knew what he meant. She'd felt the condom when he'd entered her. She sighed, knowing she had to let go for a few minutes.

"I'll be right back," he promised.

Then she opened her eyes and a gasp escaped her. He was still wearing his boots, his sweatpants down around his ankles. "Boots?" she said. "Really? Coop..." She hardly knew what to say but it seemed so out of place.

He cupped her face. "If you'd been the places I've been... Well, boots stay on until the threat is gone."

She supposed it made sense, but she had to admit it was almost funny to watch him pull up his pants halfway and hobble to the bathroom. Boots!

But even as the humor of it struck her, she was still enraptured by everything about him, from his broad shoulders to his narrow hips, from the muscles of his arms to his thighs, the kind that indicated total fitness. A finely honed piece of manhood.

Sighing contentedly, she pulled a corner of the blanket over herself and tried to recall every single moment of their lovemaking, replaying it in her head as if she could prevent herself from forgetting even the least little part of it. Engraving it.

Given her apparent short-term memory problems, however, it seemed even more important to remind herself of every moment she still retained.

But in spite of every effort to relive each instant of the last hour, reality insisted on intruding.

She couldn't force back the onrush of memory, small though it was, of that knife flashing down and stabbing her, of that dead black rose that had been delivered by an innocent child.

Of the coffee pouring. Her brain fixed on that, sensing that if she could see the moments just before or just after she might answer one of the most important questions of her life: Who had attacked her?

Even the sound of Coop's return couldn't pull her out of the anxious memories.

"Kylie?"

"It's hitting me," she muttered. All of a sudden breathing seemed painful. Anxiety crawled along her nerves like a million ants. It didn't even help when Coop stretched out beside her and pulled her into his arms.

Her mind was rebelling. It wouldn't give her peace. It wouldn't give her anything.

Coop held her while she shivered and panted. At least she was letting him hold her, but he had a good idea what she was experiencing. He'd gone to this place a few times himself. Well, more than a few. He'd just had more opportunity to learn to deal with it.

He didn't know whether to hope she had remembered something new or not. Much as he had tried to keep things on an even keel, he hadn't forgotten that black rose and the threat it implied. What he couldn't understand was why her attacker would announce himself. Why not just come unexpectedly, with no one anticipating him?

Or maybe it had just been some other kind of sick creep who'd heard about the rose in Denver and was enjoying the thought of how much terror it had probably evoked.

At this point, anything was possible. They had

someone frightening people all over town by speaking to children, yet no child had been threatened, other than by being approached by a stranger. So why not someone who loved scaring people to death and had used the rose to do the same thing he was doing to the kids?

Psychologically it might fit nicely. What did he know? All he was certain of was that he had to protect Kylie if anyone threatened her. And he admitted he was worried about the kids around town. Who knew when or if this creep might decide to attack? He felt particular sympathy for his cousin, Connie. She'd been through this ten years ago when her ex-husband had unexpectedly taken their daughter. She'd walked in this hell, and wondering what might happen now had probably started that hell all over again for her. At least she had her job to reassure her that she could do something, and Ethan to support her emotionally.

Part of him felt like he ought to be looking out for Connie's kids, but it was Connie who had deputized him to look after Kylie. She had appointed him to this task and it was clearly what she most wanted from him.

Not that he felt he was doing the best job of it. He couldn't promise her she'd be okay. He couldn't take away the fears that stalked her. He couldn't help her get her memory back. He couldn't do anything at all except hold her until she got through the nightmare that would probably spring on her without warning for a long time to come.

So he held her, and stroked her back, and waited for her tremors to fade, waited for her to come back to him. She would, but it might take a while. Only someone who had been traumatized could understand the emotional grip of reaction, even if you couldn't remember what had happened.

Some guys he knew got angry and dangerous with that anger. Some hid away, not wanting a single soul to see them, touch them, speak to them. Some went to places they couldn't even describe when they emerged hours or days later. It was a grip, all right, a vise that clamped over thoughts and feelings and wouldn't let go. Reality could scarcely reach through it; sometimes it couldn't at all.

He didn't know where Kylie was, but at least she hadn't rejected him or tried to escape his touches. She just shivered, locked in the clutching talons of fear and perhaps more. He couldn't imagine all the emotions that had been seared into her by that attack, and he hadn't asked.

Talking about it had to be her choice. Prying would only make her uncomfortable. He prepared himself to be as patient as necessary.

It seemed like a long time, but it was probably only a half hour. He felt her shivering weaken, felt her body beginning to relax. He continued to stroke her back soothingly, waiting for her return.

"I'm sorry," she whispered.

"No apologies. It's not like you can help it. Did you remember something else?"

"No...no. It was the same memories but all of a sudden they felt like I was there again. I don't know why, it just came over me."

"There doesn't have to be a trigger." He pitched his voice low, trying to avoid disturbing her. He was certain she wasn't fully back in the present moment.

"Coffee and a knife," she murmured after a while. "What useless things to remember."

Like anyone got a choice. "Think you can sleep now?"

"I don't know. I do feel exhausted."

He wasn't surprised. Reluctantly he let go of her and rose to pull blankets over her. Then he pulled on his sweatshirt.

She watched him with pinched eyes. "What a way to thank you for our lovemaking."

He flashed a grin, though it didn't feel easy. "No thanks necessary. I was there, too."

But her face still didn't relax. He thought he understood. He eased himself back onto the bed beside her and scooped her close along with the blankets to keep her warm. "I'll be right here. Not going anywhere at all. Sleep if you can. Talk if you want. I'm here for you."

Those words sounded like a promise. He considered them as he waited for her to finish unwinding and drift toward sleep. He was in no position to be making promises of any kind.

But somehow the sound of that was good. He'd be here for her.

The pressure inside Todd was becoming intense. He sat in his kitchen drinking coffee while the night deepened outside, and considered the changes in himself. Until he'd snapped and attacked Kylie, he'd daydreamed about taking vengeance, but he'd never felt almost physically pushed to do it.

Now that he'd done it once, he could almost feel as if he were being kicked in the ass by the need to finish the job. And he'd started thinking about the next woman, a woman he hadn't chosen yet, but one he was evidently going to need.

The changes he recognized in himself at once astonished him and pleased him. He had become an actor, an important actor, in a life that had always made him feel like part of the scenery.

For the first time in a long time, if ever, he stood back and took a long look at himself. He'd been living mostly by rote his entire life, doing what was expected of him, first by his father, then by his employers. He had lived believing that something good would come along if only he played it straight.

But now he realized that he'd been letting life and others drive him. Kylie, the one thing he had wanted that was just for him, had scorned him more than once. Even after he'd grown up and had become reasonably successful financially, and had met up with her in Denver, she still wasn't interested. In fact, she was less than interested, although he couldn't begin to understand why.

Now, even without her memory, she still didn't seem interested. She'd accepted his token gift pleasantly enough but, other than an offer of coffee, had given him no sign that she had become interested.

Not that it mattered. If she got her memory back, her lack of interest would become a lot worse.

But all of this was irrelevant now, he told himself. Except for the part about taking care of her for good before she remembered him. No, now he was filled with power—power he had tasted when he'd thought he had killed her. The power of life and death.

That was so much more intoxicating than money. In fact, that experience had been the most real and intense one of his entire life. He had a taste for it now.

He wasn't going to blend in and disappear again. Oh, he wasn't going to let anyone know about his new powers. He'd keep all that secret from everyone. But *he* would know, and that was the most important thing of all.

He had found the true Todd at last. The real one. The one who could hold a life in his hands and extinguish it.

Feeling the power course through his veins, he decided tomorrow would be the day, as long as Connie and Ethan Parish were working. The older girl would be as inattentive as usual, and the boy would probably soon be alone in his sandbox. It could all go down in a matter of minutes.

Coop would join the search party. If he left Kylie home alone, that would be an easy takedown. If he didn't leave her alone, it would be easy enough to release the Parish boy and try another angle.

But time was short. With each passing day he worried more that Kylie would remember him. Each passing day enhanced his risk.

And each passing day also enhanced his hunger to finish the job.

Chapter 13

The news that little James Parish had gone missing from his own backyard spread through the town like a wildfire. He'd last been seen by his sister playing in his sandbox shortly after dinner. The next time she'd looked he was gone.

After calling for him for ten minutes or so, Sophie had phoned her mother. The sheriff's department had arrived in huge numbers, both on- and off-duty members, and began walking an ever-widening search perimeter. Other police had set up roadblocks at quite a distance from town on the only roads leading out of the county.

Kylie and Coop heard about it when Glenda called shortly after arriving on her shift at the hospital.

"God, can you imagine it?" Glenda said. "Once was bad enough but now that has happened to Connie again?"

A few minutes later, Ashley arrived at the door and they invited her in. Kylie could feel the tension in Coop ever since they got the word. She didn't need him to spell it out that he wanted to be out there looking for his cousin's little boy. But here he was, stuck with her because he'd made a promise and had been deputized.

God, this made her feel awful. She watched him clench and unclench his hands repeatedly, and saw how hard it was for him to hold still.

"I can't believe this has happened again to Connie," Ashley said, refusing an offer of coffee. "I'm going to join the search parties, but…well, I just needed a minute to vent."

"I understand," Kylie answered. Indeed she did. Though she'd been in high school herself when it had happened and hadn't known Connie well at the time, she vividly remembered when the whole town had been on alert because a stranger had talked to Connie's daughter. And then Connie's daughter had disappeared. Kylie was quite sure that the fact that the girl had been taken by her father didn't ease the panic or the memory of what Connie had endured over Sophie. And now it was happening to her again? To the same woman?

"It's unbelievable," Kylie said, finding herself helpless to come up with any other words. The same woman twice? How unlikely was that? The odds were probably astronomical.

She glanced at Coop and saw him standing stone-faced, arms crossed, a million miles away. Thinking about James, no doubt—about a little boy he was just getting to know. The last of his family, Connie and her children. They had drawn him all the way out here.

She'd gotten the measure of this man, and didn't need him to explain that he was being torn in two by his desire to help find James and his promise to keep her safe. He was standing in the very definition of a rock and a hard place.

She did the only thing she could. "Coop, go help look for James. I'll be perfectly safe here in a locked-up house."

He gave a small negative shake of his head. "I promised. I'd be derelict…"

"Oh, don't give me that military stuff, Gunny," she said sharply, even as fear began to make her heart hammer. She didn't want to be alone. But she also didn't want to be responsible if something bad happened to James and Coop had been stuck here with her. She could live with her fear; she'd had plenty of practice. She'd never forgive herself if Coop ever blamed himself in any way for something happening to James. "You need to go help with the search. You owe it to Connie and James, and I'll be fine. Lord, with all the cops crawling all over this town right now, it probably wouldn't be safe to jaywalk, let alone try to pull a major crime."

The faintest of smiles flickered over Coop's mouth. She'd made her point. But his answer was stubborn. "I promised."

"Oh, for heaven's sake," Ashley said, butting in as she looked from one to the other. "This is ridiculous. Coop, you'd be more help out there than I would. Go look for James. I'll stay here with Kylie. Does that work?"

Coop hesitated, but Kylie gave him a gentle shove. "I couldn't live with myself. Please. Go. Help Connie and James."

He hesitated. "Make sure everything is locked up. It might be best to do all you can to make it look like no one's home. If I didn't think it might expose you to more risk, I'd take you with me." He scowled, clearly still torn. "No, I can't take you. It's getting really dark out there. We could get separated. If someone wants to take advantage of you being out there in all the confusion…" He left the rest unsaid.

"Nobody's going to try anything," Kylie said again with more surety than she felt. "One scream and fifty cops would descend. I can dial 911 faster than someone could break in. Yes, I'll check the locks."

Coop finally nodded. He picked up a sheathed knife from the backpack he kept on the hall table and stuck it in his boot. There was also the Glock and clip holster that Connie had given him when she'd deputized him to look after Kylie. This was the first time Kylie had seen him put it on. Then he picked up the radio and the Taser gun.

He was expecting trouble. But of course he was. People didn't kidnap little kids for a lark.

Heedless of Ashley, he pulled Kylie to him and kissed her hard. "Don't open the door, even if you know who it is."

She looked at him feeling a bit dazed by the kiss, and confused by the direction. "Okay," she said. Then he was gone.

Before she could move, Ashley locked the front door. "Whew, I could feel that kiss all the way over here. Got a little heat going there, girl?"

"Just a little," Kylie admitted, but couldn't quite suppress a smile. The smile didn't last long, though. Thoughts of Connie and James filled her with anxiety and more of the fear that never quite left her.

"You can go search, too," Kylie said. "This watching over me every minute…well, who's going to break in here tonight of all nights?"

"That rose was scary, though," Ashley argued. "Somebody might be watching you."

"Then maybe we ought to be out there with the search party and every other able-bodied person in the county."

Ashley frowned, but after a minute or so, her expression began to lighten just a bit. "I want to help."

"So do I. James must be terrified out of his mind. Let's go. If we stick together, I'll be safe. Right now I'm thinking of a child. Compared to that, I don't care what happens to me."

Ashley nodded. "Okay, then. Let's go."

Fierce anger burned in Kylie. It turned all her fears to ash. She'd had enough. Her entire life was being controlled by a man she couldn't remember, a man who had attacked her for no good reason, a man who was a demon in her memory but a ghost in real life.

Fear for James Parish had pushed her over the edge. She hardly knew the child, but Connie was one of her best friends and had been for years, ever since she had come home from college. Her own fears vanished in the gale winds of fury that swept through her now. She didn't care if she was being foolish; she didn't care if she died tonight. She cared only that not one hair on that child's head be harmed, that Connie didn't have to face a future without her son.

Feeling as if she were finally taking her life back from the man who had tried to steal it, she checked the charge on her phone and stuffed it into her pocket. A light jacket seemed like a good idea, too.

"I don't have any weapons," she remarked to Ashley.

"Neither do I. I wouldn't know how to use them. Would you?"

"No."

"We're just going to look, right? I have no intention of going anyplace where we'll be out of earshot of the rest of the searchers. We're just going to help turn this town upside down."

Kylie nodded. "Whatever it takes. All I care about is Connie and her son. And I'm tired of making every decision based on some creep who tried to kill me."

Ashley smiled faintly. "You go, girl. But later *you* get to explain it to Coop."

Getting the boy James had been easy. For all the nervousness around town about strangers, the kid didn't seem affected. Todd was absolutely certain that his mother must have warned him repeatedly. After all, her oldest girl had been kidnapped once. But there he was, playing in the sandbox he loved with the little cars and trucks he loved even more, and his sisters were both inside.

Todd had watched for a while and realized the oldest girl, who was supposed to be watching him, only looked out the back window every half hour or so. Must be that in her mind, the backyard was a safe place for him to be.

But it wasn't entirely safe, not against Todd, who simply walked in, wearing heavy glasses, a blond wig and a T-shirt with famous cartoon characters on it.

"Hey, James," he said. "I like those cars, too."

James had looked up without suspicion. "Wanna play?"

"Not here. I've got a bigger collection of them and more room to play. It's just a minute from here. Wanna see?"

The boy didn't even hesitate. He scooped up a couple of his cars and stood. "Where?"

"Just down the alley."

As easy as that. The only problem came when he wanted James to get in his car. And that was easily handled. "Look, I know your mom. Let's go see her so she can tell you it's okay to play with me."

Problem solved.

Twenty minutes later, James was locked up in a closet in a house that had been empty for three years. Todd wasn't heartless. He left the boy water to drink and candy to eat. As soon as he had Kylie where he wanted her, he'd call an anonymous tip to the sheriff. James would be in his own bed by midnight.

If everything went according to plan, that was.

When he closed the boy in, he left the overhead closet light on, told him it was a game of hide-and-seek and he needed to be very quiet to tease his mom.

That wouldn't last forever, so he taped the edges of the door to muffle sound.

But it wasn't going to be for long. No way. He had nothing against the kid or his mother.

He just needed to get Kylie. Just Kylie.

With that in mind, he went back to her house to wait. He was as positive as he could be that Cooper would want to look for his cousin's son. And that he'd make the mistake of thinking Kylie was safe in a locked house.

But then that Ashley broad arrived, and when Cooper finally left to join the search parties, Kylie wasn't alone.

Red rage nearly blinded Todd, and he had to calm himself down. It was okay, he reminded himself. All he had to do was transform himself into the lifelong friend. He ditched the wig and glasses, and pulled on a business shirt with his jeans while standing in the deserted alley behind Kylie's house.

Then he worked his way around to the front door. He'd tell them he was part of the search party. Maybe he could get inside. One way or another, he was going to take Kylie tonight, even if he had to kill Ashley to do it.

Somewhere in his mind, little warnings began to pop up. Warnings that he wasn't thinking clearly, warnings that he hadn't planned well enough. But he was past listening to them. He'd find a way because he couldn't stand another minute of wondering when Kylie would remember him.

All he had to do was kill her, throw her into that hole in his barn, and she'd never remember him. And if anyone suspected him, he was ready to leave town, too.

Driven by urges he couldn't control, needs that overpowered him, he no longer cared about anything except ending the threat Kylie posed to him.

Her very existence had become the biggest threat he faced. Nothing else mattered any longer.

Kylie and Ashley were just stepping out the front door to join the search when Todd appeared. Smiling, he climbed the steps. "Hi, ladies," he said pleasantly. "Joining the search?"

Ashley smiled. "Absolutely. You, too?"

"That's what I came to town for. Mind if I go with?"

Standing on the threshold, something inside Kylie turned to ice, as if a glacier filled her entire body. Terror clawed at her, and anxiety weakened her.

God, she couldn't even step outside with friends? What was wrong with her? She'd made up her mind that James was more important than her own stupid fears, than her life even. She'd decided she wasn't going to let that nameless, faceless attacker run her life one more minute, and certainly not with a child at stake.

And now she froze? She simply couldn't make herself move. Never before in her life had this happened to her, and the reaction in its own way was as terrifying as all the rest of it.

In an instant she had become trapped in a waking nightmare over which she had no control. She tried with every ounce of will she had to take that step, to join Ashley and Todd on the porch, and her body would not budge.

"Kylie?" Ashley said.

Kylie tried once more and couldn't even lift a foot. It was as if she had become paralyzed.

Stiff words emerged from her mouth. "You go without me. I'm…feeling sick."

Ashley instantly became concerned. "Need me to stay with you? That's what I promised I'd do."

"No…no." That much was clear to Kylie. Everyone who could needed to be searching for that child. If she was paralyzed by her terror, that didn't give her a right to keep someone else from looking. They needed everyone they could get.

How could she think so clearly when her body had gone into a state of utter rebellion? It was exactly like a nightmare, unable to move as the danger approached.

"You go," she said. "It's important."

"I'll check back in a little while?" Ashley said uncertainly.

"Yeah. But all that matters is James. Just go."

So she stood there still frozen until Ashley and Todd disappeared down the street to the gathering point. When they vanished from sight, she found she could move again.

Shaken by the experience, she stepped back inside and closed the door. What the hell had caused that?

Well, she decided, she'd calm herself down and try again. There were plenty of searchers she could join up with. Or she could just follow orders and stay safely inside.

Right then, she doubted her own sanity. How could she have frozen like that? She'd walked through that door before.

But then the images returned. The flashing knife. The pouring coffee. Without knowing it, she curled up on the couch, lost in a repetitive series of flashes, the same things over and over again.

The present vanished.

Todd shed Ashley with no difficulty once they reached the staging point. She immediately fell in with her friend Julie and her husband, Trace Archer. Todd didn't know Julie as well as some of the others, and Trace Archer just made him plain uncomfortable. It was easy enough to sidle away without being noticed. All his life he'd been able to do that and no one ever asked, "Where's Todd?" Useful, perhaps, but it had made him feel invisible at times.

Then, as everyone was dispersing, he slipped away and headed back for Kylie. She was his now, but he still needed to move fast. He saw Coop over by the deputies who were directing the show, and assumed he'd been given some kind of command role here. Good. That would keep him away.

He ran all the way back to Kylie's house, afraid someone would see him. But the search parties were just beginning to spread out and most of the alleys were still vacant.

He didn't know what the search plan was and he didn't care. His car was parked in the alley behind Kylie's place, out of obvious sight. All he had to do was persuade her to go with him. He had his knife, but if necessary he'd clock her again in the side of the head. That had worked pretty well the first time. Brass knuckles had their uses.

* * *

Kylie emerged from the nightmare relatively soon. As she came back to the present, those ugly memories receding, she sat up and looked at the clock. Fifteen, maybe twenty minutes had passed. Not so bad.

But what had triggered all of this? Remembering not being able to step out the front door worried her at least as much as her memory loss. What had caused that? Did she have a new problem to deal with? How could she return to work or move forward in any meaningful way if she could be overwhelmed like that and unable to move? What if she'd been treating a patient in severe trouble?

God, she wanted to just cry. Her entire life messed up by one madman they couldn't even find. Each time she began to see a way forward, something threw her back again.

Someone knocked on the door. She peered out the peephole and saw Todd. What was he doing here? Had something happened to Ashley?

Forgetting all the warnings Coop had given her, she flung the door open.

And felt again that sense of creeping horror. What was wrong with her? Her body seemed to have developed a mind of its own, backing up and away from Todd.

"Where's Ashley?" she asked hoarsely, her heart galloping wildly.

"She's still searching. She was worried about you, though, so she sent me back to check that everything's okay."

"I'm fine. You can go back to searching." She brushed up against the hall table and looked down, seeing the tarnished arch that Todd had given her. For some reason, she picked it up, aware that she was breathing too rapidly, that darkness seemed to be hovering around the edges of her mind.

None of it made sense. She shouldn't be reacting this way. Desperate to appear normal, she held up the arch. "I like this, Todd." She sounded as if she had just run a marathon.

He smiled. "I'm glad." Then he closed the door behind him.

"You can...you can go back to searching," she said again. All of a sudden the image of the flashing knife entered her mind again. Without even understanding why, she threw the arch at Todd and caught the side of his face. A streak of blood appeared almost instantly.

Some functioning part of her didn't even wonder why he failed to look startled. Why he smiled.

"I guess you've remembered," he said, and swung his arm.

Her entire world turned black.

A half hour later, Coop saw Ashley with Julie, whom he'd met only once. What was Ashley doing here? He trotted toward the two women, worry for Kylie beginning to blossom alongside his fear for Connie's son.

"Ashley?"

She paused and looked at him. "Hey, Coop." Then she appeared to squirm a little before he could even ask. "I swear, Kylie told me she'd be fine and I should come down here with Todd. She insisted. She's in a locked house, isn't she?"

Of course she was. He tried to let go of the crawling sensation that *everything* was very wrong—this hunt for a child, Kylie being left by herself... "Where's Todd? How did you link up with him?" Some alarm at the back of his mind began clanging.

"Oh, he just stopped by. Kylie had decided she wanted to join the search and insisted we'd be fine if we stayed together. But then Todd dropped in to say he was also going, and Kylie backed out at the last second. She told me to come with Todd." Ashley shook her head. "I don't know where he is, though. I guess he joined another group."

But Coop hadn't seen Todd anywhere, and he'd been patrolling the streets as rapidly as he could, keeping an eye on searchers, helping to direct them to the places the sheriff's people wanted them to go first.

And he hadn't seen Todd.

All of a sudden things slammed together—Kylie's hesitancy around him, the little ways she seemed to avoid him. Todd dropping by to tell Kylie he was searching. How nice if he could have persuaded her to search with him, but Ashley had been there. As soon as the ugly thought appeared, he wanted to wipe it away. It couldn't possibly be...

Opposing needs began to shred him—his need to find James and his need to protect Kylie. This whole situation stank. The likelihood that two creeps were working this small town at the same time?

He turned from Ashley and Julie, and pulled the radio off his belt, calling in. "This is Coop," he told the sheriff. "I need to go to the house to check on Kylie. She's alone."

"Go," said Gage Dalton's rough voice. "Want any help?"

"You need everyone on this job. I'm just checking."

"Okay, then. Call if you need us."

He ran. *Not right, not right...* The words hammered in his brain with his pounding feet. Why had Ashley walked away after promising to stay with Kylie? Because she didn't believe Kylie could be at risk in a locked house and apparently Kylie had assured her she'd be safe. That was probably true, but something he wasn't prepared to trust, torn as he was by this whole situation. His cousin needed him, but so did Kylie. Hell, he should have brought Kylie with him to search, but he was afraid they might get separated, leaving her alone and unprotected. A locked house and a friend had seemed like a better choice.

Until this very moment.

Then there was Todd. He scanned every face he passed, hoping to find the man. He'd come out here to search, too, Ashley had said. But even though Coop was seeing many faces more than once, he had yet to see Todd.

He could run fast when he needed to, and he ran fast now. Like the wind. All he could think of was Kylie's sweet face, her terror, what that beast had done to her. She filled his brain.

But sitting firmly on the burner beside her was little James. Two lives at risk, and he was only one man. With any luck he'd get to the house to find Kylie was fine, and he could resume the hunt for Connie's son.

He'd been caught between conflicting concerns many times. In this case he judged the hundreds of people hunting for James would hardly miss him for the few minutes it would take to check on Kylie.

But if Kylie was in trouble, right now she'd have no one to pin her hopes on except him. That definitely tipped the scales, no matter how uncomfortable it made him to think of that little boy.

But his situational awareness, honed in many tough places over the years, goaded him. Something was very, very wrong. Something that extended beyond James's disappearance. He managed to push out another burst of speed, wishing he hadn't been at the far end of town. But there he'd been, like some kind of sap, assuming Ashley would take him seriously about not leaving Kylie alone. Or that Kylie would. She probably felt safe behind locked doors. And maybe she was.

Then he'd go back to helping with the hunt for James.

He took the front steps in one leap, his hand reaching for the key in his pocket. But then he saw something that froze everything inside him.

The door was ever so slightly ajar.

Todd loved those plastic handcuffs. He'd bound Kylie's wrists and ankles so she couldn't give him any trouble when she came to. And he wanted her awake. She didn't remember the first attack, which he hadn't worried about at the time because he was sure he had killed her.

But now he wasn't going to make the same mistake. He wanted her awake so he could enjoy her terror and pain, and then he was going to make sure she was in a deep hole she would never emerge from. Never.

He glanced at his watch and at the unconscious woman beside him. Maybe it was time to let the sheriff know where the kid was stashed. He had what he wanted, and he knew from experience how scary it could get for a little boy left in a closet alone, even with food and a light turned on. It had been cheaper than a babysitter when his parents wanted to go out for a night of drinking and dancing, but a little boy's mind could fill all that silence and an empty house with all kinds of horrors.

Yeah. Once he got to his place, he'd call with that burner phone he'd bought a while back in Denver. Not traceable.

The rest, though... A traitorous thought popped into his head again. Maybe he hadn't thought this through well enough.

Except time had proved him right. He had Kylie, and no one would know where to look.

Because everyone knew he was her friend.

What now? Coop wondered. An empty house, no idea where to begin looking. Everyone who might have seen anything moving up and down the streets of this town calling for a little boy, checking vacant houses for him.

Surely if someone had seen something unusual happening here, they'd have called it in. Few people were stupid enough to ignore something suspicious even if they were wrapped up in looking for James. They knew Kylie's story.

They also knew she'd known Todd all her life. But Todd was suspiciously absent from the search he'd said he was joining. Except how the hell could he be sure of that? He might have missed seeing any number of people out there tonight. Todd could be anywhere.

He swore and looked around, hoping for any clue, however small.

Then his gaze lighted on that tarnished arch Todd had given her. It lay in the entryway, on the floor, too far from the table where it had been earlier. Someone had thrown it.

Bending, he picked it up and saw faint traces of blood and skin.

Dear God!

Closing his eyes a moment, he settled his mind as best he could, pushed his roiling emotions to the side and gathered the bits and pieces into a partial picture. Todd, whom Kylie had said was always on the fringe. Which meant something about him bothered people, even those supposedly his friends.

Two dates and then she called it off. She couldn't

quite say why. The refusal to go to the prom with him. Todd showing up here almost the instant she got home, then later with flowers. Kylie's subtle avoidance, her carefully hidden distaste for him. Oh, she'd been good at covering, but Coop had felt it. Todd coming by again with a lame gift after his trip to Saint Louis. Almost as if he were checking up on something.

Checking up on whether she had remembered anything? Coop searched his brain, and realized Todd had asked her if she'd begun to remember anything. Far from confiding, Kylie had said no. Even though she had.

She didn't trust him.

That was enough for Coop. He pulled the radio and called the sheriff. "Have you seen Todd Jamison tonight?"

"Give me a minute." The sheriff clicked off, probably checking on the frequency the deputies were using. A couple of minutes later he came back. "No. He could be around, but no one recalls seeing him."

"Then tell me how to find his place."

Gage Dalton's voice sharpened. "Why?"

"Kylie's not at home and...I got a feeling."

"You want me to send someone?"

"I want you to find Connie's son. I could be all wet. Just let me check it out. And radio me if anyone sees Kylie."

So the sheriff gave him directions and made him swear he'd call if he needed help.

Yeah, thought Coop, like there was anyone left to help. Feeling grimmer than he had since coming home from Afghanistan, he set out to find Todd Jamison. And maybe that's where he'd find Kylie.

As he drove toward Todd's place, a certainty fell like

a pall over his heart. If anything happened to Kylie, he'd never be able to live with himself.

Kylie woke long before she stirred. She could tell she was in a car and bound, and she remembered Todd being there just before she blacked out.

Todd? Really?

Icy realization settled over her. Memory or no memory, her old friend had probably been behind everything that had happened to her. She didn't need to remember anything because the truth of it filled her heart and stomach with lead.

In fact, she didn't want to remember, for fear memory would paralyze her as it had before. She couldn't afford that now. She needed her every wit about her to try to get out of this mess.

She felt really stupid, however, for not heeding Coop's concerns more closely. Safe in a locked house? Not when you opened the door to a friend. Not when you acted impulsively because you saw the guy out there and wondered why your best friend wasn't with him.

Worry about Ashley had opened that door. Instead of answering it, she should have gone to the phone and called someone. Coop would have come instantly. Ashley would have answered her cell. There were a dozen smarter things she could have done.

But she had opened the door to a familiar face, ignoring the very instinct that had inexplicably caused her to freeze on the threshold.

And now she was in serious trouble. No one would know she was gone or where she was. If memory overtook her, she'd be worse than useless, a helpless quivering lump ready to be slaughtered for good.

She hoped her quickened breathing hadn't given her

away, hoped it was drowned in the sound of the car engine. Todd's aftershave filled the confined space, nauseating her. Why had she never before noticed how much she hated that aftershave?

But with her awareness of it came a memory of having smelled it before. In Denver. During the attack.

No! No memories now. She had to be able to deal with this situation somehow. At the very least, she had to try. No one was going to save her, no one could find her. That left her.

Maybe she could talk him out of this somehow. Maybe she could even lie and say she *had* remembered and she'd written it down, so everyone would know who to look for if she disappeared. Or maybe that she'd sent an email to the police that they'd read before long.

Each idea sounded thin, but if that was all she had…

God, she wished he hadn't bound her ankles, as well. At least then she'd have a chance of running. Whatever, she had to find a way of making this as difficult for him as possible, because the longer it took for him to kill her, the more chances she would have of finding some way to prevent it.

Think, Kylie. Think!

By the time Coop reached Todd Jamison's place, murder filled his heart. An errant part of him hoped he was wrong about all this, that he'd just find the two of them having coffee, but no part of him really believed that.

At this point, he was willing to bet that Todd had something to do with James's disappearance, as well. It had crossed his mind before, that scaring the kids might be a diversionary tactic, or that sending the black rose to Kylie might serve the same purpose. One actor who wanted forces divided and attention misdirected.

He hadn't quite succeeded. But before he killed Todd he was going to make sure the man revealed where he'd put James. And God help him if he'd hurt the boy or hurt Kylie. No mercy flowed in Coop's veins right then. None at all.

His consciousness had shifted to battle mode. The rules of the civilized world no longer held sway. He had two people to protect, a mission to accomplish and absolutely no compunction about how he accomplished his goals.

He parked a hundred yards out from the structures and switched off the radio the sheriff had given him. The last thing he needed right now was for the damn thing to squawk. Then he hurried across open ground, a dark sweatshirt and jeans his only concealment. A knife in his boot, a gun on his hip. It was more than he had sometimes carried.

He reached the house. Lights were on, a car was parked out front, but he quickly circled the building and realized no one was in there. That focused his attention on a barn about fifty yards away, and he saw the slivers of dim light seeping out between some of the aging boards.

There. Using a broken step, so as not to sound like a person approaching if anyone heard him, he hurried across the greening grasses of spring and the brown earth that had been worn by the years.

When he reached the barn, he put his ear to the wall. He heard voices. Todd. Kylie.

He slid over to a dirty window and used fingertips to wipe clean a peephole. They were both in there, and

Kylie was bound at her wrists. Worse, there was a hole in the barn floor right behind her.

Rage overtook Coop then, the rage that had been useful so many times in his job. It was clear-sighted, but an irresistible propellant.

He was going to kill that guy.

Kylie had remembered, and what she remembered was making her furious. The terror and the paralysis that had hit her before didn't come as memory returned. All that came was an anger she could barely contain.

This was the man who had tried to kill her, who had nearly destroyed her life, and now she could see the images in her mind, remember the awful moments. No longer did she wonder, she *knew*.

As he cut the ties around her ankles and dragged her out of the car toward the barn, she remembered. She remembered being grabbed from behind, stunned by a hard blow to her head. She remembered the world fading away, then slowly awakening on her back. Gravel bit into her, the stench of nearby Dumpsters nearly concealed the familiar aftershave.

Some of her clothes were already off. A knife flashed and rested against her throat. A face she knew all too well hovered over her, adding shock to her confusion. A gruff voice warned her not to fight. What…?

She recalled the awful moments when he had tried to rape her and failed, recalled holding perfectly still because of that knife at her throat, wondering if she would even survive. Then the terrifying knife, rising and falling again and again, feeling like hard painful blows to her torso. Thankful, so thankful, when the darkness closed in again.

Now she faced him again in that barn. Aware that

he meant to end it all here. He was afraid of her, she realized. Afraid that she would recall he had been her attacker.

Well, now she had and this time, instead of being frozen, she was enraged. But first things first.

"Why'd you take the boy?" she demanded. "He had nothing to do with this."

"He got Cooper away from you. I knew he would." But Todd wasn't smiling. He was licking his lips, looking edgy, troubled.

"Let him go."

"Aren't you the bleeding heart? I'm going to kill you and you're worried about a kid. He's okay, not that it should matter to you. And as soon as I'm done with you, I'm calling the cops to tell them where he is."

Then he stilled, his dark eyes becoming like twin chips of obsidian. Soulless. "You remembered."

"Yes. All of it. And it doesn't matter if you kill me now because I wrote it all down. By tomorrow, someone will be reading it. They're going to get you, Todd."

"But you won't be around to testify and I'll be long gone." He licked his lips again. He appeared to be losing his sense of control. Kylie didn't know if that was good or bad.

"Just tell me why. Why did you attack me in Denver? What good does it do to kill me if I don't know why?" Never taking her eyes from him, feeling the rage turn icy, she edged away from the pit, using her peripheral vision to find something, anything, she could kick at him. She seemed to remember glimpsing some tools hanging on a post nearby. If she threw him off balance, maybe she could run.

She didn't have much hope that she'd get far, but she

had to try. Everything within her rebelled at the idea of making this easy for him.

"Because you always treated me like something you wanted to shake off your shoe. Staying home was better than going to the prom with me, as far as you were concerned. Then when I ran into you in Denver, you had one excuse after another. No time. Too much schoolwork. The job. But I saw you go out with your other friends!"

A shiver of shock ran through her. "All of this because I didn't date you? You've carried a grudge this long?" At least he didn't seem to notice she was moving away from her intended grave. He seemed to be sure once again that he had full control. Farm implements appeared in the corner of her eye, and since her hands were bound in front of her instead of behind she might be able to grab and use one.

But how long did she have? He was looking wilder and crazier by the second. She had to move fast.

"You were never really nice to me," he said. "None of you were, but you were the worst. Dating me twice and then telling me to get lost."

"How was that worse?"

"I know you laughed about me with all your friends. I remember how they looked at me after."

She had never done that, and any looks he thought he'd gotten had probably been the same looks he'd been getting all along. But she couldn't argue against that. She racked her brain for a way to buy more time. "I didn't tell you to get lost. My Lord, Todd, we were in high school. Almost nobody dated anyone else for very long."

"What was wrong with me?" he demanded.

"Nothing," she said, sidestepping toward the implements hooked on the post. "Not one thing. It just didn't feel right to me. Have you forgotten I dated a couple of other guys? Some of them only once. There was nothing wrong with you."

"What about Denver?"

"What about it? A job and a graduate school program? I wasn't kidding about time. Did you think those study groups were social?" She knew he wouldn't believe her but apparently he'd watched her sometimes. The thought might have sickened her except for the icy fury that filled her. This guy had terrified Connie and her son because he was hung up on *her*?

He stepped toward her, and her heart leaped into her throat. She had to get to those implements.

Just then, a window to the side broke. Todd whirled to look. Kylie jumped to grab some clawlike thing that looked like it could do a lot of damage.

And then the marines arrived. One, anyway. He came charging through the barn door, vengeance personified, and jumped on Todd before he could do more than half turn.

Coop wanted to beat Todd to a pulp. He wanted to wring his neck. He wanted to kill him for all he'd done to Kylie and evidently to James.

But cool reason edged his anger. He laid a few good blows before the creep covered his face and started to cry. Damn, what a coward.

"Coop! He knows where James is."

"I heard," Coop growled. "See any rope?" When Todd wiggled under him, he punched his shoulder right in the brachial plexus. The man froze with agony.

He listened to Kylie scurry around, and then an adequate, dirty piece of rope fell in front of him. Straddling the man, Coop quickly bound his wrists, then flipped him over, hog-tying the guy's feet.

Spying Todd's knife, he kicked it to the side, safely away.

Only then did he do the thing he most needed to do. Pulling his own knife, he cut the wrist cuffs off Kylie. Once he'd shoved the knife back into his boot, he wrapped her in his arms and held her so tightly she squeaked.

Thank God. Thank God. He didn't know what he would have done if he hadn't found her in time.

Much as he wanted to savor the moment, however, there was other business. He let her go and went over to Todd. He nudged him with his boot. "Where's James? You've got ten seconds to tell me or I'll start kicking you."

Chapter 14

The bright morning sunlight hurt Kylie's eyes as they emerged from the sheriff's offices after a long night. Connie had gone home long ago to be with James, who didn't seem awfully traumatized by his experience. At least not yet.

His grandfather, Deputy Micah Parish, stayed at the office, however, as they sorted through all the facts Kylie could give them. His Cherokee face looked older than Kylie had ever seen it.

But while a team scoured Todd's homestead for evidence, the real story was unfolding in a conference room where Kylie told the sheriff, Gage Dalton, Micah and soon a cop from Denver everything she knew and remembered. It was a long night, but she could understand why they didn't want to let her go.

And truthfully, she wanted to tell them everything she could. Todd had not only tried to kill her, but if one thing had gone wrong with his misbegotten plan they still might be looking for James. She shuddered to think of it.

Todd was under guard at the hospital. The detective from Denver was already talking about extradition so he could face charges for what he'd done to Kylie there. Dalton and the county attorney figured he'd be facing serious charges in Conard County, as well. Two kidnappings. Quite a record for one night.

But at last they told her she was free to go. Get some rest. She wondered if she'd ever sleep again.

Wound up, edgy, not ready to settle as the night and the events in Denver kept playing through her mind. She was glad to let Coop take her home. Glad to feel his big hand tight around hers. Glad that he apparently didn't care what Glenda might think as he took her upstairs and put them both to bed. Together.

Somehow curling up naked with him punctured the nervous energy that had kept her running. Almost as soon as he wrapped himself around her, urging her head onto his shoulder, she fell asleep. Deeply asleep.

When next she woke, it was late afternoon and she was looking into Coop's smiling eyes. "Welcome back," he said.

She felt a sleepy smile come to her own face. She knew he'd be leaving soon, but that shadow didn't enter the room. Not yet. She wouldn't let it.

Then he said utterly without preamble, "I love you. I love you more than life. I realize everything's been messed up for you, so I'm not asking you to say anything in return. I just want you to know. I love you. And whenever, if ever, you're ready to consider it, I'll be waiting for you. In fact, I'll come running."

She drew a sharp breath as joy began to fill her, driving away the demons that had haunted her days.

"I know it's a lot to ask," he said. "You'd have to put up with a few more years of me being in the corps. You might wonder sometimes why you're with a guy who leaves you alone so much. Maybe you could never do it. But I had to tell you, even if it's selfish of me. I love you."

"Coop…" She could hardly find the breath to speak. Happiness beyond description squeezed out every other thought or feeling.

"You could go on with your own plans," he said. "Finish your master's, or go to medical school. I'd be proud to help with that. But you don't have to give up your life if you decide to be with me. I want to be sure we're clear on that. Like I said, you'd have to put up with my job. Why wouldn't I put up with yours? They're your dreams and that makes them as important to me as they are to you."

When she didn't answer immediately, his smile softened. "Take your time, Kylie. As much time as you want to be sure I'd be right for you."

But she already knew. Deep in her heart she knew. This was the man who had stood as her protector before he had even known her, who had comforted her during her flashbacks, who had been willing to devote himself full time to watching over her. He had shared his dark cemetery with her, a trust she fully valued.

But mostly, she realized that she loved everything about him, from his quiet strength to his willingness to be gentle. An avenging angel with a heart of gold.

And she wanted him in her life for every day yet to come. "I love you, Coop," she said softly, then repeated it more strongly. "I love you."

At once he laughed and rolled over until he was half

on top of her. "I love you, Kylie Brewer. And right now I want to show you how much."

Bending his head, he kissed her deeply, and swept her away to the distant mountaintops of desire.

Her heart sang with more joy than it ever had. He loved her.

* * * * *

Don't miss the next
CONARD COUNTY: THE NEXT GENERATION
book, coming in January 2017.

And don't forget previous books in this thrilling series by New York Times *bestselling author Rachel Lee:*

CONARD COUNTY SPY
A SECRET IN CONARD COUNTY
CONARD COUNTY WITNESS

SPECIAL EXCERPT FROM

HHARLEQUIN®

ROMANTIC suspense

Jolie Peters's daughter has witnessed a murder and now they're both targets. She has nowhere else to turn— except back into the arms of T. C. Colton, the man she left years before without a word of explanation.

Read on for a sneak preview of
COLTON FAMILY RESCUE
by Justine Davis, the next book in
***THE COLTONS OF TEXAS** continuity.*

For a moment longer she just gazed up at him and looked nothing like the fierce protector who had been ready to shoot to protect her child.

He wanted to protect her. And Emma. He wanted them both safe and able to grow and blossom as he knew they would. He'd never felt the urge this strongly in his life.

Except with her.

He couldn't stop himself; he reached for her. She came into his arms easily, and he realized with a little jolt she was trembling.

"Jolie?"

"I'm scared," she whispered.

"They're gone, whoever it was," he assured her.

She leaned back again to look at him, gave a tiny shake of her head. "Not that. You."

He went still. "You're scared of me?"

Again the small gesture of denial. "Of how I feel about you. How you make me feel."

Making her feel was exactly what he wanted to do right now. He wanted to make her feel everything he'd felt, he wanted to make her move in that urgent way, wanted to hear the tiny sounds she made when he touched her in all those places, wanted to hear her cry out when she shattered in his arms.

On some vague level he knew she was talking of deeper things, but that reasoning part of his brain was shutting down as need blasted along every nerve in his body.

"I think we should check on Flash," he breathed against her ear.

He felt a shiver go through her, hoped it was for the same reason he was practically shaking in his boots.

"You think he might be getting in trouble out there?" she whispered.

"I think I already am in trouble."

"No fun getting in trouble alone," she whispered and reached up to cup his face with her hand. He turned his head, pressed his lips against her palm. And read the longed-for answer in her eyes.

He grabbed a blanket from the storage chest at the foot of the bed. Last time he'd been picking straw out of uncomfortable places. He supposed she had, too, but she'd never complained.

Jolie never complained. She assessed, formulated and acted on her best plan. It struck him then that she was exactly the kind of person he preferred to deal with in business. No manipulation, no backroom maneuvering, just honest decisions made with the best information she had at the time.

Like she had made four years ago?

Love the Harlequin book you just read?

Your opinion matters.

Review this book on your favorite book site, review site, blog or your own social media properties and share your opinion with other readers!

Be sure to connect with us at:
Harlequin.com/Newsletters
Facebook.com/HarlequinBooks
Twitter.com/HarlequinBooks

HREVIEWS